# KILL
# SWITCH

Also by Freddie P Peters

HENRY CROWNE PAYING THE PRICE Thrillers

INSURGENT

COLLAPSE

BREAKING POINT

NO TURNING BACK

SPY SHADOWS

IMPOSTOR IN CHIEF

RED RENEGADE

NANCY WU SMART WOMAN CRIME Thrillers

BLOOD DRAGON

SON AND CRUSADER

SAVAGED INNOCENCE

# KILL SWITCH

*A River Swift Vigilante Thriller*

## FREDDIE P PETERS

Shadow Network Press

*London*

Print ISBN: 978-1-0686722-4-8
eBook ISBN: 978-1-0686722-3-1

Cover design by Lizzie Gardiner
Typesetting by Susan Hood

# Prologue

## Sunday, January 16

The sound of footsteps coming from the far side of the underpass woke up Charlie. He hadn't owned a watch for a long time, but he knew it was very late. He turned on his side to check whether Dumbo had heard the noise, too. His companion was still fast asleep, snuggled on the cardboard they'd spread on the ground a few days ago, when they'd decided to settle under the John Philip Sousa Bridge in the Washington Highlands neighborhood of DC. It was almost too cold to sleep outside, but the footpaths that led to the bridge provided some shelter, and no one had yet sought to chase them from the location. Charlie surveyed his companion's leathery face. Dumbo hadn't woken up.

Charlie pushed the rags away from him and shivered. He grabbed the old duvet he used to cover the rest of his bedding and moved noiselessly toward the intersection of the footpath and the underpass leading to the bridge. He approached with caution and risked casting a glance farther down the path.

Two men dressed in black and wearing balaclavas were dragging a third man down the underpass. Charlie couldn't be sure, but he thought they were also wearing some sort of body armor. The third man had his arms slung loosely over their shoulders, and the other two seemed to be supporting the bulk of his body. His feet twisted and dragged along the ground, unsteady.

Charlie retreated around the corner of the footpath as soon as they stopped. He heard the distinct sound of a body being dropped as one of the men said, "Is he coming around?"

"Perhaps another half hour or so. It won't be long," a second voice replied.

"Should we wait to make sure?"

"No need. The hotel receptionist has called the police. They must already be on their way. I want us out of the area before they start searching for him."

There was silence and then the sound of footsteps echoing off the walls of the underpass. Charlie didn't move. A loud groan broke the silence, and then a cry. Dumbo was having one of his nightmares. Charlie froze for a moment and then ran back to the place where Dumbo lay. The older man's eyes were now wide open yet unfocused. Charlie clamped his hand over Dumbo's mouth. Dumbo thrashed around and then woke up.

"Shhh," Charlie murmured. "Some bad people around."

Dumbo didn't seem to understand, and Charlie said, "Must make it look as though we're asleep."

Dumbo nodded, and Charlie slid back into his makeshift bed and pulled the duvet over his head. This time the footsteps weren't fading away but getting closer. They stopped a yard away from the cardboard mat where Dumbo had curled up to sleep, and the first man Charlie had heard said, "Just a couple of vagrants."

The second man moved right up to Dumbo. Charlie could just about make out what was happening through one of the holes in his duvet. The man used his foot to push Dumbo awake and said, "Been here long?"

Dumbo opened his eyes again, but this time they were fixed on the two thugs who stood over him. He mumbled something incomprehensible even to Charlie. The man who had nudged Dumbo said, "I don't like these two being around. We don't need witnesses."

"We don't need to leave two dead bodies behind, either, and we don't have time to dispose of them. The police will track down

Wayne to this place, and that's all we want them to find. Let's not move away from the plan."

"I still don't like—" The man was interrupted by the sound of a police siren in the distance.

He took a phone out of his pocket and snapped a photo of Dumbo as the old man lay on his dirty bedding, eyes wide open in fear. Charlie watched the two men from inside his old duvet as they finally left. Their footsteps receded until the underpass fell silent again.

Charlie waited a moment, and when he was sure they were not coming back, he threw the duvet off and sat up. He laid a hand over Dumbo's chest. The old man whimpered and turned his face toward Charlie.

"It's okay. They've left, but we need to go."

Dumbo sat up slowly, and Charlie started to gather their meager possessions. He helped Dumbo stand up, and the old man shuffled toward the shopping cart they used to carry their belongings. Charlie hesitated. Perhaps this wasn't a good idea, but he wanted to check on the man who'd been dumped just a short distance away. There might be something he could take from him—a little money, maybe. Charlie turned around and started to walk back toward the underpass. Dumbo pulled Charlie toward him and shook his head.

"Be only a minute, maybe get a bit of money," Charlie said, rubbing his thumb and index finger together.

He gently freed himself from Dumbo's grip, adjusting the woolly hat his companion had pulled down over his wispy gray hair, and rounded the corner of the footpath. The man who had been dropped a few minutes ago was there, his body slumped to one side. The few overhead lamps that hadn't been vandalized were providing just enough light for Charlie to see that the man was covered in blood. Charlie doubted he would survive much longer.

He crouched next to the man and waited. On closer inspection, the man looked out of it rather than on the verge of death. He was wearing an aviator bomber jacket that looked old yet in good condition. It was open, and Charlie slid his hand slowly inside it, looking for the man's wallet. He fumbled around a little and found what he was looking for.

Charlie's fingers had just clasped the wallet when the man jerked up, and his hand grabbed Charlie's wrist. The man's eyes fluttered open, and Charlie fell on his back as he pulled his wrist free from the man's grip. The man still couldn't focus, and his head rolled around a few times like a loose ball on a stick. Charlie crawled backward, not wanting to lose sight of the man, who was just about to wake up. When Charlie reached what he thought was a safe distance, he stood up, turned around, and ran.

"Wait," Charlie thought the man tried to shout, the word garbled.

Charlie rounded the corner again. Dumbo had done a good job at loading their bits and pieces into the shopping cart. When Charlie reached him, he pushed the old man perhaps more brutally than he'd meant to and said, "Must go now—bad people around."

Charlie started walking as fast as he could, pushing the unwieldy cart, Dumbo struggling to keep up. They reached the top of the footpath, ready to turn onto the main road. Charlie looked back to see the man he thought he'd left behind leaning against the wall, a hand stretched toward them. Charlie let go of the cart and pushed Dumbo forward along the road. Traffic was starting to build up. He crossed the highway to the sound of car horns and drivers' swearing. He didn't care. The man in the underpass was alive, and the blood that covered him wasn't his. If it were, he would be dead.

Jason Wayne, his head still swimming, stood up to follow the man who'd tried to rob him of his wallet. He struggled to reach the corner of the footpath around which the would-be thief had vanished. He leaned against the wall for balance as he saw the vagrant and an older man disappear in the distance. Bile rose in his throat, and he thought he might be sick. There was no point in trying to pursue the two men now. His wallet was still in the inner pocket of his aviator jacket, and he needed to make sense of what had happened to him.

As his eyes started to focus and the sick feeling subsided, he looked down at his hands and gasped. He'd seen enough blood in his time as a SEAL operative to know that not only his hands but also his shirt and jacket were covered in it. Jason's instinct was to check his own body first. He placed a hand over his abdomen and then his chest, but there wasn't any pain, and the amount of blood that was soaking his clothes would have meant a serious wound.

Jason shivered at the memories of what had been his last mission in Afghanistan—the one that had cost the life of three of his teammates and forced him to quit a world he had thought he would be part of for the rest of his professional life.

*No one realizes they are coming until it is too late—the Taliban fighters who are waiting for them when his unit enters a village where two American hostages are held. The mission is clear despite the high risk. Get to the village, deep in the central highlands, under the cover of darkness, free the hostages, return to Camp Leatherneck, in Helmand Province. The number of fighters guarding the hostages shouldn't be a problem for his Alpha team, but an ambush has got them squeezed between two lots of fighters and the steepness of the terrain on two sides . . .*

Jason leaned against the wall and breathed deeply. The gaping wounds in his right leg had healed, but the pain still flared up from time to time, and today was one of those days. He straightened up and despite the suffering returned to what had caught his attention in the first place—the blood on his clothes.

His watch indicated it was 3:47 a.m. Jason tried to recall where he'd been for the past few hours, but his mind was blank. He tried to focus, but nothing came. He'd never experienced this before. It wasn't the foggy brain of someone who'd overdone the booze. There was nothing there, not a faint image or bodily sensation that indicated he might later remember . . . nothing.

He retraced his steps and went back to the place where he'd

woken up. Perhaps this might jog his memory, but instead he heard distant voices. He noticed a trail of blood on the ground leading toward the entrance to the footpath. Police sirens were screaming in the distance but approaching fast. He heard shouts and now footsteps pounding through the underpass. That's when he did something he'd never done before—he turned around and ran.

# Chapter One

NOTEBOOK–AFGHANISTAN DEPLOYMENT

June 2021
SEAL Team 1

The team's last assignment was harder than I'd expected. Some of my teammates are getting on my nerves, so I've gotten into the habit of listening to some music instead of joining them after the debrief. I don't want a beer. I want the anger to stop.

I've taken the new meds that the medics have given me for headaches. They do the trick for a while, but once they wear off the thing comes back with a vengeance. I'm not sure how long I can go on like this and do the job without endangering the op. This is causing even more tension for me, which I just about manage.

I don't want to write this down, but I must. I'm scared and frustrated about what's happening to me because I don't know what to do. I'm reading a lot about PTSD. The books are at home, and I've tried to be honest with myself, but I don't understand why post-traumatic stress would have suddenly caught up with me, although the description of what I'm experiencing fits.

I just don't know, and that's the most infuriating part.

J.

## Sunday, January 16

The flames crackled, and sparks spit into the snow that they had pushed into a circle to accommodate their campfire. River stood up slowly, grabbed a log, and added it to the pile. Karen poured another two cups of coffee from the Thermos and handed one to River.

Since her good friend Karen Robinson had left the air force, River had kept in touch with her. Karen had gone back to her hometown, doing what she'd done brilliantly when she was in the same battlefield medics unit as River—treat life-threatening injuries. Now it was River's turn to join her in Kotzebue. Karen had welcomed her almost eleven months ago, when River didn't know where she'd go next. Today they were enjoying a moment in the Alaskan wilderness to witness one of the most magical events River had ever seen—the northern lights. Neither spoke, simply enjoying the mesmerizing spectacle displayed across the sky in the camp they'd set up in the forest to greet it. The dogs Karen had been taught to mush by her father, Chief Robinson of the Kotzebue police department, had settled alongside them for the night, and they would soon fall asleep in the snow.

River sat back down, sipped some coffee, and whispered, "Tell me again what your mom used to say about the aurora when you were a little kid."

Karen smiled, her broad, round face exuding kindness. But then she grew serious again. "We Inupiat have a story about the *kig e uh*. Whenever we walked home and saw the aurora, my mother used to say, 'You must be quiet!' and I would ask, 'Why?' Mom would reply softly, 'Those are your ancestors up there, and a bad spirit is chasing them.' And she would continue, 'You must keep quiet, or else the bad spirit will notice you and cut off your head.'"

River nodded, waiting for the rest of the story.

"At that point, I would get scared and say to Mom, 'C'mon, let's hurry,'" Karen continued. "We would then both scurry home. I can remember to this day the relief I felt when we reached our house."

"The lights are magical," River said. "I've read about the science behind them, but I'm still in awe when they appear. I used to love it when my mother was telling me all these folk stories about spirits and demons. She used to pick them up from the local people wherever we traveled."

"We've known each other for a while, Riv, but you never told me how many countries you visited with your folks," Karen said, turning her head toward River.

River frowned. "My God—I don't think I've kept a tally. Mom and Dad started working for Doctors Without Borders even before my brother and I were born, and we traveled all the time. So I don't know. Guesstimate, perhaps twenty countries."

Karen shook her head. "That's crazy. I might not have moved from Kotzebue had I not joined the air force."

"It was a bit crazy, I've got to admit, but it was fun. And now I can blame our bohemian lifestyle for the fact that I can't settle anywhere."

Karen shrugged. "So what? You don't want to have a guy, a house, and two kids."

"Except that I thought I did, and I ended up hurting someone in the process." Deep down, she knew she deserved the pain that still so often ran through her for having left a man she'd thought she loved and possibly still did.

"How long are you going to torture yourself for making an honest mistake?" Karen asked. She stood up, went to the sled, and took out the two sleeping bags she'd folded neatly a few hours ago, when they were preparing for their aurora-watching night.

"For as long as it'll take," River said.

Karen handed one of the bags to River, who shook her head and squeezed Karen's shoulder quickly. "So sorry, my friend. It's been almost a year, and I still can't believe I walked out on him."

"Perhaps you should think about joining the air force again—"

"No can do. They'll know within a millisecond what happened between me and Jason. I don't think I would ever be trusted again after that."

"But Riv, you were one of the best trauma resuscitation specialists in the SOS teams."

"It makes no difference," River said.

She spread the sleeping bag next to the fire and sat down on it. The thick down filling shielded her from the cold of the snow. River no longer wanted to talk about her ex-fiancé, Jason Wayne, whom she'd met on one of her Afghanistan tours. He had been caught in a deadly ambush that had cost the lives of three of his teammates. He had barely survived and might not have done so were it not for the deployment of River's Special Operations Surgical Team alongside his SEAL extraction team. They'd managed to reach Jason's squad after hours of fighting hostiles in a dangerous terrain, and by the time they arrived, three SEALs lay dead, and two others had to be operated on on-site.

River took a deep breath and released it slowly. She'd come to Alaska to heal her wounds, not reopen them. She had torn herself away from a job she'd loved doing for more than twelve years in order to embrace a more conventional life with Jason—move to DC with him, get married, have a family. It had been the plan until she realized she wasn't the conventional type. And now she'd lost it all.

River took her shoes off, wrapped them in a pouch to keep them from freezing, put on a spare pair of socks, pushed her thick hat further down her shoulder-length blond hair, and slid into the sleeping bag. She shuffled a little to make herself comfortable near the fire. Karen had done the same, and they both turned their gaze skyward.

The display of colors shifting in long tendrils across the dark sky drew River out of her somber mood. They were lucky today. The usual green hues dancing in the sky were joined by dark pink and the occasional blue or purple. She'd never seen such an exceptional array of colors. River always needed to understand the mechanics behind whatever scientific phenomenon she was interested in. She'd read that when electrons and protons, minuscule atomic particles discharged by the sun, collided with the gases in the earth's upper atmosphere, they produced tiny flashes that filled the sky with color. Usually those flashes were green, but the other hues shimmering across the vastness of the sky today announced that the sun had just had a large solar flare and fired off many more particles toward the earth than usual.

The other thing that fascinated River was that the aurora stretched across the sky in all directions. It wasn't like a show on a TV screen; rather, it enveloped her. River smiled at Karen's memory of her childhood. She could understand why the elders felt in awe of what they saw. She felt it, too, and let herself be carried by the moment, hoping that sleep would catch up with her and that she would slide into it without reminiscing about her past.

She stayed motionless inside the sleeping bag for a while. Her eyelids drooped a few times, but every time she thought she was nodding off, they opened again, teased by the spectacle overhead. She turned her attention to Karen. Her friend had drifted into sleep, and she could hear the light sound of a soft snore. River lifted her head to check on the dogs. Like their musher, they'd fallen asleep, snuggled together against the cold.

*SEAL Team 6 has gone ahead with the extraction of their wounded comrades of Team 1. The first chopper that carries them has landed. River has seen it disappear over the mountain and the narrow valley beyond. She hears over the radio comms in her helmet that the Taliban fighters are retreating, no doubt helped by the launch of four Hydra 70 rockets that have cleared the higher ground and eliminated the possibility of a rocket launcher downing one of the helicopters.*

*The chopper she's on has now been given the go-ahead. It breaks its holding pattern and climbs over the mountain. There is still fighting going on. River sees the discharge of gunfire in the fading light. Soon it will be dark, and they need to extract the dead and wounded as soon as possible.*

*She checks her equipment one more time—the resuscitation kit, the equipment she needs to treat life-threatening wounds and increase the chance of survival. She straps on her backpack, secures it, and slides to the side of the chopper, ready to jump out. The rotors raise so much dust that she can hardly see the ground, but the pilot gives them the thumbs-up, so she and the other two combat medics leap out and stay crouched until the chopper has risen enough above them for the dirt to settle again.*

*One of the SEAL Team 6 men has moved closer. He signals they need to stay low. In the distance, River sees bodies on the ground. Based on her experience, she can almost always accurately guess whether a man is dead or alive. She knows that two men are dead but that the third one is still clinging to life. She crouch-walks to the SEAL operative and hand-signals that she needs to get to the third man. He hesitates for a few seconds, checks the immediate perimeter, and nods.*

*River uses a couple of boulders that stand between her and her charge for cover. The man is slumped on the ground, a gaping wound to his leg that shows the shattered bone inside the flesh. He's used a strap as a tourniquet to stop the bleeding and the shot of morphine that SEALs carry with them in case of emergency. River can see he's in and out of it.*

*The hand she places on his shoulder makes him twitch, and she says, "What's your name?"*

*He struggles to lift his head and says, "Jason."*

River sat bolt upright, her heart pounding against her chest. She hadn't had the dream for a while, and she cursed herself for bringing back the subject of her ex-fiancé. She had so wanted to fit in, to be a tight couple just the way her mom and dad had been . . . loving, having fun, and doing things together to make the world a better place. Her father had once said to her, with the utmost seriousness, "Love does not consist of gazing at each other but in looking outward in the same direction." He hadn't told her where the quotation had come from, leaving it up to her to find out. She'd forgotten all about it until she'd met Jason, but by then both her parents had passed and there was no one left to talk about her feelings with.

She checked her watch. It was 6:10 a.m. There wouldn't be any daylight today, as there hadn't been yesterday and wouldn't be tomorrow. In January, Kotzebue was in the polar night zone, and it wouldn't see a glimmer of sun until early February. River turned her attention to the fire. Karen must have woken up during the night, added a log or two, and made sure it was still burning to keep them warm.

River took her time getting out of the sleeping bag. She had no one to rescue today, although she'd promised Pauly, one of the local nurses, she would lend her a hand that morning. She took her shoes from their protective pouch, put them on, and stood up. The sky was still dark, but the aurora had disappeared. The lead dog stirred, lifted her head, and yawned. But it was River and not Karen coming toward the sled, so she dropped her head between her paws and went back to sleep.

River opened the plastic basket in which she'd stored a battered old kettle. She poured water into it, returned to the fire, picked up the branch they'd used the day before, and placed the kettle on the branch above the embers. She returned to the sled to retrieve instant coffee and sugar from the basket.

Karen returned from a quick walk around the woods for morning exercise, and she started preparing food for the dogs. By the time River and Karen had their breakfast, fed the dogs, harnessed them for the return journey, and arrived in Kotzebue, it would be mid-morning. River hadn't checked for a cell signal. Out in the wilderness, there was often little or no coverage, but they had only ventured twenty miles away from town. If she had a signal, she might give Pauly a call to tell her she would be a little late.

River took her cell phone out of her duffel bag and checked. There was only one flickering bar, not enough to make a call but enough to send a text and hope it would go through. She then noticed she'd received a text herself a few hours back. She pressed the icon and almost dropped her phone as she read.

**I've been arrested for murder. You're the only one who can help. Jase**

13

# Chapter Two

River was still on the tarmac when she turned around and gave Danny a wave. He waved back and gave her a thumbs-up. She'd been lucky to find a ride in his ATR 42 Cargo aircraft from Kotzebue's Ralph Wien Memorial Airport to Anchorage. Danny and Karen had been friends since they were kids, and River always wondered whether they had ever been more than just friends. She had broached the subject with Karen, but her friend had been a little cagey. River hadn't pushed. Who was she to give grief to anyone about their love life?

She turned back one more time, but Danny was now talking to one of the airport staff, no doubt about the cargo he was about to offload. So she shouldered her military-issue duffel bag and entered Ted Stevens Anchorage International Airport through one of the side doors. She found her way through the main terminal and looked for the United Airlines desk.

She spotted the distinct blue-and-white logo and waited for the passenger before her to be served. He wasn't traveling light, it seemed, and yet he wasn't happy with the surcharge the airline was wanting to charge him. The ticket agent wasn't budging, and River glanced at her watch nervously. She didn't need the man to create delays when she was trying to catch the 8:15 p.m. flight to Dulles. She was about to complain when the man relented and paid.

She flashed a smile to the harassed rep and presented her ticket. He smiled back, handed over her boarding pass, and moved to the next customer. River didn't bother to check her bag. She wanted to be off the plane as soon as possible and hit the ground running. She hadn't been able to find out which precinct Jason was being held in, but she'd been in touch with a veterans rehab organization she knew well, and Father Hopkins, the man in charge of the center, had assured her he would find out by the time she arrived in DC.

River went through security. Her military duffel bag attracted attention, but she was too busy thinking about what was awaiting her in Washington to take much notice. The gate number had just been displayed on the departures board. She sped toward it, reached it after a five-minute walk, and found a secluded place, where she dropped her bag. She sat on it and called Karen.

"You're through?"

"Yep. It's odd to be all packed up with my bag and yet not going to a war zone," River replied.

"Look at it this way—you are going to a war zone of sorts," Karen said. River imagined her friend seated in the living room of her small wooden cabin with a cup of coffee and the stove burning bright in the corner of the room.

"I know what you're getting at. But I'm not sure how suited I am to be playing detective. I'm a medic, not military police."

"But you've done some pathology work when the MPs needed you, and you got results."

A few images flashed through River's mind. She'd never been squeamish and could deal with any wound on a soldier. It was always a matter of life and death. And she'd learned to put herself in what medics called the golden-hour zone, in which all she saw was an injury and worked with every tool at her disposal to make sure the wounded soldier survived long enough to be transported out of the battlefield. But it was something different to have to autopsy a dead body—perform the Y incision and take the organs out to inspect them. It somehow felt wrong to her.

Karen's voice brought River back.

"I know I have, but I never enjoyed the autopsy work much, although it might be useful in this case," River said.

"Have you spoken to Father Hopkins?"

"I managed to get hold of him . . ."

"But?" Karen said in her don't-try-to-hide-what's-on-your-mind voice.

"He's going to find out where the police are holding Jase. I have a feeling he wanted to speak to me about something else but held back at the last moment."

"So you're worried he's got some bad news?"

"It's always been complicated for Jase since his injury. He loved being a SEAL, and he was so good at it. He's now doing another great job—helping veterans and even guys who're still serving when they have issues—but it's not the same, of course."

There was a silence that River didn't feel like breaking. Karen had seen her fair share of injuries and death, too. She'd joined the air force as a medic almost ten years before River, and when she retired it wasn't to marry and have a family but to return to her ancestors' small-town home in Alaska and help.

"You don't have the facts to start worrying about something that may not be there in the first place," Karen said eventually. "Get some rest while you can. You know that's in short supply when you're on the front line."

The PA system started to crackle, and people stood up slowly as an airline employee was preparing to make an announcement.

"We're about to board," River said. "I'll be landing at 7:55 a.m. and go straight to see Jason if I have the address of the precinct."

"Keep me in the loop, and don't forget I'm only a few hours away from DC, too. Good luck—*ullaakkut.*"

"Appreciated, Nayuuq." River managed a smile. She'd spent enough time with Karen to know that she'd be supportive. Somehow, using Karen's Inupiat name, a name that was only entrusted to friends, reinforced their bond.

River picked up her duffel bag and made her way to the gate. She presented her boarding pass and was allowed onto the tarmac. She boarded and found her allocated window seat. She managed to squeeze her bag in the overhead locker, apologized to the man who was sitting next to her, and slid into her seat.

She found a position that accommodated her appreciable height and then removed her winter jacket to use it as a blanket. She fastened her seat belt and let her head drop against the side of the seat. She'd try to get some sleep, as Karen suggested. But her mind was buzzing with questions and memories. She let them pop up without holding on to any of them, the way she'd taught herself to let go of unwanted thoughts when preparing for a mission. She'd perfected her technique over the years, and it had never failed her.

But today, the inner calm she was seeking was elusive. River couldn't help wondering whether Jason had been pushed to the edge. Her initial reaction had been one of disbelief and outrage. The fact that he'd been responsible for terminating hostiles when carrying out his missions had nothing to do with the likelihood of his killing a noncombatant in cold blood.

River shifted around. She opened her eyes and realized that the plane was already in the air. Her neighbor, a large man with a salt-and-pepper beard and hair reaching his shoulders, was reading a book. She was grateful that he seemed engaged with the story and made no attempt to have a conversation.

The flight attendants started offering food. River wasn't hungry, but she would eat whatever was in front of her, not knowing when she'd have time to grab her next meal.

She opted for a hot reindeer stew, bread, and a side salad, accompanied by a large cup of coffee. Just like her parents, she was always able to sleep if she drank coffee before bed. Her neighbor eyed her food with something that resembled contempt and produced his own sandwiches, large and aromatic. River avoided looking at him, but she had to admit that the smell of his food was much more appetizing than the bland taste of the airline meal. She forced herself to eat, chewing each mouthful for far too long before swallowing it. She washed it all down with water from the bottle that had come at no charge with her food and settled back in her seat.

The food helped her doze off. She drifted into a light sleep, like the ones she used to have when the medics' camp was close to the front line and the exchange of gunfire could be heard in the distance all through the night.

*She's seated in the living room of her parents' rented house in KwaZulu-Natal, South Africa. They moved there only a few months ago to help Doctors Without Borders' ambitious HIV detection and treatment program. River arrived a few days back. She's almost completed her own medical school studies and should be now applying for a residency, but she's chosen another path. She's decided to become a battlefield surgeon and has already enrolled in the air force.*

*She's just told her parents, and there is dismay on their faces.*

*"Why would you want to do that?" is all her mother manages to say.*

*"Because that's where I can be the most useful. I know I work well under pressure, and I can help save lives by intervening fast within the golden hour—you know, the first sixty minutes after an injury, when a fast medical intervention—"*

*"We know what the golden hour is," her father interrupts angrily.*

*"But you can be just as useful elsewhere around the world. There is still so much that needs to be done for civilians, for people . . ." Her mother sounds as though she's pleading.*

*River throws her hands in the air and then runs her fingers through her hair. "You guys are unbelievable. Get real. We're no longer in the '70s, and this isn't the Vietnam War. The guys who go to Afghanistan are helping build a democracy."*

*"Don't be so naive, River," her father says, standing up. "This will only go on until America gets fed up with sending boys to the slaughter, and then they will leave—like Vietnam and Somalia."*

*"Dad, I might be naive, but you can be so cynical. I think the United States is doing a great job fighting terrorism, and I want to support that effort." River stands up, too, and she squares up to her father. Not the first time, but today will be the last.*

18

*Her mother, who usually intervenes and calms them down, eventually getting them to make peace, hasn't budged. River wasn't expecting this. It stings more than she can say, and her eyes well with tears.*

*"I'm not changing my mind," she says with a wobble in her voice.*

*"Have you spoken to your brother about it?" her father asks.*

*"Leave Luke out of this," River shouts. "I know you think he's the stronger of the two of us, but I stopped looking up to him a long time ago."*

*"That's not fair—we don't think that," her mother says, shaking her head. She looks more upset by River's remark than by her daughter's joining the 24th Special Operations Wing at Hurlburt Field, in Florida.*

*"Perhaps you don't, but he does." River points a reproachful finger at her father. She leaves the room, slamming the door behind her.*

## Monday, January 17

The sound of the door slamming in her dream woke River up. She opened her eyes and for a few seconds wondered where she was. The rumble of the aircraft engine reminded her that she was on her way to DC. She turned her head to check on her neighbor. He was reclined against the headrest, fast asleep. River checked her watch, trying to focus on today's task. The plane would be landing in an hour and a half. The crew would soon switch the cabin lights on and offer breakfast to the passengers.

River half lifted the shutter of the porthole. The sky was still dark, but a glimmer of light was trying to pierce the scattered clouds. As expected, the lights flickered on in the cabin, and the captain made an announcement. The flight would be landing at Washington Dulles International Airport at 7:55 a.m. Her neighbor shifted and opened an eye. He grunted and settled back into his seat. Breakfast wasn't in the cards for him.

River couldn't force herself to eat the food and simply grabbed the coffee that went with it. When she was done, she managed to get to the aisle without disturbing her neighbor and went to the bathroom to make herself look presentable. She combed her hair, arranged it into a ponytail, put a little mascara on, and added a dash of lipstick. She needed to make the right impression at the police station and didn't want to seem disheveled and on edge.

The seat-belt lights came on just as she was returning to her seat. Her neighbor wasn't there, and River took her seat for landing. She retrieved her cell phone from the pocket of her jacket, which she'd placed underneath the seat in front of her, and slid it into her pants pocket. Her neighbor returned. He glanced at her and pointed toward the porthole and the city that spread out below them.

"Don't like this place . . . too many people, too many intrigues, and far too much money swirling around," he said moodily. He didn't seem to expect an answer, so River just nodded.

She couldn't disagree with him. She'd spent almost a year in DC, and she hadn't enjoyed it. She hadn't admitted it to herself until the day she decided to tell her husband-to-be that she couldn't go through with their wedding. Jason hadn't said anything to start with. It was as though he'd always known. But then they argued. It was hard to explain why she was certain she couldn't commit, and when she tried to put it into words, she ended up sounding selfish and fickle.

The plane touched down and taxied to the gate. As soon as it stopped, passengers stood up despite the seat-belt sign still being lit. River switched her cell phone on. She had only one missed call, and it was from Father Hopkins. She didn't bother to wait until she was out of the aircraft. She sat down again, turned toward the window, and listened to the voicemail.

"Hello, River. I managed to get the information you need. Jason is held by DC PD, Seventh District, PSA 706. It's on Alabama Avenue Southeast. I'll be at the center early. If you'd like to see me before going there, just show up. No need to call."

Passengers were starting to leave the plane. River took her duffel bag from the overhead bin and shuffled with everyone else down the aisle and out of the aircraft. She made her way to the main terminal, where her next stop was. She had found out that EagleRider had a rental counter at Dulles. She'd made up her mind she would rent a motorcycle to move around DC rather than a car. It was faster, and even in bad weather she thought she would be better off. She'd been riding ever since she was fifteen, and she would enjoy riding again without having to wait for Kotzebue's spring and the big thaw.

The EagleRider counter was empty when she arrived. She called for help, and a young woman ran toward it, cup of coffee in hand.

"Apologies," she said. "How can I help you?"

"I rented a Yamaha Super Ténéré online yesterday. I've come to pick it up."

"Yes . . . I saw that this morning." The young woman sat at her computer, and her hands flew over the keyboard. "River Swift?"

River nodded, took her driver's license out of the bag, and presented it to the EagleRider rep.

"It's a good choice, especially with a bag to carry. But could I interest you perhaps in a Harley Road Glide?" the woman said with a wink.

River couldn't help a smile. "That's a very tempting offer, but I'm not sure a Harley-Davidson would be safe where I need to go, so better not."

*And I'm not here to show off.*

River turned to the helmet rack. She spotted a Shoei Neotec 3.

"That's the latest," the young woman said. "It's the best flip-front model I've ever worn."

River picked it up. It was the right size for her. She tried it, flipped the visor up and down a few times. It felt easy, and the fit hugged her face without being uncomfortable. She took off the helmet and signed for the rental. The young woman gave her a set of keys and a parking card. River thanked her and turned toward the main concourse. She followed the exit sign toward the parking lot, duffel bag on her shoulder and helmet in hand.

She found the bike easily once she entered the parking lot. She fixed her bag on the luggage rack and straddled the bike. She fired it and waited for a few seconds before revving it. She felt the engine responding and nodded. Just the sort of beast she needed to travel around DC.

She put the helmet on, adjusted it, and fastened it. She took a pair of thick leather gloves from her winter jacket, which she set on the bike's fuel tank. She took her cell out of her pocket and entered the name of the street where the PSA 706 station was located. She had spent enough time in DC before she decided to leave for Alaska to know her way around. From Dulles, which was west of DC, she'd have to travel east, cross the Potomac River near Arlington, and then get close to Capitol Hill before crossing the Anacostia River. Once she was on the other side of the Anacostia, she was in unknown territory.

River eased the bike out of the parking lot and onto the road. She joined the traffic and concentrated on her driving. She hadn't ridden a motorcycle for a while, because the snow had become too deep and ice too frequent in Kotzebue for her to handle her own Yamaha. But she'd been riding since she was in her teens, and the familiar moves came back soon enough.

Traffic was building up on the highway, and River weaved through it. She cursed as a truck driver changed lanes without signaling, and she wondered why she ever though the city—particularly DC—was for her. She'd been brought up in places barely touched by the modern world, where people were close to nature and lived in tight communities. That's where she wanted to be riding—on an open road with no vehicle in front or behind.

The journey lasted the predicted forty-eight minutes, even though River had to stop a few times once she'd crossed the Anacostia to check that she was going in the right direction. She parked in front of a rather futuristic-looking building that sprawled along the street, and for a moment thought she might have gotten the address wrong. She dismounted and walked to the front. The building's metallic curves glimmered in the weak sun of winter, and when she raised her eyes, she saw a board indicating she was standing in front of the Metropolitan Police Department Seventh District station, on Alabama Avenue.

The contrast with Kotzebue's city police couldn't have been starker. Karen's father was the head of that department, and River had visited the one-story concrete-block building a few times. Unsurprisingly, she was now dealing with a completely different animal. River gave a short exhale and steadied herself. She needed to make sure she got Jason's side of the story and then go from there.

She removed her helmet, pushed open a heavy steel door, and entered a large lobby that housed a waiting area and three counters protected by what River suspected must be bulletproof glass. River chose one of the counters and stepped in front of the microphone embedded in the glass. Her throat was tight, and she croaked a barely audible "Hello."

A plump woman in uniform greeted her with a smile and replied, "How can I help you?"

"I'd like to see Jason Wayne, please."

The woman's face grew serious, and she said, "Wait a moment."

She switched off the intercom and made an internal call. River couldn't hear the conversation, but she tried to lip-read the officer. She thought she recognized a few words: *murder*, *woman*, *visit*. The officer listened attentively to what her colleague had to say, then hung up.

"Detective Parker will see you shortly."

River nodded and went to sit on one of the chairs that lined the lobby reception area. She didn't have long to wait. Detective Parker appeared through the door and made a beeline for her—a tall, lanky man with a slight stoop and a sharp, angular face.

"Detective Alex Parker," he said as he extended a hand. Parker was exactly what she'd expected—courteous, it seemed, but intense. His manners weren't brusque, yet there was an inflexibility in his stare that told River he might not be the ally she needed to get justice for Jason.

"River Swift."

They shook, and he indicated with an outstretched hand that she should follow him. They moved to one of the interrogation rooms. Parker pulled out a chair from underneath the table that stood in the middle of the room and invited River to sit.

"I'd rather stand," River said. "I'm here to see Jason, and that's what I'd like to do first."

"I'm sure you would, but I'd like to understand who you are before you're allowed to see him. In any case, you're lucky he's still here. He'll be transferred to the DC Jail any moment."

River bit her tongue and stopped herself from asking whether Jason didn't have the right to receive visitors. She wasn't family or even his wife. Perhaps she needed a little goodwill from Detective Parker.

"How do you know Jason?" Parker asked as River sat down.

River's back stiffened, but she gave Parker a quick smile and said, "I am an ex-girlfriend, and we've stayed in touch."

"You live in DC?"

"No. I came down from Alaska. I arrived this morning."

Parker raised an eyebrow. "That's a long way to come for someone with whom you've only stayed in touch."

River shrugged. "Not sure I follow you, but here I am, so perhaps you could let me see Jason now."

"When was the last time you saw him?" Parker said, elbows on the table that separated them.

"About eleven months ago. Here in DC. Then I moved to Alaska."

"And what do you do for a living?"

"Look. I understand you need to gather information about Jason, and I also gather he's accused of committing a pretty terrible crime, but I need to speak with him so that I understand what happened."

"He killed a woman—or, rather, he savaged a woman and then fled the crime scene." Parker spoke without feeling—just the facts. He had a way of looking at River that made her want to slap his face.

"What about being innocent until proven guilty?" she replied calmly.

Parker dropped his chin to his chest, thinking.

"Fine," he said after a moment, "but I'll want an address in Alaska and in DC and a number I can reach you at."

"Sure. I'll let you have that as soon as I've seen Jase." River stood up and moved to the door of the interrogation room. Parker stood up, opened the door, and led the way down a corridor. They arrived at an entryway blocked by steel bars and a security gate. Parker called an officer on his cell phone, and someone showed up almost instantly. River was invited to put her bag through the scanner first as well as her helmet, keys, and phone. The guard then scanned her with a handheld metal detector and nodded. Parker nodded back. The guard held up a set of keys, chose one, and opened the door.

"You've got ten minutes," Parker said.

He again took the lead and entered a small room that stank of sweat and cheap food. River moved to the table at the center of the room and hesitated. Should she sit down or stay standing until Jason arrived? Her stomach somersaulted at the thought that she hadn't seen him for almost a year. They had had a few conversations regarding things that now felt so trivial that River couldn't understand why they had argued. Who cared who kept the set of DVDs they used to watch together or the mugs they'd purchased from the thrift shop?

The door creaked open, and a man in an orange jumpsuit, handcuffed and flanked by two guards, shuffled in. If she hadn't known it was Jason, she wouldn't have recognized him.

# Chapter Three

They both froze, and River bit the inside of her cheek to stop herself from screaming at the two guards who were handling her ex-fiancé. Jason's slight limp seemed to have worsened. His dark hair had grown much longer than his usual crew cut, and his blue eyes had lost their spark. As he reached the table, River and he made eye contact, but the moment was painful and embarrassing, and River looked away. She felt a storm of emotions rage inside her chest—if she'd still been with Jason, all of this might not have happened.

One of the officers led Jason to the table in the center of the room. He picked up a chain a couple of feet long that was attached to the tabletop and clamped the loose end to Jason's handcuffs.

He turned toward River and said, "Ten minutes."

Both guards walked out of the room, leaving River and Jason facing each other. River came around the table in a few hurried steps and slung her arms around him. She felt his surprise in the way he tensed up, but then he slumped against her and rested his forehead on her shoulder.

"Thanks for coming," he said as they drew apart.

River gave him a quick smile. "Tell me what happened. We haven't got much time."

River pulled out a chair for him and another one next to him for herself. They sat down, and Jason tried to run a hand through his hair, but the restraint stopped him.

River cupped his face with her hands and said, "Come on, Jase. It's tough, but you've got to tell me."

He closed his eyes for an instant, then said, "Okay. Yesterday morning I woke up in an underpass underneath Washington Highlands' Route 295."

Jason hesitated, and River squeezed his hand. Dark rings sat underneath his eyes, and the side of his face looked bruised, as though he'd been in a fight. His throat sounded sore when he spoke.

"I was covered in blood. Not mine; someone else's."

He told River about the way he'd felt when he'd woken up. He told her about running away as soon as he heard the siren of a police car closing in and footsteps coming down the path.

"I didn't want to flee the scene as they say I did, but at that point, I didn't know there was a scene to flee. The blood that covered me was worrying me, of course, but then I couldn't remember anything."

"And you still can't remember a thing?"

"Nothing. My recollection of yesterday stops when I entered a bar in Arlington. After that, it's a complete black hole."

River thought for a moment and said, "The obvious cause of memory loss is a severe trauma to the head, but I guess you would still feel the blow if you'd had one. I presume Parker got you checked by a medic."

"There is nothing wrong with me."

River drew her chair nearer and gave Jason a closer look. There was a mark that resembled a scratch on the side of his neck. He saw where her eyes were lingering and turned his face.

"But he got a medic to check you, and I presume someone took blood?"

"Yes. They're testing for illegal substances."

River willed herself to stay calm. It was hard to see a man who had always been so together, honest, and courageous chained to a table.

"I don't want to sound like Parker, but did you take anything?"

"Like what? Drugs? I've never done drugs, and that's not gonna change now, even with"—Jason's jaw clenched before he continued—"my old wound."

"Sorry," River said, squeezing his hand harder. "I don't want to be asking all these awful questions, and I know you've been through this with—"

"Look." Jason stood up and moved as far away from her as the chain would allow. "Perhaps it wasn't a good idea to get you involved," he continued, his eyebrows knitted. River could sense his anger bubbling under the surface.

"It must be tough to be accused of something you haven't done, so why don't I shut up and let you tell me what the cops say you've done? Please." River stood up, slid her hand around his arm, and tried to lead him back to the chair.

Jason resisted. She caught his eyes and said, "I believe in you."

He sat back down slowly and took a moment to think. River came to sit down next to him again.

"Parker showed me photos of a woman. She was dead." Jason stopped. He cleared his throat and continued in staccato. "She'd been murdered. From what Parker showed me, I'd say savaged. Her throat cut. She'd been tied to a bed. Parker then gave me the name of a small hotel in Washington Highlands. The receptionist apparently remembered me and her walking in and asking for a room. This guy said I looked a bit out of it. I don't recall the woman or the hotel."

River waited to let Jason catch his breath. He was staring at his hands as though they might reveal the truth to him.

"Do the police know who she is?"

"Her purse was still in the room. So, yes—she's called Jane White. According to Parker, she's some sort of escort who operates in lobbyist circles. They showed me a picture of her. I don't recognize her, but of course they didn't believe me."

River watched him as he was telling her what had happened. Jason was in pain, not so much physical—although she suspected that his arrest hadn't been a simple put-your-hands-in-the-air job—as emotional. His suffering was real.

"So what's Parker's conclusion?" she asked. "He thinks that because you're a former SEAL with hand-to-hand combat training, you're the best suspect for this"—she hesitated and then chose not to call it murder– "homicide."

"My prints are all over the room and all over her body, Riv. It's easy to see it from their perspective. I'm just a veteran who's flipped his lid."

"But you and I know this is not the case, right?" River said, determined.

"What really gets me is why I don't remember a thing."

"You could have been drugged. I know this sort of stuff tends to happen more to women than men, but there is no reason why Rohypnol couldn't have been used on you."

"You mean I've been roofied?"

"Why not? Rohypnol is as powerful on men as it is on women. It's just a question of dosage."

Jason thought for a moment. "And it would result in complete memory loss?"

"Absolutely. And the woman would have been able to get you into a cab and make it look as though you were drunk or high."

"How long does Rohypnol stay in the blood?" Jason asked, turning to face River.

"About twenty-four hours, I think. As long as Parker does his job properly and asks that it be tested for, it should show on the tox report."

"But wouldn't he have to request it?" Jason asked. "It's not the sort of thing you automatically test for on a guy, right?"

"Well, I'll be asking him that question after we've finished."

"You're not my lawyer, though," Jason said.

"Let me worry about that and see whether Parker's going to be an ass about it," River said as she checked her watch. "We've only got a few minutes left, and we haven't even spoken about the main question. Why do you think someone framed you?"

Jason returned to staring at his hands and the chain that tied him to the table.

"I think I might have stumbled onto something a few people in DC would rather keep hidden."

River frowned. "Jase, you're not the stumbling type."

"Okay . . . you're right." He seemed to be deliberating, then said, "I've been asking questions about the suicides of two of my teammates."

"Suicides—"

River's question was cut short by a door banging open.

"Time's up," one of the guards said as he entered the room. He moved toward Jason and jerked his head in the direction of the door. "You're not going be trouble, are you?"

River stood up and grabbed Jason by the arm. "Who do I speak to?" she asked him.

A second guard entered the room. He put a hand on River's shoulder. "You heard my colleague—time to go."

River shrugged his hand off. "Who?" she said with the guard hovering over her.

"Don't touch her." Jason stood up.

River sensed danger and stepped away from both men, hands in the air. "I'm fine, Jase, and yes, I'm leaving," she said to the guard.

She left the room slowly, walking backward. The guards had relaxed a little, but she saw on Jason's face that he wouldn't go back to his cell without putting up a fight. She crossed the threshold, and Jason shouted.

"Father Hopkins. Speak to Father Hopkins about—" was all River heard before the door of the interrogation room slammed shut.

River hesitated, but she knew there was no point in going back into the room. She would only make things worse. She retraced her steps and found Detective Parker waiting for her beyond the security gate. When she got there, she retrieved her duffel bag, helmet, and keys and was let out by the same officer who'd let her in. Parker didn't say a word but indicated through an extended hand that she should follow him. They went into the same interrogation room he'd used before, and Parker closed the door.

They sat around the same table as before, and Parker picked up a jug of water and poured some into each of two paper cups that lay on the table. He let River reach for her own, then took his and waited for a moment before speaking.

"Did Jason tell you about the murder?"

"No," River shot back. "We held hands and reminisced about old times."

"Was Jason ever violent toward you?" Parker asked, ignoring River's sarcasm.

"Never," River said her voice trembling, furious. She noticed she'd spilled water onto the table as she squeezed her paper cup. Was she sounding too defensive?

"Did you notice a change in Jason's attitude when you last spoke to him?"

River half closed her eyes and recalled her training. Raw anger was of no use. It must be channeled. She took her time answering, recognizing that she needed to speak to Jason's attorney, whoever that man or woman might be, before she answered Parker's questions. Now, perhaps, a little horse trading was warranted.

"Jason said the police took a blood sample. Will you be testing for Rohypnol?"

There was an almost imperceptible movement in Parker's eyebrow. "You mean testing *the suspect* for rape drugs?"

River cringed at the way Parker had put it, but she held her own and said, "No. I mean testing Jason."

This time Parker crossed his arms over his chest. "You're not Jason's legal representative. Just answer my question."

"That's true, and I haven't spoken to his lawyer to understand what position Jason is in, so I'll do that, and then we can talk again."

Parker seemed to think about that, then asked, "Why would we want to test him for Rohypnol?"

"Because he has lost memory of the events, and the use of that sort of drug would explain why."

"I would have to buy the idea that he doesn't remember any-thing in the first place," Parker said with a dismissive shrug.

"But if you don't test for Rohypnol now, it will disappear twenty-four hours after the sample was taken," River said.

"When you last spoke to him, what frame of mind was Jason in?"

River clenched a fist underneath the table. Parker was a pig-headed SOB who wouldn't follow through with her request unless she gave him more of what he wanted—details. "He was fine. He just wanted to know what to do with some old DVDs."

"How long have you two been apart?"

"Almost eleven months." River's voice quivered a little, but she swiftly followed with the answer to the question she knew would be coming next. "We both agreed that it was better if we separated amicably before making the mistake of getting married and then getting an acrimonious divorce a few years later."

She'd rehearsed that sentence and recited it many times to friends and acquaintances. She'd convinced herself it was a credi-ble line—certainly a much better one than admitting she couldn't cope with being tied to a home and family for the rest of her days.

"Still, in my experience, even an agreed-upon split isn't that straightforward."

"Really, Detective Parker. How about you? Are you on your fourth marriage?" It was a silly estimate, but River couldn't hide her anger this time. Parker was getting too close for comfort, and he must have sensed it.

"Never mind my marital track record, Ms. Swift. I'm more in-terested in yours and Jason's. You're both in your midthirties: Time to think about marriage and family."

River closed her eyes for an instant. She didn't need to be drawn into a conversation that would harm Jason in any way. She stood up slowly and then said, "There is nothing to add but what I said to you. Still, you said you were transferring Jason somewhere else."

"That's right. I'll be taken to court for arraignment shortly. I take the view that he's a flight risk, so I will ask for the judge to decline setting a bond. He'll then be transferred to the DC Central Detention Facility, not far from here."

"Doesn't he have the right to representation?" River asked, anger rising again.

"He'll have it. Someone has been appointed for him from the CJA lawyer pool, but you can replace him if you find someone who is willing to act pro bono."

"Then I'll find someone," River said, bending down to grab her personal effects.

"I still need a phone number and an address in DC." Parker stood up, too.

"I don't know where I'll be staying, but if you give me your card, I'll let you know as soon as I know myself."

Parker drew a card out of his jacket pocket and slid it across the table. River took it without looking at it and placed it in her pants pocket, then walked out of the room. She crossed the lobby and went out of the station, where she took a few steps into the cold and breathed deeply of the frigid air. If she was to help Jason get out of this mess and not make it worse, she'd have to up her game, but for the time being she needed to get to Arlington and to Father Hopkins. Jason had spoken to him about the suicides of two of his teammates and perhaps confided in him about his suspicions. And then she'd ask Father Hopkins whether he might help her find a tough lawyer who'd give Parker a run for his money.

### NOTEBOOK—AFGHANISTAN DEPLOYMENT

June 2021
SEAL Team 1

My mind was clear for most of the day today. The martial arts training with the younger members of the team made me feel as though I still have some time to go before calling it a day. But then the name of the young guy I was sparring with just vanished from my memory. I think I checked it afterward but still can't remember.

River zipped up her winter jacket and reached her Yamaha. She put on her helmet, straddled the motorbike, and fired it. It responded instantly. She flipped the peg away, held the bike motionless, and looked one last time in the direction of the police station. Anger flared up at the thought of Jason's being locked up in that soulless place.

A moment later, she joined the traffic on the main road leading across the Anacostia River. She wove her way around cars and trucks, passed the Capitol, then crossed the Potomac and sped toward Arlington. She tried to concentrate on the road, but it was difficult not to replay in her head the short time she'd spent with Jason and the interview with Detective Parker. She swerved around a large truck, and the driver sounded his horn. She waved her hand in the air dismissively.

She revved the engine, and the bike jumped forward. She flew by Pentagon City and, at the second junction of the highways that encircled Arlington National Cemetery, took the exit heading toward Penrose. She hadn't visited the Ashton Veterans Center in almost a year, but nothing seemed to have changed when she arrived. The place looked exactly as she remembered it.

Father Hopkins had managed to persuade the owner of an apartment building to let him have a space on the first floor where he could open a drop-in facility that would welcome all veterans, regardless of their military background and rank. He'd asked for volunteers to help set it up, and both River and Jason agreed to be part of his team. She was a medic and understood the trauma of injuries, both physical and mental, suffered on the battlefield. Jason's wounds were life-changing—he went from being a top SEAL operative to someone who could barely walk, undergoing months

34

of rehab after sustaining the injury that almost cost him his leg and his life.

River approached the center slowly. She found a spot to park her bike. She waited for a moment while two men entered the center. She could see through the glass front door that they were talking to the receptionist, a young woman with short hair and a kind smile. It took only a moment, and then River moved toward the main door. She walked in, managing a smile of her own.

"I'm here to see Father Hopkins. My name is River Swift."

The young woman nodded. "Father Hopkins told me you might visit. I'll let him know you've arrived."

She picked up her cell phone, slid her fingers a few times across the screen, and pressed a button.

"River has arrived, Father Hopkins."

She listened to what River suspected were instructions and then hung up. "Father Hopkins is in the chapel. He's asking whether you wouldn't mind getting there yourself. He says you know where it is."

"I do, and thank you," River said.

As she was about to turn away, the young woman stood up. "Why don't you leave your bag and helmet with me?"

"That's a good idea." River walked around the wooden desk and dropped her bag and helmet to the floor.

"I'm Maria, by the way," the woman said, extending a hand.

"Nice to meet you, Maria." River shook hands with her.

Maria seemed to want to engage in conversation, and River would have liked to oblige, but her priority was to speak to Father Hopkins. She followed a long corridor and arrived at a small atrium. The place had grown over time, benefiting from Father Hopkins's unceasing work and donations from a few generous sponsors.

The chapel was at the far end of the building. It was only a small room, but it had been beautifully put together. The stained-glass work of some of the veterans and their artist friends made the place vibrant yet calm. River arrived in front of the wooden door and stopped. She spent a moment gathering her thoughts. She hadn't obtained much information from Jason, and the reference to suicide made her want to tread carefully. The Catholic Church didn't look kindly upon the act, and she'd never ascertained Father Hopkins's views on the subject.

She pushed the door open and walked in. The place was quiet and empty. Father Hopkins had his back to her. His slim yet tall body was bent over Bibles he seemed to have gathered in a pile. River noticed that his hair had turned a little grayer than she remembered. She coughed discreetly. He straightened up, turned around, and smiled.

"I knew you would come to talk to me. It's so nice to see you again," he said as he walked toward her with open arms.

Yet his round, amiable face looked a little flustered, and River wondered whether Father Hopkins had something to tell her that might make him uncomfortable. Or perhaps it was the memory of the reconciliation he'd tried and failed to broker between her and Jason that made him look agitated.

They hugged each other briefly, and he led her to the part of the chapel that was dedicated to the Virgin Mary. Someone had brought a fresh bunch of flowers that were now standing in an old vase River recognized.

"I presume you've gone to see Jason," Father Hopkins said as he invited her to sit down in one of the pews.

"I did. I just had to speak to him to try to understand what happened and now need to find an attorney."

"He called me to tell me he'd been arrested and that he needed, as you said, a lawyer," Father Hopkins said as he sat next to River.

"How much did he tell you?"

"I got the feeling he was worried about saying the wrong thing over the phone, so he simply said that he had been accused of murder, that he was innocent, and that he needed legal representation."

"And have you found someone good?" River asked. Jason didn't have the money to afford one of DC's top criminal attorneys, but she hoped that one of the veterans organizations Father Hopkins worked with could help find someone who was competent.

"I called some of my contacts in a couple of the top law firms in DC. People who have volunteered before to help with this place," Father Hopkins said with a sweeping gesture.

"But working pro bono for your organization isn't the same as representing someone who's been accused of murder," River said.

"These firms have departments that deal with criminal law, so I'm sure we'll find someone."

River nodded. She didn't want to contradict Father Hopkins, but she imagined that the attorneys who worked at those top law firms would be trying to determine whether the client could pay—unless they were after a high-profile case to boost their reputation. The thought sent a shiver down River's spine. Perhaps this would be it—a Navy SEAL murder case might appeal to some fame-seeking lawyer.

"Jason mentioned something to me as I was leaving, but he couldn't tell me more. He said that two of his teammates died by suicide."

Father Hopkins shifted in his chair, and River thought she might have perhaps brought this up a little more delicately. "I'm sorry, Father. I don't want to sound insensitive or ask you to reveal details that may have been given to you in confidence, but Jase seems to believe those suicides have something to do with the murder and his arrest."

Father Hopkins took a moment to gather his thoughts. "Two of Jason's former teammates came to see me quite a while ago. They came within a week of each other. I'd never seen them before." He stopped and picked up a Bible, then continued. "They were desperate, suffering from mood swings, headaches, spurts of anger, anxiety, and even paranoia."

River frowned. She recognized these symptoms from her time in the field. "It sounds like PTSD to me."

"That's what I told them. I also told them that PTSD could be successfully treated with trauma-focused psychological therapy or with medication if they didn't want to go that route."

"Did they take your advice?"

"One decided to try medication immediately. He was

prescribed a new drug that's supposed to have excellent results. I think it helped for a while, but then matters got unexpectedly worse very fast. I used to visit him regularly, or he would pop in to see me." Father Hopkins shook his head. "Then one day he walked through the doors of our building and stood there, bewildered. He didn't know where he was or why he'd come to see me."

"What happened next?"

Father Hopkins opened the Bible. He flipped through the pages, then closed the book. "He died by suicide a few days later." His chin dropped to his chest, and it stayed there for a while. He then turned to River. "I wished I'd found the words to help, and I know that suicide is rejected as an abomination by many religions, including the Catholic faith, but I had this horrible feeling that whatever this man did, he did it to protect his family and his community."

River sat back. She had seen the devastation that untreated PTSD could have on military personnel. She'd spoken to Vietnam vets when she was doing her medical training, and the stories of years of mental torture were harrowing. But the issue was much better understood these days. No serviceman or servicewoman should ever die because of it.

"Do you think he wasn't taking his meds properly or that he wasn't being counseled adequately?"

"I don't know," Father Hopkins said, shaking his head again. "I've helped a lot of soldiers over time. And I'm usually pretty good at it, too."

River nodded. She'd seen the patience and kindness of the man. There was nothing you couldn't talk to him about.

"But this time, I just couldn't figure it out," Father Hopkins finished with a heavy sigh.

River waited before asking her next question. She understood the sadness of losing a soul. She'd felt the same whenever she wasn't able to bring someone out of a war zone alive.

"What about the other man?" she asked softly. "Was it the same?"

Father Hopkins nodded. "Same pattern, but it happened over a much longer period of time, and in that case . . ."

Father Hopkins hesitated, and River sat on the edge of her pew. She needed as much information as possible. "Please, Father. Jason has been wrongly accused. I need to understand why if I'm going to help set him free."

"Well, this other person assembled a lot of material about how the brain functions, and then there were some odd notes." Father Hopkins's gaze dropped to the Bible he was holding in his hands.

River thought about pushing for more details but decided it wouldn't do any good. She'd never seen Father Hopkins so reluctant to share his thoughts with her. The moment she left military service she'd volunteered to work with his organization. Jason had spent a lot of time at the center when he was in rehab and learning to walk again. He thought this was one of the best places he'd ever visited.

"I don't want to push you if you think you shouldn't talk to me about what you've learned or witnessed, but perhaps you could do one thing for me, Father. Would you mind contacting the families of the two SEALs who came to you and telling them that I'd like to speak with them? If they don't want to, then fine, but perhaps I could get the story from them, and that would be less of a worry for you."

"I'm sorry I'm sounding reluctant, but these men were"—Father Hopkins seemed to be looking for a word—"ashamed. I know they shouldn't have been, but they were."

"I understand." River nodded. And she did. "So let's see whether the families will want to talk to me. But for the time being, we need to find Jason a lawyer."

Father Hopkins rose slowly and said, "I'll make some calls, but be aware that the latest suicide happened only a couple of weeks ago. And yes, let me call the law firm I spoke to about providing legal support."

# Chapter Four

River left her duffel bag at the center and walked to Ruthie's All Day Diner, which she'd spotted when she arrived. It was a brand-new place that hadn't been there when she worked at the center. At 1:30 p.m., the diner was half full, and a table near the window had just become free. A young waitress was cleaning the tabletop.

"Do you mind if I sit here?" River asked.

The waitress smiled. "Sure thing. Food or simply coffee?"

"Food, please."

The waitress nodded and handed over a menu she fished from a small shelf near the entrance. River cast an eye over it and decided on a Cuban sandwich with a side salad. The friendly waitress left to place the order, then returned to the table with a pitcher of coffee and a cup in hand.

"On the house. You're new around here," she said as she poured a cup for River.

"That's sort of true," River said.

"Most people here are regulars, and with the veterans' center next door, we have a steady stream of people," the woman said with a soft southern drawl.

River brought the cup to her lips and took a sip. She groaned with contentment. "Great cup."

The coffee was strong, and it was exactly what she needed. "I'm River, by the way, and no, I'm not a stranger to these parts. I simply haven't been here for a while."

"I'm Betsy," the waitress said with a gracious smile. "I started working here a year ago, just as Ruthie opened this place."

"Then maybe you know my friend Jason Wayne," River ventured. She might perhaps glean some information.

"Jase." The young woman sighed and gave River a grin. "He's great, but I haven't seen him for a while."

River had just found a fan of Jason, it seemed, although she had to admit there was a tinge of uneasiness in that—a little jealousy, perhaps.

"He's not been well" was all River could think to say.

"I hope it's not something bad. He hasn't been his upbeat self for a few weeks."

River pushed the cup of coffee forward for a refill and asked, "In what way?"

Betsy started to sway a little, thinking. "Worried, and uh . . . I don't know . . . maybe a little moody."

She stopped abruptly. She must have felt someone observing her. River didn't turn around to check but gathered that Betsy's boss must have glanced at her and signaled for her to hurry up. Betsy turned away and walked briskly back to the kitchen.

River wrapped her hands around the mug Betsy had given her. It warmed her fingers, and she then realized she hadn't yet taken her jacket off. She released the cup and slid out of the jacket. She took a couple of sips of coffee and turned her mind to what Betsy had said. *Worried . . . moody.* These were not words she associated with Jason. He had been upset and angry at their separation. But even when he was, he would almost certainly not have shown it to someone else. Unless Betsy was a bit more to Jason than a waitress from the diner next door. River shrugged. She was the one who gave him up and set him free to date other women. There was no time for regrets or resentment.

"One Cuban sandwich," a voice announced as a large plate appeared in front of River.

A woman was standing over her with a pot of coffee, pouring into her nearly empty cup. River suspected it must be the diner owner.

"I'm sorry it took time to take your order. Betsy can be a little too chatty sometimes."

"No problem," River replied before she started to tuck into her food.

The woman hesitated but must have thought better of asking any questions. She moved away, leaving River to eat in peace and think about what her next move would be. She picked up her phone and thought about calling Karen. It was morning in Kotzebue, and Karen would be busy helping her community, but she wouldn't mind a call from her *uuma*. River found her friend's name in her list of recent calls and pressed the number to call back. The phone rang a few times, and it flipped to voicemail.

"Hey, Karen. Just thought I'd check how Kotzebue is coping without me," River said. "It's bleak here, and I'm making very little progress."

The sound of a call coming through interrupted River. "Call coming in. Got to go."

She terminated the call and picked up the incoming one.

"Hello, River. It's Father Hopkins. I have some news for you."

"Already?" River answered. Perhaps she was in luck after all.

"It's not about my call to the families of the two SEALs who have lost their lives, but I have the name of a lawyer with a well-established DC law firm, Thompson & Meyer. His name is Reginald Cameron. I'll text you his number and the firm's address as soon as we hang up."

River could have punched the air, but instead she put her sandwich down and checked her watch. She could be with Reginald Cameron within thirty minutes, assuming his firm was close to the Capitol. "That's great, Father. Do you know this guy? I guess he must have a lot of experience."

"I'm sorry; I didn't ask. I thought I needed to tell you as soon as I had a name."

"That's okay. I'm on my way." River thanked Father Hopkins again. A text pinged on her phone: It contained Cameron's law firm's address. She took a final bite of her sandwich, wiped her lips, took a couple of sips of coffee, and stood up. She walked to the counter to pay. Betsy looked worried that perhaps the food wasn't to River's liking.

"Something urgent has come up—I have to run." River smiled and left a generous tip to avoid any misunderstanding.

She hurried to the center again to retrieve her helmet and duffel bag, then made her way to the bike. She secured the bag hastily, donned her helmet, and fired the engine. The address she'd been given meant that she had to cross the Potomac once more and drive deep into Capitol Hill to reach Maryland Avenue.

River zipped up her jacket. The weather had suddenly turned much colder, and she feared it might snow before the end of the day. She turned into the road and sped toward her destination, keeping her thoughts at bay so she could concentrate on the traffic. It was light enough, and she arrived on Capitol Hill much earlier than she'd anticipated. She drove past the Library of Congress and the Supreme Court. The density of buildings and the pristine appearance of it all made her feel uncomfortable. She'd spent so much time as a child and an adult living close to nature or in military barracks that the Hill seemed artificial to her. It wasn't, necessarily, but she'd struggled to adapt to an environment in which Jason seemed to flourish. He was on a mission to make the plight of veterans known. He didn't care what his surroundings looked like or how hostile the people he met might be as long as he could achieve his goals.

River slowed down and turned into Maryland Avenue. She spotted the building from afar and found a space to park close enough to it. She ran across the road diagonally, without waiting for the light, and only stopped when she reached the entrance of the Thompson & Meyer offices. She removed her helmet and hastily ran a hand through her hair.

A couple of women in dark business attire walked out of the building. They each carried a briefcase and were engaged in a lively conversation. River observed them as they walked past without noticing her. Their hair was cut short and looked perfectly combed. Their black winter coats were stylish, perhaps a designer label, and their handbags looked expensive. River spent a moment considering her own appearance. A thick pair of winter pants, motorcycle boots, a winter jacket that looked well worn, and underneath it, a thick pullover. She'd picked it at random yesterday as she was getting ready for her flight to DC but was now pleased that at least it was brand-new and matched the color of her steel-blue eyes.

She once more ran her hand through her hair and made herself ready. She then walked through the revolving doors, slipped inside the turnstile, and went in. A security guard looked her up and down, and she nodded with a smile. When she reached the reception desk, one of the two women manning the desk half lifted her head and said, "For deliveries you need the door to the left of the atrium."

"I'm not here to deliver anything. I'm here to see Reginald Cameron."

The woman who had addressed her lifted her head all the way. She didn't disguise her surprise and asked, "Do you have an appointment?"

"No, I don't, but—"

"Then I'm afraid you have to make one," the woman replied coldly.

"Look. I've just flown from Alaska this morning to see Mr. Cameron. Can't you at least check whether he's around?"

The woman turned to her screen. "I can give you the number of his team's administrative assistant, and you can give her a call."

River closed her eyes for a moment and then decided that perhaps a little anger might be warranted. "I might not look the part . . . Whitney," River said, just as she noticed the woman's name tag pinned to her dress, "but I'm here to ensure that a veteran, a former Navy SEAL who's selflessly served his country, won't be convicted of a crime he hasn't committed. So perhaps you, too, could play your part and make a call."

The woman's eyes flashed in anger as her cheeks reddened and her colleague looked up from her screen. River stood her ground.

She wanted to get right in Whitney's face, but she judged it might perhaps be a little too forceful. Whitney was about to answer, but her colleague had already placed a call and was apparently speaking to someone in the criminal law department of Thompson & Meyer.

"Is Reginald Cameron around?" she asked.

Someone answered her query, and she nodded. "There is someone in the lobby who'd like to speak to him about one of his clients." The woman looked at River, who understood immediately and said, "Jason Wayne."

"The client is called Jason Wayne."

The woman listened again, then put the phone down.

"Mr. Cameron is on his way down," she said.

River smiled. "Thank you. Your help is very much appreciated." She turned away from the reception desk and moved to the waiting area, where expensive settees and chairs were set out for the firm's clients. There was only one older man reading *The Wall Street Journal* in the lobby's far corner. River didn't feel like sitting, so she moved close to the large bay window that formed one of the building's external walls and started watching the passing traffic and pedestrians outside.

Soon the reflected silhouette of a man appeared in the glass. He stopped behind River, a few feet away, and seemed to be waiting. She studied him from where she stood—small, thin, hair cut close to his skull, a man of color as far as she could tell—but, most strikingly, young.

River turned around, and what she saw confirmed her worries. Reginald Cameron was young—very young.

He extended a hesitant hand and gave River a broad smile. "I've just been appointed to represent Master Chief Wayne. Very nice to make your acquaintance."

They shook hands, and River was surprised by how firm his grip was. "River Swift. I'm Jason's ex-fiancée." The word stuck in her throat, and Reginald Cameron seemed to notice. She carried on hastily. "Jason texted me as soon as he was arrested. I arrived from Alaska this morning."

Cameron looked puzzled. "So how is it going to work? I mean, you're not together, but you're sort of here, and—"

"We'll work that out later. What you need do right now is visit Jason, speak to Detective Parker, and ask for a revised blood test."

Cameron scratched his head and said, "Isn't it standard procedure to take a blood test when someone is suspected of murder?"

"I'm sure it is, but we need to ask that an additional substance be tested for," River said. She eyed the man reading his newspaper at the far end of the lobby. Should they really be having this conversation in the middle of the reception area?

"The tests are extensive—I think," Cameron said.

"Do you have an office or somewhere else we could talk?" River said, impatient. "It might be better to discuss this in private."

"Oh—of course." Cameron looked around as though he wasn't sure where to go and then walked to reception. He spoke to the woman who had called him. She checked her computer and seemed to be giving him directions, then passed him a badge. River started walking toward him.

"We've got a room over here," he said as she reached him. He handed her the badge, and they both went through a second set of turnstiles. They turned to the left and walked down a long corridor, Cameron carefully reading the number on each door. He stopped in front of one, pushed the door open gingerly, then thrust it wide open and extended his hand, inviting River in.

"Please," he said with more confidence. He moved to a side of the room where there was an impressive display of coffee, tea, and various snacks. "Can I offer you anything?"

River leaned against the large table at the center of the room. Any minute now she was going to lose her temper.

"No. I don't want a goddamn coffee, or a cookie, or anything else. I need you to get to the police station on Alabama Avenue or to the DC Jail if we're too late for that arraignment hearing and speak to your client, my ex-boyfriend, and make sure he doesn't get convicted of a crime he did *not* commit." Her voice had risen gradually as she spoke, and Reginald Cameron stopped in the middle of the room, not knowing what to do.

"I . . . I'm going to do that as soon as I can," he said. "I mean find out about the arraignment and—"

"No, Reggie– you don't mind if I call you Reggie, do you?" River didn't wait for a response. "You're gonna do it now. It's already three thirty. I've got a motorcycle, so I can get you there by four. You speak to Jason to get his side of the story, and then you ask that he be tested for Rohypnol. Can you do that?"

Reggie straightened up and said, "I'm an attorney with the District of Columbia. I know what I need to do."

"And how many times have you done this before?" River asked, locking eyes with the young man.

Reggie's sudden confidence melted away as he said, "Once." He shifted on his feet and then continued. "But it was a difficult case, and—"

River lifted a hand to interrupt him. "I don't want to know. We'll talk about your track record later. Let's get to Washington Highlands first. Then we can talk."

River turned around, got to the door, and opened it. "What are you waiting for?" she asked a stunned Reggie.

He shook himself out of it and hurried toward the door. "I need to get my coat."

"And if you could borrow a motorcycle helmet, that would be good," River said, then added as he was walking toward the elevators, "Don't do a disappearing act on me, Reggie, or I'll come and find you no matter where you're hiding."

Reggie stepped into one of the elevators. River followed the floor numbers displayed on a screen next to the Up button as the elevator rose. It stopped on the third floor. She decided she'd wait ten minutes, and if he hadn't come back by then, she would go up there and find the young man herself.

The security guards who'd been standing at the door of the building stopped in front of the turnstiles. River wondered whether

Reggie had called security and asked them to remove her from the building. Her stomach tightened. What would she do if she lost Reggie's help?

But soon another elevator door opened, and Reggie stepped out of it. He'd already put his coat on. In one hand he held a helmet and in the other a brand-new briefcase. River managed to hide her relief and said, "Let's go. We've already lost fifteen minutes."

The young man nodded and followed her. She said goodbye with a smile to the receptionist who'd helped and walked out of Thompson & Meyer with Reggie in tow. They remained silent until they reached the bike. She turned around to check that he was following. Reggie had stopped and was grinning.

"It's a Yamaha Super Ténéré. That's a cool bike," he said as he was putting his helmet on.

"You know much about bikes?" River replied as she donned her own helmet.

Reggie shrugged. "Just a bit."

There was more to this story, it seemed, but River would have to wait for the time being. She secured Reggie's briefcase on top of her duffel bag and straddled the bike.

"You know what to do, right?" she asked him.

He gave her a thumbs-up and sat behind her. River started the motorbike with a hard kick and eased it onto Maryland Avenue. The roads to Washington Highlands were getting a little busier, but she managed to make good progress, weaving the bike through the flow of traffic. She wasn't taking any chances, though, with a passenger on the back. Reggie needed to get to the police station in one piece, both physically and mentally.

River parked the bike in the same place she had that morning. She removed her helmet and turned toward Reggie. He flipped the visor up and smiled.

"I thought you might be a bit less tame, especially once we crossed the river."

"What do you mean?" she said as she dismounted. "We're not on a goddamn racetrack."

Reggie shrugged and retrieved his briefcase from the back. "Nothing wrong with a bit of speed."

River pointed to the Seventh District station, and they walked to the entrance—River with her helmet in hand and Reggie with his briefcase.

"Remember, you need to get Parker to test Jason's blood for Rohypnol."

Reggie rolled his eyes. "I might be new, but I'm not a complete idiot."

They entered the lobby. The same woman was manning the reception desk. This time, though, she didn't greet River with a smile but immediately made a call—River guessed to Detective Parker.

Reggie glanced at River. He rubbed his free hand on his coat and cleared his throat. River bent toward him and murmured, "Don't forget that you're a hotshot attorney with the District of Columbia."

Reggie didn't reply, his eyes fixed on the door that would open any minute to let Detective Parker through. After a few seconds, Detective Parker walked out, stopped for a second, and broke into a smile.

"Reginald Cameron," he said, his smile broadening. "And how is your pop? Keeping out of trouble?"

River swiveled toward Reggie. No time to clarify the situation, though.

Reggie's face turned inscrutable. "Good afternoon, Detective Parker. I am here to see my client Jason Wayne."

Parker made a grand gesture toward the back of the building. "Just in time to get your client to court."

Reggie took his time going through the door that Parker was keeping open, and they both disappeared. River caught the receptionist's snigger. She fired her a look that caused the woman to return to her computer screen. River kept looking at her for a moment to drive home the message. Intimidation of any sort would not work on her.

River moved to a corner of the lobby in which a few plastic chairs had been assembled to create a reception area. The seats were screwed to the floor, an attempt to ensure that people visiting the station—suspects or relatives—couldn't use them as weapons. She hadn't realized until then, but a young woman with a child in her arms was seated on one of the chairs. She was rocking her baby slowly, eyes cast in the distance.

River chose a seat a few chairs away from her. The woman didn't notice River, or perhaps she just chose not to. The baby made a small noise, and the woman increased the speed of the rocking. River's heart pinched. If she followed the course her life was taking, she would almost certainly forfeit having a family.

The door through which Reggie and Parker had disappeared opened. River frowned. Surely they couldn't be done yet. Instead, a tall, gangly man emerged, followed by a female officer. The young woman with the baby stood up, and she started walking toward the door, hardly acknowledging the apparent release of someone River suspected might be her partner or the baby's father—or both. River watched as the man walked out without calling after his wife-girlfriend. It almost certainly wasn't the first time he'd walked through these doors, and it probably wouldn't be the last.

River let herself drop against the chair. She took her cell phone out of her pocket and decided to call the only person she could confide in.

# Chapter Five

"When did she arrive?" Chuck Clery asked, clutching the phone tightly to his ear. He walked away from the limousine his driver had parked a few moments ago along one of Kalorama's side streets. The person on the other end was the thug he'd hired to clean up any messes that happened to stand in his way.

"This morning. From Alaska. She and Wayne used to be an item," Manolo replied.

"What does she do?"

"Ex-military like him, but medic with the air force."

Clery looked around. He'd asked his driver to stop on a stretch of road he knew would be deserted and where eavesdropping would be unlikely. He would destroy the SIM card as soon as he'd finished the call, and the burner phone would go in a trash can.

"I don't like it. Keep an eye on her, and if she's asking too many questions, let me know."

"She's already visited Father Hopkins."

Clery kicked a can of Diet Coke someone had dropped on the ground. It rolled toward the gutter with a clattering sound. He didn't need more interference with his next project. Congress was about to review the annual budget for the US military, and his client expected it would retain the lucrative weapons contracts it had clinched from a competitor a few years ago.

"What else has she been up to?"

"Gone to see the lawyer who's representing Wayne," Manolo said.

Clery gave the news a cruel smile. "Reginald B. Cameron, pro bono attorney with one deal under his belt. A real find. I'm glad Thompson & Meyer still runs its community program. Sponsor some of the poor kids and offer them a career. Good PR. Shit results for the kids, but who cares?"

Manolo grunted in approval, and Clery's smile broadened. Then he grew serious again.

"How about the two beggars?" he asked.

"Still looking for them. Arturo and I found some of their rags, but it looks as though they abandoned them."

"You need to find those two motherfuckers. I don't want any loose ends on this job. You hear me?"

"Understood. We'll find them. I just want to make sure we do this without alerting the rest of the vagrant community we're looking for them."

Clery arched his eyebrows. "We're talking about two fucking tramps. Who cares about the community of vagrants knowing? Anyway, I bet if you offer $100 to find these two, they'll all be lining up to tell you where they are. I want you to deal with those SOBs in the next twenty-four hours."

"We'll find them," Manolo simply said.

Clery bit his tongue. He would have happily reminded Manolo that he was the one shelling out the cash, but Manolo had always delivered, even in the most tricky situations. Still, Clery was paying him more than he'd ever paid anyone before, and for that money he was expecting speed of delivery.

"Call me as soon as it's done, and let me know about the notebook, too. I know it's more complicated to locate, but I need that book."

Clery killed the call, opened the phone, and crushed the SIM card under the heel of his expensive Italian shoe. He scattered the bits with a quick kick and walked toward a large trash can. He took a Kleenex out of his pocket, wiped off his prints carefully, wrapped the phone in the tissue, and threw it in the can. He then glanced at his watch. It was already 4:00 p.m. He needed to make his way back to town for his next meeting. The lobby business was to him a continuous string of meetings interrupted by a few breaks for food, drinks, and, occasionally, sex on the side. He almost never saw his wife and wasn't sure whether that was a good or bad thing. He just didn't have time to think about it.

Clery returned to his limousine, where his chauffeur was waiting.

"Everything all right, Mr. Clery?"

Clery nodded. "Everything under control. Let's get back to DC and the Hill, using a different route."

His chauffeur glanced in the rearview mirror to catch his boss's eyes and nodded. Chuck nodded back. He picked up the briefcase he'd left behind in the car when he made his call. The same vicious smile crossed his lips at the thought of the content of the case and what he was about to do with it.

After what seemed like an eternity fidgeting in her seat, River went outside to call Karen. She updated her friend on what had happened during the day. This reinforced her feeling that it had been an unnecessarily difficult struggle. She hung up and stayed where she'd made her call, leaning against her bike and thinking about her action plan.

She'd reached DC as quickly as possible and was glad she had. But she hadn't followed one of the first rules of engagement she'd been taught during her training, which was to achieve operational readiness. An evaluation of the resources at her disposal needed to come later, but for now, she needed to make sure Reggie revealed all he'd learned from Jason and Parker—Jason's side of the story and Parker's evidence. Then she would give Reggie the boost in confidence he needed. She suspected the young man had more grit than he knew and that he might need a little push to realize this.

A gust of wind threw a loose strand of hair in her face. She shivered, stood up, and returned to the station. Reggie and Parker had been gone for almost two hours: Surely Reggie had had time to speak with Jason. She returned to the seat she'd occupied before and sat down. The receptionist ignored her.

A man in rags walked through the doors with difficulty. He shuffled to the reception desk and asked a question in a low voice. The woman gave a heavy sigh and shook her head. He turned around and shuffled out again. He leaned against the door frame as the doors opened, letting some cold air in. The receptionist lifted her face and frowned. River went to help him, but her sudden move seemed to scare him, so she stepped back and let him go.

"What's with him?" River asked, raising her voice.

The receptionist lifted an eye and said, "He's lost his friend."

"Does he have a safe place to go? It's freezing outside."

"There is a shelter a few streets away," the woman said as she returned to her screen.

River hesitated, but she needed to stay put and wait for Reggie. Just then the door at the back of the reception area opened and Reggie walked out with Detective Parker. Parker stopped just as they crossed the threshold. He shook hands with Reggie and walked back in. Reggie turned to River and hesitated. He then shook his head and walked to her.

"It was a tough meeting," he said as he reached her. "The court hearing is in a couple of hours' time."

She stopped herself from firing the thousands of questions she had and instead laid a hand on the young man's shoulder and said, "You and I need a coffee."

They left the station and walked in the direction of River's bike. "Let's get out of this place."

Reggie nodded. He and River got on the bike. She fired it and eased the bike into the evening traffic. Driving around DC proved more complicated as they hit rush hour. She still managed to make good time, and they found themselves in front of Father Hopkins's center forty minutes later.

River parked the bike near the entrance again and started

walking toward Ruthie's All Day Diner. Reggie followed, and they entered and made their way to a table at the far end of the room.

They both sat down in silence and waited for the waitress to take their order. Betsy was still around. She came to the table, pad in hand and looking serious, but she gave River a wink.

"Coffee for me," River said.

Betsy turned to Reggie. The young man was perusing the menu. He put it back where it belonged and said, "Can I get a coffee with four blueberry pancakes and a double helping of ice cream, please?"

River raised an eyebrow, and he said, "Meeting with a client does that to me."

"I hope you don't end up with hundreds of clients. Otherwise you won't last past forty."

Reggie ran a hand over his closed-cropped hair a few times and then said, "If I keep my job at Thompson & Meyer, I'll be lucky."

A flash of anger ran through River. She resisted the urge to grab Reggie by the throat and instead curtly said, "You'd better tell me what happened, then. Starting with your conversation with Jason."

Coffee arrived. They both took a sip before Reggie started.

"Jason doesn't remember anything when it comes to the woman who was murdered. Parker showed us photos of the crime scene." Reggie fidgeted with his cup and took a large gulp. River wondered whether he might have felt nauseated at the sight of blood. She drummed her fingers on the table a few times, and Reggie carried on.

"It was a very violent attack. The victim was tied to the bed with plastic restraints. She had been sexually assaulted and then . . . her throat was slit open. Parker insisted that the attack was carried out by someone who knew what he was doing. I mean a professional." Reggie took another sip of coffee. His pancakes arrived, and he grew pale. River slid them to the other end of the table, and he continued.

"Parker told me they're waiting for a tox report and an autopsy report. Tox report for the victim and for Jason, but Parker thinks she'd been doing drugs before she was killed."

"And why does he think that?" River asked.

"He didn't say."

"But surely he must disclose the reason to you."

Reggie gave it some thought and then shook his head. "Not unless it's evidence that will incriminate Jason."

"And what does Jason say about all this? Apart from the fact that he doesn't remember anything?"

"The only thing he remembers is stopping a vagrant from stealing his wallet when he woke up in the underpass."

"Did he manage to talk with the vagrant?"

Reggie shook his head. "No. He was still too woozy, and then the cops arrived, and he fled the scene."

"Did he tell you why he fled the scene?"

"He was covered in blood. He realized it wasn't his." Reggie waited a moment and said, "I buy the idea that he was roofied. I've seen a lot of that where I come from, unfortunately, and what Jason describes is exactly what happens when you take that sort of drug. The problem for him was that he'd never experienced it before, so he didn't know how to react to it, and he ran away to give himself time to think it through."

River was about to take another sip of coffee, but she put the cup down. This was an extremely insightful analysis of what a man like Jason would have done in such circumstances. He was a trained operative, someone who would always either be in control or seek to regain control of a situation. Fleeing would have done exactly that—created time to regain control.

She extended a hand toward Reggie and pressed his arm. "I'm convinced this is exactly what happened, and I'm glad you see it that way. Don't let people tell you you're not good at your job."

Reggie sighed. "But that's not the way Detective Parker sees it, and I'm not sure I managed to persuade him to test Jason's blood for Rohypnol."

"Parker is an asshole. He's probably only interested in putting someone behind bars as soon as possible to get his quota of arrests for the month."

"He's also convinced that Jason had taken hard drugs, too."

"What? He won't ask forensics to test for Rohypnol, but he's gonna test for class A drugs? And why would he do that?"

"Jason told me himself. When they arrested him, they gave him a thorough body check, and they found a needle mark between his toes."

River wasn't sure how to react to that. She could see how it might look from Parker's perspective. A man and a woman doing drugs together, and then . . . the man loses control? She tried to imagine the scene—the drugs, the victim being tied to the bed, and then the knife to her throat. This time it was River who paled. She stood up suddenly and walked out of the diner.

She couldn't bear it. It wasn't the man she knew. They'd never, ever tried drugs together, even weed, and they'd certainly never had had rough sex. Yes, Jason was a tough Navy SEAL, someone who knew how to wield a knife in hand-to-hand combat, but he would never use his skills outside a mission. River felt tears of frustration rising to her eyes. She pushed them down and waited a moment before she walked back into the diner. Reggie was standing at the window.

"Sorry," Reggie said as River sat back down at the table.

Betsy came to top off their coffee mugs. She gave them a smile and asked, "Is everything okay?"

"It's all fine," River said with a nod. Reggie nodded, too, and Betsy took the hint.

"What else did Jason tell you?"

"He doesn't even remember where he met the woman. Parker's men are going through all the bars in Arlington, and if she picked up Jason in one of them, they'll find it for sure."

"And who is this woman?"

"She's called Jane White. An assistant in a small law firm in DC by day. By night, it seems, Ms. White was supplementing her income by selling her services as a call girl. Again, Parker is checking this out, but I reckon it's true." Reggie leaned toward the plate of pancakes River had pushed away and starting tucking into them.

River swirled the liquid in her cup. There wasn't any point in saying it wasn't the Jason she knew. She had to get past her anger.

"What does Jane White's law firm specialize in?"

Reggie swallowed his second mouthful and said, "I don't know, but I'll check. According to Parker, mostly property and divorces, with a bit of litigation thrown in on the side."

"So anybody could have asked her to target Jase and lure him into a trap."

Reggie grimaced. "Except that she ended up dead."

"But she could have been told a pack of lies and forced to get Jason to the hotel in which she was discovered. If the pay was good enough, it might have worked."

"I suppose so. What I don't get is why go all the way from the bar in Arlington to Washington Highlands?"

River took a sip of her lukewarm coffee. "I can't think of any reason right now, but you're right; there must be one."

Reggie took another bite and carried on after a moment. "I asked Jason why he thought he'd been targeted. He said he'd been speaking to the families of two of his former teammates. They'd been diagnosed with PTSD in recent months before they"—Reggie searched for the right words—"took their own lives."

"And did he say why that would have resulted in his being targeted in such dramatic way?"

"He doesn't know. But both families told him they didn't see it coming. Yes, both men were having mental issues, but they were seeking help and had agreed to take medication. Everyone thought this would work."

"I've asked Father Hopkins, the padre who runs Ashton Veterans Center, to inquire whether one of their close relatives would speak to me," River said. "I'm still waiting to hear."

Reggie shook his head. "It's got to be tough."

"Yes, it's tough to not know why your loved one took his own life. It's hard to believe that men who have operated at that level of competence can suddenly give up." River thought for a moment, then said, "Did Jason add anything?"

"Nothing, but I'm not sure he told me everything he knew." Reggie took another sip.

River frowned. "Why wouldn't he?"

"I don't know. I did tell him that all he said to me was confidential and that I couldn't and wouldn't disclose it. But he just told me that was all he could think of."

River finished her cup of what was now cold coffee. Reggie had opened a world of possibilities about Jason's mindset she didn't want to face.

"Parker told me the autopsy would be done by the end of tomorrow and that he would get a prelim tox report tomorrow evening," Reggie said.

"It takes twenty-four hours for Rohypnol to degrade in the blood of a victim. If Parker didn't request a test of that substance when you asked him to, then it will be too late," River said, glancing at the clock on the wall of the diner.

Reggie chewed his lower lip, thinking. "Perhaps I could send a formal request by email, so that if Parker doesn't do it, then it can come back to bite him."

"That's a great idea, Reggie," River said. "But is there a way to get the request to the CSI lab Parker uses and ask them directly?"

"I'm not sure we can make a direct request," he said slowly, "but it might put Parker under more pressure."

"What are the consequences if you file that request with the lab, apart from pissing Parker off?"

"Might mean I have the shortest career of all interns at Thompson & Meyer," Reggie said before finishing his last bite of pancake. "On the other hand, I rate my chances of having a career there to be rather low anyway. I'll find out what lab Parker is using and pay them a visit." He wiped his mouth with a small paper napkin. "I guess I'd better be going, then. I'll grab a cab from the street. I wouldn't want to miss my client's arraignment hearing."

River hesitated, then simply said, "Thanks, Reggie."

He left the diner, and River found herself alone at the table. The place was getting busier. She spotted a couple of men who, judging by their prostheses, she assumed were veterans. Another man was in a wheelchair, yet wearing camo cargo shorts and a dark green T-shirt in the middle of winter. They were chatting and seemed in good spirits. The Ashton Center made a difference, and she was glad she'd contributed to it, even if for a short while.

River hadn't heard from Father Hopkins, and she now wondered whether that meant bad news. She could understand why families might not want to talk to her. She no longer was an air force medic. She no longer was part of the veterans' center, and, perhaps even worse, some may have heard of her breakup with Jason, which would do little for her credibility.

River finally stood up and went to the counter to pay. Betsy's shift must have been over. Another waitress took her payment, and River left the diner. She walked to the center and found Maria still manning the reception desk.

She greeted River with a smile. "He's running a session at the moment. He'll be finished in a few minutes. Would you like to wait?"

"Please, and I'd like to pick your brain about a place to stay. I haven't had time to book anything."

Maria took a moment to think. She plucked a pink Post-it from a stack and wrote a few words on it. She handed it over to River. "It's not luxurious, but it's clean. That's where servicemen go when they come here and need a place to stay."

River picked up the piece of paper and read the address. It was a couple of blocks away from the center. "That's very helpful—thank you."

The sound of voices told River that Father Hopkins's support group must have broken up. She gave Maria a quick nod and moved farther inside the building. She saw men walking out of a room, some in small groups, some by themselves. She waited for a few minutes at the door and then stuck her head through the opening. Father Hopkins was putting chairs away and didn't turn around until River was halfway through the room. He gave her a tired look, and she stopped in her tracks.

"I haven't forgotten you," he said as he laid two folding chairs against the wall. "I've left a message but haven't heard back yet."

"I understand," she said.

"Did you manage to see Jase?"

"It was so quick. We didn't have much time. But I met his lawyer."

"That sounds more encouraging," Father Hopkins said.

"Have you used Thompson & Meyer before?"

Father Hopkins shook his head. "No, but they contacted me recently to offer a large contribution. They also said they handled pro bono cases and that if some of the veterans needed legal representation, they would be happy to help."

"How recently was recently?"

"Two weeks or so ago."

River frowned and wondered—coincidence? A very generous contribution would have put the law firm at the forefront of Father Hopkins's mind and created a sense that they really meant to help. They'd be the perfect choice. Or perhaps she was being suspicious for nothing.

"Where are you staying, River?" Father Hopkins asked. "I presume Jason's apartment has been sealed by the police."

"And I don't have a spare key anyway," she replied.

"I do. Jason left a set of keys with me just in case he might need it. He locked himself outside his place a few times in the past couple of months, so he thought it might come in handy."

"I'm sure the police have done what they needed to do by now," River said. "If you don't mind letting me have his keys, I'll see whether I can use his place."

Father Hopkins nodded. "They're in my office desk."

They both walked out of the meeting room and passed a few more rooms that were in use with their doors closed. Father Hopkins went into his office and unlocked a drawer with a key he produced from his jacket pocket. He rummaged through an open box, found what he was looking for, and handed over a set of keys to River.

"Here you are. I'm sure Jason won't mind. Perhaps you should contact the police and ask."

River took the keys and pushed them into her pants pocket. "Will do," she said with a sly smile.

*I'm taking a look at what's in Jason's apartment whether Parker likes it or not.*

She thanked Father Hopkins and took her leave. She grabbed the duffel bag she'd left at reception and waved goodbye to Maria.

River wasn't sure what she expected to find in Jason's home—reassurance or evidence.

## NOTEBOOK–AFGHANISTAN DEPLOYMENT

June 2021
SEAL Team 1

The alarm went off this morning at 0500 hours. I'm sharing with Javier and could hear him getting up. He called my name a few times, but I found it too hard to open my eyes. My mind and my body don't seem to be in sync with each other anymore. It took me a while to sit up in bed and get going.

I'm glad that today was only a waiting-around day. Our next target has been elusive, and the intel we're getting from the men who've infiltrated the Taliban is contradictory. I had an argument with one of the guys about this. They think the Afghans don't push themselves hard enough, but they risk their lives and those of their families to help us . . .

I'm back in my room jotting down these notes, and my eyes already feel heavy with sleep. It's only 1900 hours, but I need the rest, although I suspect I might wake up in a couple of hours' time. Sleep is gradually becoming an issue. I won't be taking more pills to help me sleep. I must find a better way.

J

# Chapter Six

River secured her duffel bag on the back of her motorcycle. She zipped her jacket up against the cold and put her thick bikers' gloves and helmet on. The weather had turned bitter now that the sun had set and it was dark. Still, the night sky was clear, and the snow she'd dreaded when she'd first arrived in DC hadn't materialized. She hit the road and made a U-turn, changing directions.

Traffic had built up, and she felt the frustration of having to contend with vehicles standing in the way of a good run. She wished for a stretch of open road where she could let the bike loose. Instead, she allowed herself to zigzag from lane to lane. The driver of a large SUV sounded his horn. She grumbled but slowed down and spent the rest of the journey exasperated yet safe.

She finally turned onto the street where Jason and she had lived. River parked the bike a couple of blocks away and walked the rest. Nothing had changed since the day she'd left the apartment they shared. The trees were bare, and the lawns that lay in front of most houses and small apartment buildings had turned black and muddy.

River's heart quickened when she arrived at the two-story building. The red brick of the facade had been freshly pointed, and the sandstone on the sides had been cleaned up. The porch looked inviting, with its evergreen shrubs and flowerpots full of cyclamens. River didn't know a home could look so inviting and comfortable until Jason had introduced her to his place. Her parents had always favored practical over beautiful. She hadn't suffered from it and rather liked an environment where everything had a purpose. But living in a pretty place with some decorative touches had, at least for a time, mesmerized her.

River stopped for a moment a few feet away from the door. Lights were on in all the apartments except one—the one where she and Jason had lived. She climbed the couple of steps that led to the main entrance and used one of the keys to open the door and enter. The familiar aroma of the food her former neighbors enjoyed cooking slowed her down. She bit her lip and then climbed the staircase in front of her two steps at a time.

When she arrived at the top of the stairs, she turned left and hurried to the door, only to stop abruptly at the sight of yellow police tape marked CRIME SCENE—DO NOT ENTER. River hesitated for only a few seconds. She used the second key to open the apartment door, then ducked underneath the tape and entered Jason's apartment. She closed the door softly behind her, took her cell phone out of her jacket pocket, and switched the flashlight on.

Parker's CSI team had gone through the place thoroughly. She lifted her phone to eye level and ran the beam of light across the open-plan main room and kitchen. Books lay on the floor or on tables and had not been put back on the shelves. The cushions of the sofa and armchairs had been overturned and most kitchen cabinets left open. River frowned. It no longer was her home, but she still resented the intrusion into a place she had once called hers and cared for.

River pushed the anger away. She needed to remain clearheaded, just the way she would if she were treating a wounded soldier for a life-threatening injury. She had always managed to find that place within herself—the one that allowed her to remain calm and efficient. Nothing mattered but saving a life.

River went through the room methodically. She didn't replace the books or the items that had fallen from the open cabinets in case the police came back to carry out another search. Still, she couldn't help but pick up a picture frame that lay on its side. The photo of Jason and two of his teammates brought a smile to her lips. The three *J*'s—Jason, Jake, and Javier. These three were inseparable until Jason almost lost his leg and ended up with a permanent limp. Even then, Jake and Javier would visit, but it would never be the same.

She put the frame back down, but upright, and kept going through the room. There was nothing she could spot that felt helpful or telling. She stopped close to the set of French doors that led to a small balcony. The table and chairs they used to have dinner on were still out there, looking lonely and forgotten. The curtain hadn't been drawn in front of the doors, so River retraced her steps to avoid being seen and moved to the kitchen and then the bathroom. She was about to give up her search when she shone her light on the medicine cabinet, which had been left open.

The contents had been emptied. The CSI team must have decided that the various products she and Jason had stocked there were of interest, although she recalled that neither one of them was big on medication. There was some acetaminophen and antacid tablets, disinfectant, cotton balls, and a box of bandages. For a medic, River didn't keep much. She inspected the residue of what must have been a spillage and stopped dead. She ran her gloved finger over the fine white powder and rubbed it between her index finger and thumb. Although she'd never been a user herself, she'd been taught how to recognize cocaine. Being a medic also meant being alert to the use of class A drugs.

River gingerly dipped the tip of her tongue into the powder. The immediate rush it sent through her body told her all she needed to know. The police had found cocaine in Jason's bathroom. She would now have to decide whether it had been planted or whether the man she once knew as clean had turned to drugs. River shook her head and resented her own suspicions. How could she doubt? Even when he was in pain throughout his recovery from surgery, Jason had refused the use of hard drugs, fearing addiction.

*But then people change . . .*

She shook her head again. Jason's turning to drugs didn't feel credible, but Detective Parker could use the presence of cocaine in

Jason's apartment as evidence of his guilt. River, for her part, saw it as evidence that Jason had been framed. She took a bandage out of its box, removed the protective plastic, and ran the sticky part over the remaining powder, lifting most of it. She wasn't quite sure what she would do with it, but perhaps it would prove helpful. She slid the bandage back in its wrapper and stuffed it into her pants pocket.

River then moved to the bedroom. She slowed, memories of better times flooding back. She pushed them down before they could take hold. She didn't want to recall how magical their lovemaking had been or how heartbreaking it had been to fall asleep alone when Jason spent the night on the sofa. She pushed the door open and was surprised by the untidiness of the room. The bed had been stripped bare, and clothes had been left discarded on the floor. Here again, the CSI team had been thorough, but she wondered whether they'd found Jason's hidden weapons cache.

She walked to a small alcove in the wall where they'd set up a set of speakers and a USB port where they could plug in an iPhone and play music. There was also a small CD player. The CD player was a little old-fashioned, but they liked it. Below the shelf that housed the speakers, Jason had built some other shelves where they displayed their CDs. The CDs had been moved around, some falling to the floor, but no one had thought of removing the shelves altogether. River knelt and took the CDs and shelves out. She pressed hard against what looked like the wall, then felt the mechanism release and click. She slid a panel sideways, and a small opening appeared.

River directed the beam of her flashlight into the opening. A medium-size case was lying flat on the bottom of the compartment. She leaned forward and pulled it toward her. The word GLOCK was embossed on it. She entered the security code she knew by heart into the keypad, and the lock released. She held her breath for an instant and opened the case. Jason's Glock 19 was still there, complete with two clips. River released her breath and swiftly checked the contents of the compartment again. She found a box of ammunition. She then stuffed the Glock into the inside pocket of her jacket and the clips into the back pocket of her pants. She'd have to carry the ammo in her hand. She replaced the case, shut the wall panel, put back the shelves and CDs, and stood up, looking around quickly.

There was nothing left for her to do here. River went back to the entrance, stopped for a moment next to the front door, and listened for sounds in the corridor. Everything was silent. She switched off her flashlight, stuffed it into her pocket, and cracked the door open. Then she ducked underneath the police tape, locked the door, and hurried downstairs as fast as she could without looking too rushed.

She stuffed the box of ammunition in her duffel bag and was on her way within minutes, riding the motorcycle in the direction of the motel Maria had recommended. She concentrated on finding the place, but no one could miss the large neon sign displaying the name of the hotel—the Arlington Inn. River rode toward the space allocated to motorcycles in the parking lot. She retrieved a chain from underneath the passenger seat, then locked the bike to one of the bars. She removed her helmet, shouldered her bag, and walked to the front of the building. The porch that led to the entrance felt rather grand, but the rest of the place looked like it needed some repairs. Still, the old man at the reception desk confirmed that there were a few rooms left. She chose one with a twin bed and a small kitchenette.

He eyed her bag and asked, "Still in the service?"

River shook her head. "I left almost two years ago."

He stared at her and said, "How long were you in?"

River stared back at him. Despite his age, he looked fit—someone who trained or at least looked after himself. And his sudden alertness made River wonder whether he, too, had served. She resisted just picking up her key without answering. A man like him might come in handy. "Twelve years. Medic with the air force resuscitation specialists—SOS teams."

He nodded appreciatively. "Been to the field to save Navy SEALs."

"Afghanistan, three tours."

"I'm Pablo. Anything you need, you let me know."

He handed over the key, and she disappeared down the corridor. River opened the door of her room, which was on the ground floor. It looked clean, but every piece of furniture must have been secondhand. She dumped her bag on the floor, closed the door, and went to the window. It was overlooking the parking lot, but shrubs had been planted underneath it, making access to the room from outside difficult.

River shrugged her jacket off. She retrieved the Glock and the clips from her pockets and laid them on the small table next to the kitchenette. She sat down on one of the chairs and thought for a moment. She had to check what the tox report said and what the autopsy report said. Reggie hadn't called yet, and she took that to mean he'd failed to get direct access to the information. She picked up her cell phone and dialed his number. Whatever the news, she just had to know.

"I told you it has to be an emergency," Chuck Clery said through gritted teeth. Manolo's call, on his new burner phone, had forced Clery to temporarily excuse himself from a Zoom meeting he didn't want to miss.

"We found one of the beggars and terminated him," Manolo said, sounding unperturbed by Clery's tone.

"That's hardly worth celebrating," Clery whispered as he stood in a secluded part of his office, where he knew couldn't be heard. "The other piece of trash is still alive. He'll be going underground now that he knows his buddy's gone."

"It's getting colder. He won't be able to avoid shelters or soup kitchens for long. It's only a question of time before he resurfaces or freezes to death. Carlos is on the lookout as we speak. But I'm not calling you about that. The woman you asked us to follow has paid a visit to Wayne's apartment in Arlington. She spent half an hour there and then moved to a motel not very far from it."

Clery gripped his cell phone harder. "Would she have found anything there that you didn't find yourself?"

"I don't think so. But it might be worth paying her a visit."

Clery pressed the bridge of his nose with his thumb and fore-finger. "What the fuck is this bitch doing?" It wasn't a question to Manolo but rather a question to himself. Manolo waited for Clery to come to his own conclusion. "She's going to become a pain in the ass. I can see that, so let's not wait until it's too late this time. I'm not taking any chances. Get rid of her."

"She rides a bike," Manolo said.

"Excellent. Bikes are risky in DC traffic. You know what you need to do. Don't call back until after midnight. I have a dinner, and I can't be disturbed."

Clery killed the call and returned to the Zoom meeting he'd had to abandon to take Manolo's call. Nothing much had progressed, it seemed. His major client had decided to take another stand against proposed legislation regarding gun control. "The sanctity of the Second Amendment to the US Constitution has to be preserved," his contact had said, and Clery couldn't agree more. Gavin Newsom, California's governor, had proposed an amendment that would raise the age to buy a gun from eighteen to twenty-one, ban so-called assault weapons, and mandate universal background checks and a waiting period between the purchase of a gun and its delivery. Clery looked at this as an assault on the right to defend oneself, and he regarded America's forty-eight thousand gun-related deaths in 2021 merely the price to pay for that right.

Clery made a couple of points he'd prepared in advance as the meeting progressed, but his mind wasn't focused on the discussion. Instead, he kept returning to what Manolo had told him. This stupid bitch River Swift was starting to get too close for comfort. His stomach tightened at the thought that she might have found the notebook. Clery checked the old clock that sat on his desk, a gift from one of his contacts across the Atlantic. It was already 8:00 p.m. and unlikely that she would do anything with the notebook until the morning, assuming she'd found it. At least if it was she who'd discovered it, he could do something about it. Better this than Detective Parker, even though he knew that Parker was desperate to wrap up the case and improve his standing in the Seventh District.

The meeting kept going for another half an hour. Clery forced himself to look alert and engaged until the very last moment. As soon as the Zoom connection had been severed, he picked up the first thing he found on his desk, this time a box of Tic Tacs, and threw it across the room. The plastic box shattered, sending its contents across the floor.

"Fuck," Clery said, running a hand through his thinning gray hair.

He didn't relish having to neutralize yet another person in the Jason Wayne case; it might attract unwanted attention. Then again, a bike accident was less obvious than a bullet to the head. He hadn't asked Manolo about the way in which the first vagrant had been disposed of, but it seemed to matter less. Who would worry about a tramp's murder?

Clery stood up and put his jacket on. He kicked a few Tic Tacs that lay in the way as he reached the door of his office. His assistant was waiting for him when he opened the door. She stood up abruptly, ran to the closet, and returned with his winter coat. He grunted a form of thank you, then turned into the corridor of the building's fifth floor. The consulting firm he had founded had grown over the years to become one of the powerhouses of the lobbying industry in Washington. Clery had partnered with three other men, but they all ran their business with a large degree of autonomy, recognizing that there were times when an association of like-minded people might be beneficial but that secrecy was equally valuable.

When Clery arrived on the first floor, his chauffeur was waiting for him in the lobby. They both exited through the automatic sliding doors. His chauffeur opened the door of a limo, and Clery climbed into the car. He pushed himself deep into the back seat and leaned his head back on the headrest, closing his eyes. His day was far from over. Although he was returning home, he was due to meet one of the most powerful men he'd encountered in his long career, and that man was interested in the outcome of the Jason Wayne case.

*   *   *

The kettle had just boiled. River moved back to the kitchenette. She'd found that the previous occupant had left a half-empty jar of Starbucks instant coffee. She took one of the mugs that hung from a hook underneath the kitchen cabinet and made herself a cup of strong black coffee. She barely waited for the liquid to cool before she took a sip. She'd just spoken to Reggie, and the call hadn't been a surprise. Jason had been denied bail. She'd protested to start with, but then she realized that his chance to be granted it had always been almost nil—he'd fled the crime scene, and he was an operative trained in evasion. And then the CSI lab that was processing Jason's blood sample and carrying out the autopsy on Jane White wouldn't allow Reggie to view the results first. The man Reggie had spoken to, however, volunteered that the results would be sent the following morning to Detective Parker.

River took another sip, paused a moment to consider her next move, and then placed a call. Karen picked up almost instantly.

"What's new?" Karen's voice sounded a little echoey, and River wondered whether she was in one of her large wooden sheds, preparing food for her dogs.

"I can't be completely sure, but I think Parker hasn't asked the lab to test Jase for Rohypnol."

"So because he's a guy and a former SEAL, Jase can't be duped into taking that stuff? That Parker sounds like an idiot," Karen said.

"I've been to our—I mean Jase's—apartment."

"Should you have gone?"

"Almost certainly not. The police tape was still in place, but I managed to get a key from Father Hopkins."

"Good for you. You've got to check whether the CSI guys are doing their jobs properly. What did you find? I gather you found something, and that's why you're calling."

"I found traces of cocaine in the medicine cabinet."

"Shit," Karen said. River could hear that her friend had just interrupted what she was doing.

"I took a sample on a bandage, but I'm not sure what I can do with it."

"Stupid question, I know, but you're sure it's cocaine?"

"No mistake."

There was a short silence, and then Karen asked, "What are you gonna do?"

"I need to see the tox report and the autopsy report before Parker does, but that might prove a bit complicated."

"And how are you gonna do that? Parker will have precedence over you," Karen said.

"Reggie tried to ask for the results to be sent to him at the same time as Parker, but the lab—or, rather, a certain Dr. Amanda Pike—told him he would have to wait. I still need to find a way, though," River said.

"Right. I know that tone of yours. You're about to do something you shouldn't—again."

River sighed. "The story of my life. And I need some help in doing that thing I'm not supposed to do."

"You've gotta be a bit more specific, Riv."

"I've decided to break into the lab and see what I can gather," River said.

"Well, that's an interesting way to go about it," Karen mused.

"Your help would be very much appreciated," River simply replied.

"Riiiight," Karen said. "Should I also ask for a few tips from my dad? I mean, he's only Kotzebue's chief of police."

"I hadn't thought about that, but that's not a bad idea. He *must* know what the procedure is to obtain forensic evidence."

"Fuck it—I'm in. I need a bit of action. I love helping here in Kotzebue, but I miss the front line," Karen said.

River raised her free arm in victory. "When can you get down here?"

"I'll speak to Danny. It's an emergency, so he'll have to get me down to DC in one go."

"You mean fly you to Washington on his empty ATR?" River frowned.

"Yeah. Danny owes me, and I'm sure he'll pick up some business on the way back."

"Okay, *uuma*," River said with a smile. "See you tomorrow morning."

She hung up and took a sip of coffee, thinking. It was getting late, and she didn't relish the idea of going for a run along streets full of cars. Instead, she would do a floor routine and use the bed frame as an anchor for sit-ups. Still, she wasn't done with the last bit of work she needed to do to prepare for Karen's arrival. Reggie had given her the address of the CSI lab Detective Parker was using. River thought a reconnaissance mission was in order to determine how she and Karen might enter the lab.

River stood up and put her jacket on. She thought about the gun and ammo: Leaving the gun behind wasn't an option. She wasn't sure how safe the motel room might be. She could perhaps risk leaving the ammo in her duffel bag, though. She quickly opened the padlock securing the bag and stuffed the extra clip into it, preferring to slide the gun in her backpack. She zipped the duffel shut again.

She took her helmet and her keys. Before closing and locking the door, she slid a hair strand she'd just plucked out between the door and the door frame. She wasn't sure how effective this would be, but an unsavvy intruder might not notice a blond hair falling to the ground.

On her way out, she saw that Pablo wasn't at his desk. She walked to the parking lot, unlocked her bike, and joined DC's heavy traffic. She crossed the Potomac once more and moved in the direction of Capitol Hill to get to the lab, on Hill East.

A traffic light turned red as she was about to go through. She applied the brakes hard, and the bike slid sideways, almost hitting a car. The woman driver looked at River with petrified eyes, and River lifted her visor to apologize. The woman gave her a weak smile but let River go ahead when the lights turned green. River grumbled to herself. She'd be no use to Jason dead . . . *So get a grip.*

On the approach to Potomac Avenue, River slowed down. She'd memorized the address, which she found on Google Maps. She was getting close. She decided to drive past the lab's building and then turn back and drive past it a second time. The tall structure she'd spotted from afar looked more like a landmark than an office building—a complex construction in which several wings branched off from a main tower. River circled the block a few times. The place had three main entrances and a couple of back entrances. All of this looked promising.

She parked her bike a block away and retraced her steps. Most of the office windows were dark, but a few were still lit. River walked to entrance B, removed her helmet, and stopped. The sliding glass doors were shut, and a security guard was watching something on his cell phone, sitting at the reception desk. He briefly lifted his head when River appeared at the door, but then returned to his phone. She knocked against the glass, and this time the guard put the phone down. He got up, unhappy.

"The building is closed," he said through the doors.

River nodded. "I'm sorry to disturb, but I've got a delivery tomorrow. It's my first day on the job, and I'm making sure I know where I'm supposed to go."

The man frowned and said, "Which company are you looking for? There are ten businesses in this wing alone."

River squinted, looking as though she was making an effort to remember. "Jackson Laboratories," she said.

"They're on the second floor, open from eight to eight." The guard pointed toward the upper floors. "One of them is still up there," he said, sounding a little more amenable.

"That's really helpful. Is there a delivery entrance?"

The guard thought for a moment and then said, "Deliveries are at the back, but with Jackson Labs most people go to their front desk."

"Thanks a bunch. That's great." She gave him a thumbs-up and smiled.

The guard nodded and returned to the reception desk. River crossed the road and spotted a tree almost opposite. She hid in the shadow of its thick trunk and started to wait. She raised the collar of her jacket as the wind picked up. She'd stay put for as long as it would take.

Half an hour later, a light went off on the second floor of the building, and a few minutes after that a woman walked out. She waved goodbye to the guard as she zipped up her parka. River caught sight of a white lab coat underneath it. River waited a moment and started walking in the same direction as the woman. The woman reached the Potomac Avenue Metro station and disappeared down its stairs. River broke into a jog and caught up with the woman at the entrance. She didn't have a Metrorail card, so she had to break her tail, but she noticed the woman turning left, toward the Blue Line.

The station was empty, and she thought about jumping the turnstile. But she wasn't sure what she'd achieve by following a lab technician. She returned to the office block in search of a back entrance she might use. She spotted what she was looking for but kept her distance. The set of security cameras over the door would make it more difficult for her and Karen. River noticed that two large dumpsters had been rolled outside the back door. Tomorrow would be trash-collection day, something she would bear in mind. She spent a few more minutes surveying the area. There was nothing more to glean, and River didn't want to be noticed. On her way back to her bike, she glanced at her phone and smiled.

**Strapped to a crap seat at back of empty plane . . . Danny not happy. May have to administer TLC in the not-too-distant future! ETA 8:11 a.m.**

River still had one more stop to make before returning to the Arlington Inn to firm up her plan.

# Chapter Seven

**Tuesday, January 18**

The alarm on River's phone rang at 6:00 a.m. She rolled onto her back, eyes closed. By the time she'd returned to the Arlington Inn with her purchases, exercised, and had a quick dinner, it was the wee hours of the morning. River went to bed thinking about her first rather frustrating day in DC and had finally fallen asleep.

She stretched and got up slowly, blinking her eyes open, then went straight to the kitchenette to brew a cup of coffee and kick-start her day. She had visited a Walmart on the way home from Jackson Laboratories and bought some food as well as the items of clothing she would wear to gain access to the lab. Just as important, she found that the strand of hair she'd placed in the door frame hadn't dropped to the floor. No one had visited her room while she was away, and the box of ammunition was still in her bag.

River opened the duffel bag, which she hadn't bothered to unpack yet, and chose a thick tracksuit, a hoodie, and a pair of winter running shoes. She put on the tracksuit, tied her shoes, and went through a short stretching routine. She thought about taking the gun with her but decided otherwise. She stuffed it into her duffel bag, closing its padlock securely. She left her room, locked the door, and walked out of the hotel. Pablo again wasn't at the desk. River gave the lobby a cursory check. She spotted two surveillance cameras and assumed he was in the back, keeping an eye on the reception area from monitors installed there.

She started what she hoped would be a three-mile run along streets she no longer was familiar with and veered toward veterans' center. She wasn't sure why she needed to have a destination. Perhaps running in the city meant running to or from something. The year she'd spent with Jason in DC had been made easier for her because Jason had settled there before her and become familiar with the place.

River accelerated along a stretch of sidewalk that was almost empty, concentrating on her run. She kept going steadily after that until she reached the center. She slowed down to a walk and then stopped in front of the main entrance. It was early, and the place was still closed.

River walked around to the back of the building and found the small green space she remembered there. The shrubs had been trimmed, and the two benches that formed a semicircle inside the small garden looked exactly as she recalled them. Despite the cold, River sat down. Her heart rate slowed, and her mind grew still. She could never explain to friends or even her parents what it meant to spend time on her own. She'd been branded odd and selfish. She didn't think she was either. She just was different, yet she'd been tempted to try to fit in, get married, have a family . . .

Movement in one of the rooms inside the center caught River's attention. The place was still dark, but someone was walking around. She stood up and approached the window of the room where she'd spotted a shadow. She stood on her tiptoes and looked in. It was Father Hopkins's office. But the place looked empty. She walked around the building, peering through each window. The rooms were quiet. She came to the front door and gave it a push. It was locked. She tried the doorbell on the side of the main entrance, but no one answered. She took her cell phone out and called Father Hopkins. Her call went to voicemail. River didn't leave a message but instead went around the premises again. All was calm. She shook her head. Perhaps she was just imagining things.

She waited for another minute or so and then started her jog back to the motel. She'd check on Father Hopkins in an hour's time.

When she entered the Arlington Inn, out of breath from the last push on her run, Pablo was there. He nodded a good morning, and she waved back. Once in her room, she took a shower, then changed into the pair of dark pants and the dark pullover she'd just bought from Walmart. It looked cheap, but it would do the trick. She checked her phone and noticed a text from Karen.

> **Just landed . . . Danny has surpassed himself or else he just wants to get rid of me. Either way, I'm early. New ETA, 8:00.**

River turned to the large bag that held her purchases from the night before—two pairs of coveralls and caps that looked like the kind worn by sanitation workers, two white lab coats, one short black wig, a lighter, a small bottle of isopropyl alcohol, and a couple of newspapers. They were all set for their "incursion" into Jackson Laboratories.

The pot of coffee River had just prepared was on the table, ready, when Karen knocked at the door. River opened it, and they gave each other a bear hug followed by the requisite slap on the back.

"You look sharp for someone who's spent the night strapped to an old seat on Danny's ATR," River said with a grin.

Karen yawned and stretched. "I made myself comfortable at the back of the plane with some old rags. Danny and his copilot didn't appreciate that. Apparently I hogged all the blankets, and they had none left for their own half-hour rest."

She went to dump her own duffel bag in the far corner of the room, then took off her bulky winter jacket and woolly hat. She ruffled her thick dark hair a few times and joined River in the kitchenette.

"They thought you were going to play flight attendant and serve them coffee and food?"

Karen only laughed as a reply. River poured two cups of coffee and pushed one toward Karen. They both sat down, took a few sips in silence, and then Karen asked, "What's the plan?"

They decided against taking the bike. Instead, they rode the Blue Line up to Potomac Avenue. They both wore the coveralls and caps River had bought the night before and slowed down as they approached the Jackson Laboratories building. River had checked the trash-collection times for the area, and they were just in time for the sanitation truck's arrival. Karen pushed her cap further down her forehead. She should have looked nervous, but instead River thought her friend was enjoying herself.

The truck turned the corner of one of the connecting streets, and they both stopped to observe the men moving around the truck and think about how they could follow them without being spotted.

"Let's cross the street and wait at the back of the A wing," River said. She'd surveyed the entire building on Google Street View the night before and realized that the dumpsters were all gathered near the back door of the wing closest to the road—the B wing.

They moved swiftly, crossing the road just as the truck was approaching. They huddled in the recess of the A wing and waited. Three men came to the B wing back door and dealt with the largest dumpsters first. River murmured, "They've got to collect the hazardous waste from the lab separately. That type of waste won't be left outside. One of them will have to call for someone to open the back door. That's our chance."

Just as River had predicted, one of the men pressed an intercom button, waited for a response, and bent forward to acknowledge he'd heard it. The back door clicked open, and he moved in. He rolled a couple of smaller garbage bins out and held the door open with his foot. One of his colleagues picked up the bins and rolled them forward toward the slowly moving truck. It stopped for a moment as the bins from the laboratory were hooked to its side to be emptied. The man who'd emptied them returned to the back door. His colleague pushed them inside and walked out again, letting the door slowly close.

River left her hiding place and ran silently to the door, darting in before it closed completely. The men were still close by but busy chatting as they jumped on the back of the truck. She slid into the corridor and waited for a moment. She made sure the men had gone, then held the back door open for Karen. Inside, they stopped, taking in their surroundings.

The place was silent apart from the buzz of the overhead lights that ran along the corridor. They moved farther down the passageway and stopped at one of the doors that seemed to lead inside the main building. They took a moment before going any farther, but then Karen nodded, and River opened the door. The smell of coffee and food told River that they must be close to a kitchen. She could hear voices in the distance. Perhaps some of the security guards and receptionists were taking a break. Karen moved next to River, letting the door close behind her.

A door to what she thought must be the kitchen opened. A woman in a gray suit appeared on the threshold. She was laughing and holding a mug in her hand. She turned serious the moment she noticed the two women.

"Can I help you?" she said, glancing toward the inside of the kitchen, perhaps preparing to call on one of the security guards.

River said, "I'm sorry to trouble you, ma'am, but we were told that there is more hazardous waste to be collected from Jackson Laboratories. We were told they didn't have time to take it down before the dumpster came to collect."

"No one told me," the woman said, suspicious.

Karen shrugged. "We've just been told by the guys that we had go inside and check, but if it's inconvenient we'll tell them it's gonna have to be done tomorrow."

One of the security guards appeared at the kitchen door. "What's that?"

"More waste to be collected from Jackson."

"Not surprised. These guys can never get their act together," he said. "Just call the second-floor receptionist and tell them we're send-ing two people to collect some waste."

The woman turned around and started walking toward the lobby. "Follow me." She pushed open a door and walked to the re-ception desk, River and Karen in tow. Her colleague at the desk looked a little surprised, but the woman simply laid her mug down, picked up her headset, and dialed a number.

"I have two people down here to collect hazardous waste," she said. She nodded at the lab's answer and hung up. "I'll open the turnstile for you. The lab's on the second floor."

River and Karen went through the turnstile, took an elevator to the second floor, and got out. The Jackson receptionist was busy on a call when they reached her desk. She gave them a quick smile and mouthed "Sorry." River gestured to the woman that she needed to use the bathroom. The receptionist nodded and pointed the way toward the far end of the lobby.

River thanked her and disappeared through a side corridor that led to the restrooms. She dashed into the last stall, opened her cov-eralls, and took out the small bag hidden inside. She wiggled out of the coveralls, took a lab coat out of the bag, and put it on. She'd al-ready arranged her hair into a low ponytail. She fitted the wig on, picked up a small mirror, and adjusted it further. It wasn't perfect, but it would have to do.

She then retrieved pieces of newspaper, a small bottle of isopro-pyl alcohol—a good fire accelerant—and a lighter from the bag. She gathered the paper on the floor at the center of the stall. She listened for a moment to make sure she was on her own. She couldn't delay any longer. She doused the paper with alcohol, then replaced the bottle in her bag. The smell of the liquid hit her nos-trils, and she recoiled.

She opened the stall door, lit a piece of paper with the lighter, and threw it onto the newspaper. A flame jumped up immediately and spread to the rest of the pile. It all would burn quickly without reaching the walls of the stall, but the acrid smoke it produced should be enough to trigger the building fire alarm.

Within a few seconds, the strident noise of the alarm resounded through the second floor. River left the bathroom and moved to the corner of the corridor that led to the lobby. Karen was talking with a man who looked like one of the lab technicians, but the fire alarm interrupted their conversation. The receptionist stood up, speaking with urgency to Karen and the man. The smell of smoke was now spreading to the lobby. The receptionist released the turnstiles. She ran to a closet and put on her fire warden jacket and moved inside the office. The man walked to the fire exit, and Karen gave a short nod toward the bathroom, indicating she wanted to check on River.

As soon as he disappeared, River ran to Karen and threw a white lab coat to her. Karen stripped off her coveralls and put the white coat on. They then both walked into the lab as some of the staff were preparing to leave.

"It's not a drill," a young man said to them as they entered the main office.

River nodded and said, "Just need to secure the evidence I was running tests on."

The young man didn't bother to argue. He was already out the door. River and Karen attracted a few looks as they walked against the flow of foot traffic. Karen spotted a meeting room that had just emptied, and they went in, crouching behind the door, waiting. The flow of traffic dwindled within a few minutes, and the office became eerily quiet. Karen stood up slowly.

"I'll do reconnaissance first. If I get caught, that'll divert attention, and you can still go ahead."

She left the room, and River listened, worried Karen might meet someone on the way out. But Karen gave a low whistle and called to River, "Coast is clear—let's go."

River stepped out of the office and joined her friend in the largest of the corridors. Jackson Laboratories was laid out as a series of rooms along two long passageways. River turned toward the left and said, "I'll take this corridor. You take the other one. We're looking for Dr. Amanda Pike."

She walked fast along the hallway and found the nameplate she was looking for at the far end. She pushed on the door handle, fearing it might be locked, but it wasn't. She ran to the desk, sat down on the large office chair, and immediately checked the computer screen. She was in luck: The screen hadn't locked down yet. The file that was open wasn't Jason's, though. She closed it and accessed the list of files Dr. Pike was working on.

Karen appeared at River's side. "You found it?"

"Not yet," River said, "but perhaps you could take a look at the files she's got on her desk while I try to find Jase's file on her computer."

Karen started opening and closing the various files that lay on Dr. Pike's desk. Either the woman was disorganized or busy, but the untidiness of her office didn't tally with the image River had of a CSI technician. Next to her, Karen was replacing the files in the same position as she'd found them after perusing them, but then stopped.

"Is the name of the victim Jane White?"

River replied without looking away from the computer screen. "That's right. What does it say?"

Karen read a summary of the findings: "Death by exsanguination. Her hands and legs were tied to the bed on which she was found. She'd taken drugs by injection, cocaine. She'd put up a fight, and there were signs of bruises on her forearms and lower leg."

River turned to Karen. She felt bile rising to her throat but swallowed it down. She just nodded, indicating that Karen should carry on. "Her throat was cut open with a long blade, estimated at seven inches in length and 0.165 inches in thickness. The blade would be consistent with a KA-BAR knife."

River closed her eyes for a moment as she gripped the arms of the chair. Karen waited and finally said, "A KA-BAR knife is not the only one that can inflict that sort of wound, Riv. You and I have seen enough knife assaults in the field to know that."

River opened her eyes and murmured, "But Jase's KA-BAR wasn't in the cache when I got the gun out of it. I didn't think about that at the time."

"You don't know what he did with it after you left for Alaska. Perhaps he used it for something unrelated."

"Parker hasn't told Reggie about the murder weapon, so I guess they're still looking for it," River said as she forced herself to resume her search for Jason's file.

Karen took her phone out and started to take pictures of Jane White's file.

"I've got it," River said as she clicked through the documents. She found the toxicology report quickly, and she printed it immediately.

The printer on the side of Dr. Pike's desk started spewing out papers. Karen went to pick them up as River was going through the rest of the file.

"That's odd," she said as she flicked through the papers that lay on the tray. "Dr. Pike has already printed two copies of the same document—and there's more. Jase's tox report, the analysis of other samples taken the night he was arrested, and . . ." Karen rotated a document and opened her eyes wide. "Photos of the crime scene and the tox report of the victim. All printed twice."

River frowned. "Was she preparing a file for someone else?"

"That's a thought," Karen said as she replaced the wad of papers in the printer's tray. "Let's see whether there's any other clues on her desk."

Karen started to move files around the desk again. River was printing the second report in Jason's file when the printer churning the document out suddenly sounded louder. River and Karen looked at each other and said, as one, "The fire alarm is off."

The blaring sound of the fire alarm had stopped, and neither of them knew whether this meant that the source of the fire had been discovered or that firefighters would soon be swarming the premises. River grabbed the documents she had printed and stuffed them in her bag. Karen pushed a few more files around, hoping to find something with a name. She spotted a note at the bottom of a messy pad full of scribbles and took a picture with her phone.

River walked out of the office first. Karen followed a few seconds later. They retraced their steps along the corridor through which they'd come, but then stopped dead. Voices were coming from the lobby, and they both hugged the wall as they resumed their progress toward the fire exit. Two firefighters in full gear had arrived in the lobby and were making their way to the restrooms. As soon as they turned the corner, River and Karen dashed to the emergency exit and ran down the stairs. More firefighters were on their way, but instead of turning back, River pressed on, screaming at the top of her voice, "The fire is starting again."

The two firefighters who'd slowed down, perhaps to question them, looked up. The tallest of the two asked, "Where?"

"On the second floor," Karen replied as both women ran past.

They kept going until they reached the first floor. The fire exit had been propped open. River stopped and peered outside quickly. She hand-signaled Karen that they were good to go, and both women followed the wall of the building until they reached the A wing. No one was paying attention to them. They took their lab coats off and stuffed them into River's bag.

Karen spotted a group in the distance and said, "The fire wardens have moved people to the assembly point. Perhaps we should pay them a visit."

"You want to find out who Dr. Amanda Pike is?"

Karen nodded. "And if we find that Dr. Pike is releasing evidence to the wrong people, then perhaps we could have a conversation with her."

River bumped fists with Karen. "You do miss the action."

They walked around the building's B wing and moved toward the large group that had gathered at the assembly point. There River and Karen got to chatting with people and asking questions. They separated and made their way toward the people who interested them.

Jackson Laboratories employees were huddled at the far end of the group, not mixing with the other workers. River reached them first and turned toward the receptionist who'd welcomed her in the first place. Her initial disguise must have done the trick, because the woman didn't recognize her.

"I hope you're all accounted for," River said.

"Yes, we are. I'm so glad. It's my first time as a fire marshal. I checked the floor three times."

River nodded, looking concerned. "So glad to hear. And any idea what caused it? I suppose there is a lot of flammable stuff in a lab."

As she was talking, River spotted the woman she'd seen leaving late the night before and tried to determine whether she was wearing a name tag, but she couldn't quite tell. The receptionist's cell phone rang, and she turned away from River. River smiled and waved a friendly goodbye. She wove her way through the crowd and brushed past the woman from the night before, almost bumping into her. The reaction was immediate—a mix of anger and fear. River spotted the name tag on her white coat. She'd just met Dr. Amanda Pike.

River ignored the reaction and moved away, taking her time. People were starting to make their way back in. She went in the other direction, toward the Metro station, and was soon caught by Karen, who fell in step with her.

"Did you find her?"

"I did, and you know what? She's the same person I saw leave the lab late last night."

"My dad would say there is no such thing as coincidence," Karen observed.

"Speaking of your dad, does he know you're helping me?"

"I just told him you'd gone to sort out some business in DC and you needed a bit of moral support."

"Right . . . then he knows you and I are up to something."

Karen feigned a look of shock. "Am I that obvious?"

"To anyone else, no, of course. But he is your dad, *uuma*. He knows," River said.

She'd met Karen's dad, the chief of police in Kotzebue, a few years ago when she and Karen were on leave, and River and Karen's dad had gotten along from day one. He didn't mind her talking enthusiastically about her job or even comparing notes about firearms, something her own parents had never understood. She hadn't been able to explain why serving in the military had been so important. Now that she was older, she knew, and perhaps she could articulate it more clearly. But her parents were gone, and she would never have the opportunity.

Karen must have sensed that River had drifted and said, "We've got work to do when we get back to the motel."

"I'll get hold of Reggie, too. He's been very quiet, and I'm not sure this is good news."

They joined the commuters on the Blue Line and got to Arlington faster than expected. They remained silent for the journey, and Karen seemed to be uneasy, but River couldn't figure out why. They left the Metro at the Arlington Cemetery station and were walking back to the motel when Karen suddenly nudged River, forcing her to cross the road suddenly.

"What's up?" River said, surprised.

"I think we're being followed," Karen replied.

"Shit. I should have been on the lookout for that. If we've been followed, they must know where our motel is. I didn't think about using the old strand-of-hair trick this morning."

"If we haven't clocked them so far, they must be pros. In which case they'll check for exactly that trick and make sure they put the hair back where it was." Karen shrugged. "We're medics, not spooks."

They both accelerated their pace. A bus had just stopped and was taking on passengers. They ran after it and hopped on just as it was about to leave. They paid the fare and sat down. It didn't matter what the destination was. They would get off in one or two stops.

River didn't look back as the bus pulled away. She took her cell phone out and placed a call to Father Hopkins, hoping that this time he would answer.

# Chapter Eight

The phone rang for a minute or so before a breathless Father Hopkins answered.

"Is everything all right?" River asked with a frown.

"I'm fine," Father Hopkins said, taking a few more breaths before he continued. "I've been running around this morning since Maria hasn't turned up. It's very unusual. She didn't call in sick, and I can't get hold of her."

River thought about the silhouette she believed she'd seen that morning in Father Hopkins's office and cursed silently.

"Has anything gone missing from your office, Father?"

Father Hopkins's voice sounded shocked. "What are you implying? Maria is—"

"Sorry," River interrupted. "I didn't mean to imply anything, but my daily run took me to the center this morning, and I thought I saw movement in your office. I looked around and tested the door. It all looked fine, and I thought I might have dreamed it, but maybe I hadn't."

"I saw a missed call from you, but by then I was already at the center and dealing with the lack of a receptionist. I haven't checked my office closely, but nothing seems to be missing, and all sensitive information is kept in my locked cabinets." Father Hopkins thought for a moment. "I'll check again, though, and let you know. Anyway, I wanted to speak to you about your request to meet with the SEALs' family members."

River's stomach clenched at the news. *Please let it be a yes.*

"Lorrie Carlton is willing to speak to you. Her husband, Jethro Carlton, passed three months ago. I'll text you her address."

"I'm so grateful for your help, Father. I'll tread carefully."

"One thing that may also interest you, which I didn't know. Lorrie spoke to Jason shortly after her husband's"—Father Hopkins seemed to find it hard to bring himself to say the word—"passing. She didn't elaborate, but I have the feeling she's got something to share with you."

"Thank you. I'll let you know how it goes." River hung up and turned toward an intrigued Karen.

"I'll tell you more when we've reached the motel."

Both women waited for a couple of stops and left the bus. River hailed a cab. The less time on the street, the better.

By the time they arrived back at the motel and were headed to their room, River had received a text from Father Hopkins that gave her Lorrie's address and phone number. Karen got her key out and opened the door. River was already searching for Lorrie's address on Google Maps. The Carltons' house, in Virginia, was only thirty minutes away by motorcycle. She checked her watch. It was lunchtime—not the best time to call, River thought. She'd have to wait.

Karen had gone to the refrigerator to check what River had bought the night before. She picked up a bag of prepared salad between her index finger and thumb and pursed her lips.

"What do you call this?" Karen asked, doubtful.

River raised her head from her iPhone screen. "Salad," she said. "It's supposed to be good for you. But if you look closely, you'll see it comes with a thick, creamy dressing."

"That's better." Karen turned to the open fridge again, pulling out a large container of chicken drumsticks and thighs covered in Mexican seasoning. "I'll heat this in the microwave. You do the salad, and let's get to the evidence we gathered."

River took the wad of documents they'd printed in Dr. Pike's office out of her bag. Karen swiped her cell phone open and handed it over to River. They sat at the table, and River started reading.

She first went through the printouts of Jason's toxicology report and slammed her hand on the table.

"That SOB Parker didn't ask for a Rohypnol test."

"Are you surprised?"

River threw the pages down on the table. "Not really, but I guess I had held out some hope." She turned to a batch of images and tests that had been run on her ex-fiancé. The photos showed his clothes and body covered in Jane White's blood. The tests showed that the substance taken from underneath his fingernails contained some of Jane's skin cells. River read the report aloud and then turned to Karen. "But if he was drugged, someone could have dragged his fingers over Jane's skin, so we're back to the question of Rohypnol."

"I know Rohypnol vanishes from a blood sample after twenty-four hours, but what about a urine sample?" Karen asked.

"Sixty hours, sometimes more, depending on the quantity administered."

"We're getting close to that cutoff as well, aren't we?" Karen said.

"It's been two days since Jase was arrested, but if we hypothesize that he was drugged, say, six hours before the arrest, then it's been fifty-two hours."

Karen simply nodded. She fished a dish out of one of the cabinets and took two pieces of chicken out of a plastic tray. "How about cocaine?"

"Jase is positive, although it's a small amount."

Karen stopped what she was doing. "Just enough to make him out of it but not enough to endanger his life."

"That's a thought," River said, picking up the pages and reading the results again. "If someone is out to frame him, they want him found guilty, not dead."

"Why not dead?" Karen asked as she arranged the chicken on the dish and stuffed it into the microwave.

"Perhaps they need him alive to discredit him as well as frame him," River mused.

She read the other documents she'd printed. There was nothing she could find that would help Jason. She then turned to

Karen's phone, which held pictures of Jane White's file. She forced herself to once more read the description of the assault. It had been brutal, even frenzied.

"Do you remember the case in Afghanistan in which a local accused one of our translators—a local as well—of murdering his daughter?"

Karen stopped to think, then shook her head. "I can't say that I do."

"The military police got involved, and I assisted with the forensics. It was my first time. You hadn't arrived yet, I don't think—but anyway, the point is that this was also a knife assault. What exonerated the suspect was that he was left-handed, whereas the perpetrator had been right-handed."

Karen put a cup of coffee in front of River and asked, "You mean the pathologist could tell by the shape of the gash whether the killer was left or right-handed?"

"Correct."

"And Jase is left-handed," Karen concluded with a smile.

"It was all about the depth of the wounds and the blood-splatter direction, I recall. If the cut is deeper toward the end, and if the blood splatter goes from right to left, then the killer is probably left-handed."

"And I presume there is nothing about that in the report."

"Nothing." River kept scrolling down the document. "Reggie has got to ask whether this has been considered, but the notes do mention that the splatter goes from left to right."

Karen bumped her coffee cup against River's. "Hey, one positive outcome at last."

"It's small, but it's something."

River finished reading Jane White's file, but there was nothing more she could find that helped. The thought that Jason was accused of murder—let alone carrying out a frenzied attack—made her sick to her stomach. She ran a hand over her face and picked up her phone to call Reggie, but Karen put a plate of food in front of her.

"Let's eat something first. Remember what the old sergeant used to say: Grab it while you can."

NOTEBOOK—AFGHANISTAN DEPLOYMENT

June 2021
SEAL Team 1

Javier had to drag me away from the body of the Taliban I'd terminated. We'd just cleared the space and planted explosives around their weapons cache when this one appeared from nowhere. I know I used my sidearm to take him down, but after that it's all a blur. Javier tells me I went berserk and jumped the guy using my knife when he was already down and dying.

The story has shaken me. I know Javier is telling the truth, and I remember the feeling of rage, but I can't seem to put images to the feeling. Or, rather, it's like a series of disjointed clips that make no sense. All I recall is that I seemed to want to kill someone who was already dead.

I'm glad it was only Javier and I in that room and that the rest of the operation went smoothly. But now that I'm back at base, it seems surreal. I still don't understand what happened.

J.

"I'm not taking any calls for the next hour, unless it's POTUS," Clery said as he dumped his coat on his assistant's desk and walked into his office.

"Certainly, Mr. Clery," she replied with a little bow of the head.

Chuck Clery didn't like to fraternize with the staff unless they were young, pretty females with the right bust size. None of that liberal nonsense of being called by his first name. "Chuck" was reserved for a chosen few, and his assistant wasn't one of them.

He went to the safe in his office. Not the official one, which was easy to find, but the one he'd gotten a team of specialists to install in the wall of his office a few years back, when his lobbying business reached a whole new level. Chuck removed one of the tall wooden panels that ran around bottom part of his office walls and uncovered the safe. He entered the six-digit combination, applied his thumb to the keypad, and waited for the lock to release. He took a laptop out of the small vault, went to his desk, and laid it there. Clery returned to the opening in the wall and closed it. His assistant had clear instructions, and she would be guarding access to his office with the determination of a tigress looking after her cubs. Her job was always on the line, and so was a positive referral in case she decided to leave. But it paid to be extra careful with the documents that lay in his second safe.

Clery opened the laptop and logged on. It took him a few minutes, but for once he didn't grumble, welcoming the added security the lengthy process afforded. He checked his watch. His contact had said 12:30 p.m. sharp, and it was 12:27 exactly. Clery opened the video link but kept the mike and the camera off. He made sure his tie was centered, and he ran a hand through his thinning hair. The clock on the side of the screen indicated 12:29, and when it moved to 12:30, the video link came alive, and he heard the voice of his contact ask his first question.

"Progress?" the man said as the screen turned a sickening bright red.

"The lab report is just as predicted, suitably incriminating."

"And the woman?"

"She's about to have a road accident."

"Why hasn't it happened yet?"

"We need to make it look like an accident," Clery said, his mouth suddenly running dry.

"Anybody else that needs to be dealt with?"

"Well . . ." Clery hesitated but thought it better to come clean. "There is someone else who's been providing us with information, but she's still of use to us."

"In what way?"

"She's helping us find the notebook."

There was a silence that felt like an eternity.

"So this is also unresolved."

A small bead of sweat formed on Clery's forehead.

"It's proving a little more complex than expected."

"I don't pay you to find excuses. I pay you to deliver. This is taking far too long for my liking."

"I can assure you I have put my best people on the case," Clery said, hovering between defensiveness and fear.

"I don't care who it is you put on this case—your dog or your Mexican maid. I want this taken care of. I'll call you back for an update tomorrow at the same time. I expect results by then."

The man severed the video link, and the laptop screen returned to the original deep black. Clery let himself sink into his executive chair. His client held a prominent position at one of the most influential gun rights organizations in the United States, and he now demanded results. Clery knew what failure would entail.

He loosened his tie, undid the top button of his shirt, and returned the laptop to the safe. He closed it, replaced the wooden panel, and stepped to the small yet well-stocked bar at the far end of his office. Clery took a tumbler from a low shelf, grabbed a bottle of whiskey, and poured himself a generous measure. He gulped down a mouthful and leaned against the bar.

"Fuck. This bitch has got to go—now."

Clery returned to his desk, picked up a burner phone from his inside jacket pocket, and dialed Manolo, who picked up after a couple of rings.

"News?" Clery asked before taking another drink.

"Another woman has arrived to help Wayne's ex-girl, and they visited the offices of Jackson Laboratories."

Clery crushed the glass in his hand almost to breaking point. "And why are they still alive? I don't pay you and your team to sit on your ass and observe." This wasn't fair. Manolo was good at making disappearances look accidental, and for that he always managed to find the right moment. And the right moment sometimes required a delay. The short lapse before the reply told Clery he'd hit a sensitive nerve. For a Latino, Manolo was one of the most controlled men Clery had ever met.

"Do you still want it to look like an accident? If yes, then I need to pick the right time. Otherwise, I can get into their hotel room and finish them off this afternoon."

Manolo wasn't trying to be pushy. He was giving Clery the option.

Clery thought about it for a fraction of a second and chose to answer with another question. "How about the other one—Maria? The one who's looking for the notebook?"

"She tried again this morning but no luck. She then bought a ticket to Florida this morning and is on her way there. I'll have her picked up by one of my men down there."

"Could she have found the notebook and hidden it with a view to blackmail?" Clery asked.

"We'll soon find out. She'll speak once my men get to her."

"Won't it show she's been"—Clery hesitated on the word—"questioned?"

"The Everglades caymans will do the rest. It won't be the first time they help dispose of a human body."

"I need these other two women out of the way."

"It will be done by the end of today." Manolo used a tone Clery recognized. He had planned the way these women would die. He was about to execute it.

"Call me when it is."

Clery hung up and finished his whiskey. He pressed the intercom button and called his assistant.

"Burger and fries and a Diet Coke from Red Apron," Clery said.

"Right away," she said after she swallowed her own food in a hurry.

Clery returned to the Jason Wayne case, wondering why it was proving more complicated than he'd first anticipated to make the evidence disappear.

*  *  *

River ate a couple of mouthfuls of food and then called Reggie.

"I've got some news," she said as soon as he picked up.

"*I've* got some news," Reggie replied. He didn't sound flippant, just perhaps a little dubious.

"You go first," River said.

"No, you go first," Reggie insisted.

River bit her tongue and stopped herself from reminding Reggie that she was, albeit indirectly, his client.

"Parker hasn't asked Jason to be tested for Rohypnol."

There was a short silence on the other end of the line, but then Reggie said, "The tox report hasn't been released to Parker yet." He spoke slowly, measuring, it seemed, the impact of what he'd just been told as well as how it was that River knew.

"Well, I just wanted to fast-track the release of information to you," River said. She dropped her fork to focus on her conversation with Reggie. She didn't need him to have a fit over what she'd just done and threaten to drop the case.

"How about we discuss things hypothetically, then?" he said. She could hear him moving around. Perhaps he didn't want to take the call in the office and was looking for a quieter place.

"Hypothesizing is fine by me." She waited until Reggie seemed settled. "Parker can't be bothered to ask. I don't know why, and I don't care why, at least for the time being, but you need to get him to ask for this test to be done. The blood test won't work anymore because Rohypnol will have degraded by now, but we can still get a urine test. We've got eight hours left."

"Otherwise it won't be present in the sample?" Reggie asked.

"That's right, and then, again assuming Parker hasn't asked," River said, "we need to make sure that the cut to the victim's throat and the blood splatter have been tested for direction. Jason is left-handed."

"Okay. I'll speak to him again, then."

"You spoke to him this morning?" River said.

"That was my piece of news. They found the murder weapon dumped in a trash can not far from the hotel where it all happened. Parker sounded very smug about it. He mentioned it's a KA-BAR knife and that it has been sent to the lab."

River's heart sank. She hesitated, but perhaps revealing to Reggie that she'd broken into Jason's apartment the night before, albeit with Jason's key, might not wash with her young attorney.

"You know that's the type of knife used by Special Forces in the United States," she said.

"I know now. Parker enjoyed explaining that to me."

"Then why don't you go and explain to *him* that if he doesn't get off his ass, you'll get the whole case thrown out on the basis that he hasn't taken into consideration Jason's dominant hand?"

"I like the thought," Reggie replied slowly, thinking. "And you know, a fire broke out at Jackson Laboratories this morning. Perhaps that lab isn't that reliable after all. Evidence can become tainted so easily."

"That's the spirit, Reggie," River said with a grin. "I've got another line of inquiry I'm following. I'll call you at the end of the day. A friend of mine has come down from Alaska, ex-military medic like me. Her name is Karen Robinson. I'll give her your number. If I can't get in touch with you, she will." River ended the call.

Karen had finished her food. "What's this new line of inquiry?"

"Father Hopkins has given me a name—Lorrie Carlton. Her husband, Jethro . . ." River's voice trailed off, but she needed to say it. "He died by suicide. Father Hopkins told me Jason had spoken to her recently. It's only a thirty-minute ride from here. I'll take the bike, but it's probably better if I go on my own."

"That makes sense." Karen nodded. "In the meantime, I'll go through the evidence we collected to make sure there isn't anything we missed."

River picked up her fork. She ate methodically, in silence, until her plate was empty.

"Reggie just told me the police found a knife."

Karen gave a short exhale. "And it's a KA-BAR knife, right?"

"And since I didn't find Jason's knife in the cache he used to keep his gun in, I'm sure it will be his."

"Now, that is jumping to conclusions, Riv," Karen said, shaking her head. "Anyone can buy a used KA-BAR knife and make it look as though it's Jason's."

"Thanks for keeping me from doubting."

"Nah . . . doubting is good. I read this somewhere—where there is doubt, there is no doubt."

River managed a little more food, then pushed her plate away and stood up. She changed into her biking gear, opened her bag, found the Glock 19 she'd retrieved from Jason's apartment, and handed it to Karen.

"I don't want to carry when I visit Jethro Carlton's widow. It doesn't feel right."

Karen picked up the gun, released the clip, and checked that it was fully loaded.

"I'm wondering whether we shouldn't be getting another one of these. I'm almost certain we were followed this morning," Karen said, laying the gun on the table.

"Let's talk about that when I come back. I'll call you as soon as I'm out."

River picked up her helmet. She left the room and walked to the lobby. Pablo, the receptionist, was there, reading his paper. He gave her a nod, and she replied with one of her own. She was about to go out when she retraced her steps and walked to his desk.

"If someone asks for me, you could please tell them I've moved on?"

Pablo raised an eyebrow. "Trouble?"

"Not sure, but I'd like to avoid it for the time being."

"Sure can," he said.

She gave him a quick salute and walked out of the motel.

# Chapter Nine

River dropped her helmet on the seat of her motorcycle, drew her cell phone out of her pants pocket, and took a moment to compose herself. She'd rehearsed a few times what she would say to Lorrie Carlton once she got to speak to her, but she still felt nervous. She didn't want to be insensitive, and the thought of talking with Lorrie about her husband's suicide upset River, but she needed the details of what Lorrie had discussed with Jason.

She scrolled down the list of names in her contacts list, found Lorrie's number, and placed her call. The phone rang a couple of times, and someone picked up. The voice sounded young, and River was taken aback.

"May I speak to Lorrie Carlton, please?" River asked.

"Okay. Mom, phone for you," the young girl shouted at the top of her voice.

River heard rushed footsteps, and someone out of breath picked up the phone.

"Lorrie Carlton?" River asked.

"This is she."

"My name is River Swift. I spoke to Father Hopkins, who gave me your name."

"And you're a friend of Jason?" Lorrie said.

River silently thanked Father Hopkins for his discretion. "That's right. I'd very much like to visit you, if it's convenient."

"I'm around today."

They agreed that a visit in an hour's time would be fine. River thanked Lorrie and hung up. She checked her phone again for the route to Alexandria, pushed the phone into the pocket of her jacket, and fired the bike. She eased it into light traffic and made her way onto the 120.

River got lost once but arrived in front of Lorrie's home with a few moments to spare. She parked her bike near the front porch of the house. She thought Lorrie wouldn't mind. There was another bike dropped on the front lawn, but this one was pink and made for a youngster. The house looked like any of the other houses along the street—well-tended, comfortable; a family home. River sat on her bike, aware that she couldn't begin to comprehend the heartache this family was going through. At the top of the hour, she took a few slow steps toward the front door, breathed deeply, and rang the doorbell.

The bark of a dog and the footsteps running toward the door told River she was about to meet the owner of the pink bike and her dog. But someone shouted "Wait" from inside. The small silhouette that River could see behind the thick translucent glass of the main door turned around and stopped, but the dog kept jumping around, keen to check on a possible intruder.

A tall woman with long black hair opened the door. She had grabbed the dog—a young Belgian Malinois—by the collar to prevent him from escaping. She smiled at River and said, "You'd better come in before he gets the better of me."

River stepped into Lorrie's house. "I'm very grateful for your time."

Lorrie's gaze shifted to her young daughter. River understood immediately and turned to the little girl, who now was acting shy.

"I'm River. And what is your name?"

The little girl gave River a toothy grin and said, "Tammy."

River grinned back. "That's a pretty name."

Lorrie went into the kitchen, still holding the dog by the collar. She called to her daughter. "Tammy, sweetie, how about you take Muffin and go play in the backyard?"

Tammy gave a small shriek of excitement and ran to the kitchen. She grabbed her coat in the process and opened the door, calling for her dog. Lorrie released the collar, and both daughter and dog disappeared out the back.

River and Lorrie stood at the kitchen window for a moment until Lorrie gave a sigh and turned to River. Her face had dropped, and her eyes had lost their spark. She obviously found it hard to keep up appearances when her daughter wasn't around.

"She still doesn't fully understand that her dad isn't coming back."

River extended a hand and pressed Lorrie's shoulder gently. "If this is too much, I'll leave you in peace."

Lorrie shook her head and said, "No, please. You took the trouble to come all this way. And in any case, Jason and I were talking about what happened to Jethro. I need to make sense of it—for my sake, for Tammy's sake, and for him, too."

Lorrie stepped to the far side of the kitchen, took two mugs out of a cabinet, poured coffee in them from a pot, and indicated to River she should sit. They sipped a little coffee in silence, and then Lorrie started to tell River her story.

"Jethro was a Navy SEAL for twenty years. He deployed twice in Iraq and three times in Afghanistan. The last tour was a lot more stressful than usual, though. He'd already started to change in small ways—less patient with Tammy, forgetting things all the time, then getting frustrated when he did. Then when he came back, it got really bad. He became . . . paranoid. And that's when he decided to seek help. He had tests, scans, but no one really had an answer for us. He was prescribed drugs for PTSD, but that didn't help. It just got worse and worse until . . ."

Lorrie closed her eyes. River took her hand and said, "Jason wanted to get to the bottom of it, and if he can't, I will."

Lorrie nodded. She pulled out a tissue she'd been hiding up her sleeve and wiped her eyes, then cleared her throat and carried on. "Jethro had gathered a lot of books on how the brain works as well as how brain injuries affect human behavior. He left a note . . . he wanted to make sure that his brain tissue was analyzed."

"Are you talking about the research center at Walter Reed hospital?"

Lorrie nodded, surprised, it seemed, that River knew of it.

"I should explain," River said. "I'm a medic, and I was part of a team that went to treat wounded military personnel in the field."

Lorrie stood up slowly and said, "Then come with me and take a look at what Jethro had gathered. These might help you to decide where to go from here."

They went back toward the front door but stopped just before they reached it. Lorrie opened a door and entered a room. River followed, and her heart sank. In the corner of the room, Lorrie had erected a small memorial to her husband. The place must have been his office. It was small but well organized. His desk still had a computer sitting on it, and an office chair was pushed against the desk, ready to be used. A uniform that belonged to Jethro with his name printed on the right-hand breast pocket hung from a freestanding coat rack.

Lorrie walked to the desk and pushed a neat pile of books toward River.

"Take a look and let me know whether you would like to borrow any."

River picked up the first book. She put it down and then scanned the titles of the twelve other books Jethro had read in an attempt to understand what was happening to him. She took her cell phone out of her jacket pocket and asked, "Do you mind?"

Lorrie shook her head. "Go ahead."

River took pictures of the books. Apart from being impractical, borrowing them seemed wrong. They belonged in Jethro's small shrine. She could purchase the e-book versions and read them on her phone.

"Is there anything else you think might help me?"

"I'll let you know the results of the brain-tissue analysis as soon as I have them," Lorrie said.

"Do you know whether other SEALs or other Special Forces families have donated . . ." It was hard for River to ask the question, but she needed to know whether a pattern had been established or whether the entire community—military personnel, senior officers, and medics—was in the dark.

"I was told that other families had donated, but not many. And it was impossible to get hold of them because of privacy laws. Their names can't be disclosed unless they specifically say they can, and I don't think anyone has agreed so far, or perhaps they haven't been asked."

River nodded. "I understand."

The back door in the kitchen opened with a bang, and the sound of a young girl and her dog filled the silence. Lorrie rushed toward the kitchen, and River stepped out of the office, closing the door quietly. Lorrie didn't want her daughter to find them there. A time would come when she would want to show it to her daughter and tell her about what sort of man her father was, but that time hadn't come yet.

Lorrie handed her daughter a drink. The dog sat at her feet, whimpering. He, too, wanted a treat. She patted his head, took a large box of dry food from underneath the sink, and poured some in his bowl.

"I'll leave you in peace," River said.

Lorrie simply nodded. Pain flickered through her eyes, but she turned to her daughter and smiled. "Say goodbye."

"Bye-bye," Tammy said with a wave of her hand.

River waved back, picked up her helmet, and walked out of the Carltons' home. She sat for a moment on the seat of her bike and sent a text message to Karen.

> **It's all about brain injury and what's causing it. We need to get to Walter Reed hospital. I'll pick you up in thirty minutes.**

**News on my side . . .** Karen replied.

River hesitated, but she didn't want to lose time chatting with

103

Karen just now. It was already midafternoon, and she wanted to get to Bethesda before the hospital closed for the day. She started the bike, rode along a string of neighborhood streets, and eventually joined the highway. She revved the engine and leaned into the bike, enjoying the responsiveness of it as she gained speed.

The highway wasn't as busy as she'd expected, and she pushed the bike a little more. She glanced in her side-view mirror and noticed a large SUV behind her increasing its speed as she was overtaking a large truck. River pushed the bike more, riding at a speed way over the limit. The SUV had overtaken the truck, too, and was gaining on her. River shook her head and smiled. It would take more than a heavy, hard-to-maneuver SUV to win a race with her.

River got into a rhythm, veering tightly between cars and trucks. To her surprise, the SUV followed, although perhaps not as closely as it had earlier. She almost relaxed, happy that she could keep up the race until she reached Arlington. That's when she spotted it—another SUV, as large and ominous as the first one but a few cars in front of her. It had just moved into the middle lane. It would either block her or graze her as she rode past, and at the speed she was going, the bike would topple, and she would end up under the wheels of the next car or truck that came along.

River moved the bike to the left-hand lane and braced herself. She slowed down a fraction, lifted the front wheel as much as she could, and rode for an instant on the back wheel. She jumped over and across the divider that stood between the two opposing lanes of traffic. The bike slid sideways, almost throwing River to the ground, but she regained control and ended up in the oncoming lane. Drivers hurtling toward her in their cars applied their brakes in desperation. She heard the screeches and revved the engine once more, turning the bike around in a tight U-turn. She started riding with the flow, leaving her pursuers stuck in the wrong lane.

She came to an intersection and hesitated. She could try to catch up with the SUVs. But she was alone and without a gun, a mistake she wouldn't make again. She took the 120 back to Arlington and arrived at the motel having lost surprisingly little time. She didn't leave the bike in the parking lot but instead drove it right in front of the reception area. Pablo was there reading a newspaper when she entered. River removed her helmet, walked straight to him, and asked, "Do you mind keeping an eye on the bike, please?"

"Problem?"

"Perhaps."

He moved his chair closer to the door and returned to his paper, one eye on the bike.

River ran down the corridor. She stood in front of the door to her room for a moment. She could hear Karen on the phone. She entered and banged the door behind her.

"I'll call you back, Dad. Riv's just arrived," Karen said.

"We need to get you a gun," River said as she dumped her helmet on the table.

Karen raised an eyebrow. "I'm cool with that but wouldn't mind knowing why first."

"Some SOB tried to force me off the road. It's just as well: I've done plenty of cross-country races in difficult terrain."

"We must be getting somewhere," Karen said, flipping her phone in the air a few times.

"And we need to get to Walter Reed hospital in Bethesda today."

"You said it's about brain injury, but why Walter Reed?"

"Because they got some tissue samples. Not only from Jethro Carlton but also from other SEALs."

"They're not gonna talk to us just like that," Karen said as she took Jason's gun out of her bag, released the clip, checked that it was full, and replaced it with a sharp slam. She stuffed the gun in her backpack. "We may have gotten away with getting into Jackson Laboratories this morning, but Walter Reed—that's a whole different ball game."

"I hear you," River said. "I want to try using Jason's name. If it doesn't work, I'll speak to Lorrie again, but I didn't have the heart to ask this afternoon."

"And how do you propose to get there?"

"I'll ask Pablo whether he wouldn't mind lending us his car."

"And why do you think he's gonna say *Yeah, sure?*"

River smiled. "Don't know, but I've got a good feeling about it. I think he's ex-military, too, although he hasn't volunteered that yet."

They both left the room and walked to the reception area. Pablo was still reading his paper. He raised an eye as River approached.

"I need a car. It's urgent—I'll pay whatever the going rate is."

Pablo dropped the paper on his desk and slowly fished a set of keys out of his front pocket. He handed them to River and said, "It'd better come back in one piece, 'cause I like the old beater."

"Not a scratch," River said as she pocketed the keys.

Pablo nodded and thumbed toward the back door.

River and Karen walked along a narrow corridor and arrived in a small yard. The black Ford pickup truck looked ancient. River could hardly believe it, but it was exactly what her grandparents drove back in Utah. Karen went to the driver's-side door and said, "Love it. This beater isn't old. It's prehistoric. Can I have a go?"

"That works for me."

They both got in. Karen found the remote that opened the back gate clipped to the visor on the driver's side. She pressed it once, and the gate opened. River sat back and said, "We've got less than an hour to get to Bethesda."

"Without a scratch," Karen said, raising her finger.

Karen decided to follow the Potomac on the 123 and reach Bethesda from DC. River didn't argue with her. If there was one thing Karen knew how to do well—apart from her skills as a first-rate medic—it was navigate. River didn't know whether this came from the time Karen spent with her father, Chief Robinson, in the wilderness, running his dogs for competition, or whether it was innate, but Karen never lost her sense of direction.

"You said you had some news?" River asked as she and Karen relaxed a little into the journey. They'd noticed a couple of cars parked alongside the walkway next to the motel entrance, but none had moved when Pablo's old truck left the yard. Either they were just ordinary cars or Karen and River had tricked the pros who were trailing them.

"I took a picture of a notepad when we were in Dr. Pike's office. She'd scribbled a few names on it as well as other things that didn't make sense to me. But I googled the names, and one sounded a lot more interesting than the others." Karen glanced in the rearview mirror a few times, and River turned around to see whether she could spot anything, but Karen shook her head. "I'm getting paranoid."

"At this stage I wouldn't call it paranoia. I'd call it self-preservation," River said.

"You might be right," Karen said. "Even more plausible with the name I discovered on Dr. Pike's pad—Chuck Clery."

She let the name hang in the air as though it were one River would recognize.

"I'd like to say the suspense is killing me, but it might become too literal, so who *is* Chuck Clery?"

"Lobbyist here in DC. He represents the gun industry and is very close to a couple of gun-rights organizations that take no prisoners."

"Shit, Karen," River said, shaking her head in anger. "I wish some of these guys were sent to war zones like Iraq and Afghanistan. That might cure their obsession."

"I'm not sure, *uuma*. I'm not sure what it'll take to stop certain people from collecting weapons as though they were Pokémon cards."

River nodded and took her iPhone out of her jacket pocket. She googled the name and started reading what she could find about Clery. It was just as Karen had said: He was a successful lobbyist who had founded his own organization with a couple of other lobbyists twenty years ago. River found a few pictures that showed him shaking the hands of prominent people—everyone from senators to captains of industry.

The photo that interested her the most was one of Clery and a man in camouflage gear posing with an M60 machine gun, handguns in holsters, and an array of long-range rifles. River suspected these were M110A1 CSASS sniper rifles—compact semiautomatic sniper system weapons designated for US Navy marksmen—and MK15 Mod 0 SASRs, special applications sniper rifles used by Navy SEALs. She recalled Jason mentioning that the latter held the record for the longest-range sniper kill. Also in the picture were boxes of ammo strewn all around the two men. Clery was grinning into the camera, but the other man was serious and focused, as though the minute the photo shoot was over, he would start an altogether very different shooting session.

River saved the photo and moved it to a folder she created for the purpose of collecting information on Jason's case. She then turned her attention from her phone to another pressing issue.

"We're getting close," Karen said after a while. "What's the plan? And don't tell me you want to set fire to the toilets of Walter Reed, because then you're on your own."

"You can be such a spoilsport." River shook her head in mock disappointment. "I spent the last twenty minutes going through the list of personnel at Walter Reed, and I found someone I think I know."

Karen glanced at River before returning her attention to the road. "That's a bit of good luck."

"Not really. I was trained as a medic before I joined the air force, so I tend to know quite a few people in the field. Still, we deserve a bit of a break."

"And who's the lucky winner?" Karen slowed down the truck and then looked for a place to park. "Let's talk about it before we get into the hospital."

"Name is Frank Bruce. I gather he's senior now. I see he's part of the Behavioral Health Clinic and the Department of Pastoral Care."

Karen looked at River approvingly. "That's gotta be just what we need."

"As long as he'll speak to me," River said, still scrolling down the medical center website in search of more information.

Karen gave River a crooked smile. "People speak to you, Riv, whether they like it or not. In Afghanistan, you got even the most hard-ass Marine to tell you exactly what you wanted to know when you needed it."

"That makes me sound like a manipulative bitch," River protested.

"I never said that. You simply can get people to trust you when their life and welfare depend on it."

Karen parked the truck in a lot for which there was no need to pay. Both women left the pickup and walked toward the imposing building.

"I'll wait for you outside," Karen said. She found a bench underneath some pine trees that bordered the road and sat down to wait. It wasn't cold enough to deter a woman who went ice fishing when it was fourteen degrees Fahrenheit.

River kept going and came to the entrance to the main building. A man in military gear stepped forward and asked her to state her business.

"I'm meeting Frank Bruce of the Behavioral Health Clinic and Department of Pastoral Care."

The title as well as the self-assurance of her delivery did the trick, and she was allowed in. River walked to reception, where a man and a woman were busy with patients. She looked around more out of curiosity than concern. She'd been to this hospital a few times before, and nothing much seemed to have changed. One of the receptionists became free. She looked up and said, "How can I help you?"

"I'm here to see Frank Bruce."

The woman nodded and checked her computer but then looked a little taken aback. "Mr. Bruce has a meeting starting in just a few moments."

"I know," River said with confidence, "but it is extremely

important. It is about the suicide of several military personnel, and I must speak with him."

The woman's face dropped. She sat down in a hurry and dialed Bruce's number. She lifted her face toward River and asked, "Your name?"

"River Swift. Special Operations Surgical Team—24th Special Operations Wing, Hurlburt Field. We trained together there."

Someone came on the line, and the receptionist relayed what River had just said. She then listened attentively to the person on the other end of the phone. She kept glancing at River and was about to say something before River interrupted.

"Someone's life is in danger, and he will die if I don't speak to Frank today."

Whoever was on the phone must have heard her. It seems that counterinstructions were given to the receptionist, and she said, "Take a seat, please. Lieutenant General Bruce will be with you in a moment."

River went to sit down and suddenly worried that she might have overplayed her hand. What if there were no issues, and the brain injuries Jethro suspected weren't there? Or what if the brain-tissue analysis revealed nothing? It was too late, though. A small man with a determined stance had appeared at the far end of the large atrium that housed the reception area. He must have recognized River immediately because he bypassed reception and went straight to her. She stood up slowly, uncertain, but as he approached, Frank Bruce started to smile and then greeted her with an outstretched hand.

"Riv. It's been ages."

"Hey, Frank," she said as they shook hands warmly. "Yes, it's been a while. Thanks for taking the time."

"I've got a meeting in about ten minutes, but my aide can start without me—it's one of these regular catchup calls where everyone and his cousin is invited and nothing ever gets done." Frank started toward the inner security gates. He nodded to the guard in charge of the turnstiles, and River was let through without needing a pass.

"You said it was urgent, a matter of life and death," Frank continued as they kept walking toward a set of elevators.

"That's right, and I need to understand why this doesn't seem to be a top priority for the new research center that has just opened at Walter Reed."

## NOTEBOOK—VIRGINIA

### June 2022
### SEAL Team 1

I haven't told anyone, but I booked an appointment at Walter Reed for an MRI. I asked a senior pal to do it, just to be sure, and he found nothing. No abnormality, no tumor—nothing that can explain why I have the impression that my mind is slipping away. F suggested that I may be suffering from depression, anxiety, or even PTSD.

That doesn't sound right to me. Combat doesn't faze me. It never did. But since seeing F, I'm no longer sure. F prescribed some drugs for sleep and mood swings. I'm willing to try again despite my previous reluctance to use sleeping pills. Even if this means I must acknowledge that my resilience in combat has diminished, I now sincerely hope these pills will help. Fear and anger are not who I am.

J

# Chapter Ten

Frank led River to a small meeting room and made two coffees for them. Meanwhile, River updated Frank on the situation with Jason and Jethro. She omitted the few details that made her look more like a vigilante than a law-abiding citizen. She wouldn't have minded admitting that she'd done what needed to be done, but perhaps not to someone she hadn't seen for almost ten years.

"You realize I can't disclose the specifics," Frank said as he sat down at the table in the center of the room.

"I don't need them, at least not yet, but I need to understand what your lab has discovered about these brain-tissue samples."

Frank took a sip of coffee and placed the cup back on the table, hands encircling it. He thought for a moment and then said, "I can tell you what we no longer think it is."

He stopped again, and River nodded in encouragement, sliding her hands forward on the table as though it might help Frank speak.

"We no longer think it's PTSD, although we're still not ruling it out completely. In other words, we no longer think it's psychological. We don't think it's the same as trauma blast from, say, IEDs, and it's not similar to what boxers and football players suffer from."

River slumped back in her chair. What did that mean? "But is the brain physically affected?" she asked.

Frank drank from his cup. She could see he was conflicted.

"The problem is that we don't yet have many tissue samples, and I don't want to generalize."

"If you're concerned about my talking to the families before you and your team have had a chance to decide what's causing problems, I understand. I won't speak to them unless you tell me I can. You have my word," River said.

Frank nodded and said, "Since you're a medic, I can be a little technical with what we found. The lab identified a couple of cases of interface astroglial scarring—"

"You mean microscopic damage?" River said. "But that has to be caused by a catastrophic event that's repeated over time."

Frank couldn't help but smile at the fact that River had caught up with what his lab findings meant.

"And the other analysis showed that the brain's helper cells had turned into a tangled mass that stopped functioning properly."

"You said you'd not found any of this in other frontline army personnel or veterans who'd been exposed to single-blast trauma. And I presume you found nothing in civilians."

"Correct on both counts. It's specific to highly trained operatives . . ." Frank's voice trailed off.

River rubbed her face with her hands. She needed to concentrate on what Frank was telling her. She suddenly stopped and said, "Shit, Frank. Are you telling me that the intense use of weapons either during deployment or during training might be responsible?"

"That's the direction of travel, but we haven't discussed it with Special Operations Command yet," Frank said, looking at his watch. He slowly stood up.

River had a chance for one more question, and she took it. "Am I the only one interested in this?"

Frank smiled, walked to the door, and then turned serious. "It was nice to see you again, Riv. You look after yourself."

River stood up and rushed to the door.

"That's why you spoke to me—people are interested in this for the wrong reasons," River said from where she now stood.

Frank didn't turn back but waved at her just as he reached the elevator and then disappeared into it. River retraced her steps toward the lobby. She nodded her goodbyes to the receptionists and walked out of the building. She found Karen still seated on the bench, reading something on her cell phone.

"Have you called your dad about getting a gun?" River said as soon as she reached her.

Karen lifted her head. "Thank you, Karen, for freezing your butt off while keeping Jason's gun nice and warm in your backpack," Karen grumbled. "I didn't know I had to call Dad for that. How about I go into a shop and get one? I don't need his advice to know which gun I'd rather shoot."

"Good. You haven't called. Perhaps we only ask for one favor at a time."

Karen stood up and made a show of wiping the few leaves that had stuck to her backside. "And what favor would that be?"

River started walking toward the parking lot where Pablo's black pickup was waiting for them.

"I need a fake ID. I'm going to get a job with Chuck Clery."

Even the usually unflappable Manolo had sounded embarrassed earlier this afternoon when he told Clery that River was still alive and that his men were still looking for the second vagrant, who'd gone underground. Clery sank in his executive chair, speechless. The only thing that had prevented him from lashing out at Manolo was that he'd been told that the KA-BAR knife Detective Parker's men had found had tested positive for Jason's DNA. Clery had to stay calm.

Yes, it was a major setback that River hadn't been eliminated, but the evidence was piling up nicely against Jason. Detective Alex Parker was on a roll—and he needed it after a deplorable performance review two years in a row. Clery knew that Reginald Cameron had cast vague aspersions on the lab's security and the integrity of the evidence. But Reggie was only a very junior lawyer, and Dr. Pike of Jackson Laboratories was senior enough for Parker to dismiss those concerns. Parker couldn't have guessed that Dr. Pike had an issue of her own she needed to keep hidden. Alcoholism could lead a person to very dark places, including the mishandling of pathology reports, but neither Reggie nor Detective Parker was privy to that information—Clery was.

He stood up, went to the bar in his office, and poured himself a large glass of whiskey. He took a sip and then walked to his office window. It had an enviable view of the Capitol on the left and the White House on the right. Clery took another sip as he surveyed both impressive buildings. He had been at the center of power in DC for almost twenty years. He raised his glass to the thought. *May it be so for another twenty!*

Clery took a few more sips before he returned to his desk. Perhaps he had miscalculated, and the one person he needed to silence wasn't River or her friend but Jason himself. He picked up the burner phone he'd used to speak to Manolo and flicked through the images Manolo had sent.

Maria Lopez, the receptionist at the veterans' center Father Hopkins ran, was lying dead in an unused factory outside Miami. She had tried to run away from Manolo's men without success. She'd been interrogated, and even Clery, who wasn't squeamish, decided he'd rather not look at all the pictures. At least he was certain she wasn't the one who held the notebook he was after. Clery stopped scrolling through the photos, and a shiver ran down his spine. His eyes drifted toward a photo he had had framed a few years back.

He was standing with his client holding a selection of high-caliber weapons. His client, wearing camo, looked serious and focused, but there was something else in the man's face that Clery had never wanted to confront until recently. He looked as though nothing would stop him from killing anyone who stood in his way—past services rendered and past friendships were just that, *past*, and all that mattered to him was the future and what he needed to do to shape it his way. Clery checked his watch. He still had time until his client called tomorrow at lunchtime, but by then he would need to show progress.

Clery called the only number that was stored on his burner phone—Manolo's.

"I have another assignment for you," Clery said. "Find Wayne's lawyer, this Reggie guy, and give him a clear message that it might be better for his health if he gave up the case. And add a message for Wayne himself, complete with a few photos from the scene in Miami. Wayne'd better give up if he doesn't want his former girl to end up like Maria."

Clery didn't wait for a reply. He killed the call and calculated that by tonight Reggie would be nursing a few broken ribs and Jason would have received the message and admitted he'd murdered Jane White. Clery finished his whiskey, gave a loud burp of satisfaction, and logged on to his computer. Time to return to the less lucrative and yet excellent cover his other business provided.

This time River was driving the pickup. She told Karen what she'd learned from Frank Bruce, and Karen listened without interrupting.

"I think this guy Clery must be involved somehow. Why would his name be on Dr. Pike's notepad otherwise? Frank didn't say it openly, but someone he doesn't think much of is trying to get information about his lab's brain-tissue analysis."

"You mean find out about it? Or interfere with it?" Karen asked. "If Frank discovers that the reason all these SEALs are affected has something to do with the repeated use of weapons, this won't go down well with gun fanatics."

"And Clery is a lobbyist for the gun industry and represents gun-rights groups," River noted. "When I was surfing the web earlier on, I saw that his office is recruiting new interns. They're interested in people with military background."

"You're seriously thinking about applying?" Karen said, turning sideways to look at River.

"It's the perfect opportunity to get close to Clery and check out what he's up to," River said as she glanced at Karen.

"I'm not going to tell you you're mad, because it's not gonna make any difference, and I get that you don't want to turn up to the interview using your actual name," Karen grunted, "but do I really have to call Dad? Seriously, how am I going to ask? *Hey, Dad. I know you usually arrest fraudsters, but would you happen to have the address of someone you haven't arrested yet? It's urgent.*"

River couldn't help but smile. "We're asking for a name in DC, not in Alaska."

"Gee—I like your way of thinking. DC is a den of political iniquity, so it's okay to use scammers."

"I'm fighting fire with fire, right?"

Karen thought about it for a moment, then picked up her phone and placed a call to her father. River could hear the ringing tone and then heard it switching to voicemail. Karen just asked her father to call back and hung up.

They were almost back at the motel. River wondered whether she should visit Father Hopkins, but it was the busiest time for the center, and she decided she'd call later. She noticed that one of the cars she'd spotted when they left wasn't there any longer. She turned onto a side street and drove around to the back of the motel. She pressed the button on the visor, and the back gate opened. She parked, and they walked around the truck to make sure it was in as good condition as it had been when they left. Satisfied, she followed Karen into the corridor that led to the reception area.

"Thanks a lot for this, Pablo. I checked the truck. Not a speck of dust on your old beater," River said as she handed over the keys to him.

"No one came close to the bike, either," Pablo said with a nod at the front door.

They walked to the room, Karen in front. She pushed the door open. "If Dad hasn't called back in thirty minutes, I'll try again, but—" The rest of the sentence stuck in her throat.

The place had been ransacked *professionally*. Both duffel bags had been opened, every item inside cut up in pieces and dumped on the floor. The mattresses had been turned over, and someone had taken a knife to them and pulled out the stuffing. The kitchenette cabinets were open, and the food stored in them had been thrown onto the floor. The intruders had spared the dishes and glassware, presumably concerned about the noise they would make when breaking. River surveyed the carnage, torn between anger and guilt. She dashed to her duffel bag and checked. The thugs had walked out with the box of ammunition she'd taken from Jason's cache.

Karen took a large plastic garbage bag from an open cabinet and started to clean up the mess.

"It's intimidation. I still don't get why they think this is going to work on us. Which part of our résumés didn't they read? The part that said *deployed in Afghanistan and Iraq?*"

"They think we're just a couple of medics who stayed at camp waiting for the casualties to roll in," River said.

She walked out of the room and into the reception area. She wondered how Pablo could have let this happen, and for a few seconds she worried he might be in on it, but if that had been the case he wouldn't have lent her his pickup truck. Or perhaps this was the opportunity to get both Karen and her out of the way.

"We had visitors," River said when she reached his desk.

Pablo frowned and then guessed what River must have been talking about. He stood up abruptly and walked with her back to the room. His gait was stilted, but she could feel the determination and anger in his stride. He banged the door open. Karen stopped what she was doing, looking worried, and then she relaxed. It was only Pablo and River.

"Motherfuckers," he said as he removed his cap and scratched his head. He started muttering in Spanish and then turned to River. "Do you know who they are?"

River and Karen exchanged a look, and River said, "I'm not sure yet, but I have an inkling. Anyway, I'll pay for the damage."

"The hell you will," Pablo replied. "What do you need from me? My back is a bit crooked," he said, patting his lower back, "but I still can hold my own."

"A gun might come in handy," Karen ventured.

Pablo nodded. "Yeah, sure. What else?"

River glanced at Karen once more. She shrugged. Nothing ventured, nothing gained. "I need to conceal my identity to get close to one of these men."

Pablo half closed his eyes as he considered the request. "You mean fake papers, like a driver's license?"

"Something like that." River nodded.

Pablo ran his hand over a leathery cheek and the stubble that had started to appear on his chin.

"Take your stuff and follow me. Leave the mess. I'll deal with it. First I'm moving you to a safer place, and then I'll give you a contact for what you need."

River and Karen stuffed their clothes into their duffel bags quickly and followed Pablo. The three of them walked past reception, and Pablo took the lead, through the corridor they'd used to get to the backyard. He opened a door with a key on a key ring he'd hooked around his belt. The door led to a small entrance, and then to an open-plan space and a staircase. Pablo kept going. He climbed the steps slowly and painfully, stopping a few times. When they reached the top, he indicated a door on each side of the upstairs corridor and said, "I've got two small bedrooms. I don't use either of them because it's tough to get up here. I now sleep on the sofa."

"Are you sure?" River said.

"You bet. There is no way these SOBs will find you here." He turned around and climbed downstairs with much difficulty. The women followed. He made his way to a large freestanding steel cabinet, stopped, and leaned against it. After a moment, he straightened up, reached for another key on his key ring, and opened the cabinet. There was a big intake of breath from both River and Karen.

"Wow. Are you expecting a revolution?" River couldn't help saying.

Pablo considered the contents of the cupboard, from Glocks and SIGs to a selection of machine guns and sniper rifles, finishing with an MK15. He then shrugged. "I guess I worked with a lot of these when I was deployed. I'm comfortable with them around."

"May I?" River asked as she got closer.

"Go ahead." Pablo turned away and went to a neat little kitchen. He checked a bank of monitors that surveilled the lobby and said, "I'm gonna have to go back." He picked up a journal that looked old, tore a piece out of it, and scribbled down a note. "That's the other thing you need. Tell Eduardo I sent you."

Pablo left to go back to the front desk. Karen and River stood for a moment in front of the well-stocked armory. "Talk about spoiled for choice," Karen said.

"And you didn't even have to call your dad."

"Get lost," Karen said with a smile, her hand moving toward one of the SIGs.

River picked up her phone and the paper Pablo had just given her with Eduardo's number on it. She thought for a moment, but she didn't have time to build a story around why she needed the ID quickly. She also doubted that Eduardo would care. He would ask for a ridiculous sum of money, and that would be that.

River went to the living room window and leaned against it. She entered Eduardo's details into her phone's contact list and then dialed his number. The phone rang three times and then switched to voicemail. She left a message mentioning Pablo's name and emphasizing the urgency, then hung up. Karen was still testing the various sidearms in Pablo's collection. River hadn't heard from Father Hopkins and toyed with the idea of calling him, but her phone rang. Eduardo was calling back.

"You need papers," Eduardo said. It was going to be all business and no chitchat.

"I need a new ID for starters."

"When?"

"Tomorrow."

There was a long silence, interrupted by the sound of paper shuffling and keys jingling.

"Female, midthirties, white?" Edwardo asked.

River was taken aback. "How do you know?"

"If that's a yes, then you're in luck. I've got what you need. I'll

120

give you an address where someone will take your picture. It'll be $200 up front and another $200 when you collect it."

"That's a little steep." River would pay up, but she still needed to complain about the cost.

"Market's hot with these things, and you want it fast. Just as well you're a friend of Pablo, otherwise I might not have been able to accommodate you."

River grumbled, "Fine." Eduardo gave her an address in Washington Highlands, then hung up. River checked the address. She noticed it wasn't that far from the hotel where Jane White, the murder victim, had been found. She shivered at the thought, and her mind drifted to Jason. She'd been so busy that she'd spent little time thinking about him.

River dialed Reggie's number. She wanted a debrief every evening, even if it was bad news. His phone rang, and the call went to voicemail. She grunted in frustration. Was everyone filtering their calls today? She chose another number from her contacts list, and this time Father Hopkins answered.

"River . . . this is terrible, terrible," he said, his voice breaking.

Her blood ran cold, and she thought for an instant about Jason. "I'm sorry, Father, I haven't heard—"

"It's Maria. The police found her dead, murdered in the Everglades." Father Hopkins stopped, and River could hear he was trying to muffle sobs.

"I'm so sorry." River couldn't quite take it in. "What happened?"

"She was viciously assaulted," Father Hopkins managed to say. "The police think it was an abduction gone wrong."

River wanted to be tactful, but she also needed to know what had happened to the center's receptionist.

"That's terrifying. Why was she in Florida? Do the police know?"

"They didn't say. The police only informed me because they found the name of the center in Maria's jeans pocket."

"She had no other ID on her?" River asked.

"I presume not."

"But why abduct her? She wasn't wealthy, and . . ." River's voice trailed off.

"I know . . . It's terrible, terrible," Father Hopkins repeated, overwhelmed, it seemed, by his grief. River wouldn't get much more out of him, and she no longer wanted to press.

She hung up, promising she'd call tomorrow. She then turned to Reggie's number again. She absolutely needed to speak to him. A voice she barely recognized answered his number. It sounded distant, as though cushioned by thick material.

"So'ee, Ri'er." There was a pause. "I wan'ed to call, bu . . . I'm in pain."

"Reggie? What happened?" River shook her head. "Don't talk—let's text each other instead."

"Goo' idea," Reggie replied slowly.

River hung up and started texting.

**What happened?**

> **Was attacked on my way to visiting Jason, just outside the Metro.**

**Did they want your money?**

> **No. It's much more straightforward, but they also took my money.**

River frowned, and then she felt Karen at her elbow. She said, "Reggie has been attacked." Another text came through.

> **The biggest of the guys doing the beating thinks a black kid like me shouldn't work on the Hill but in the cotton fields where my ancestors belonged.**

River winced at the text.

**I wish I had been there to disagree with him,** she replied.

**Very kind but you would have needed
a real arsenal to take him down.**

**Well . . . be careful what you wish for,** River wrote as she
turned to Pablo's weapons cabinet. There was a silence, and River
worried that Reggie hadn't understood and would stop texting.

**If you feel threatened, come and join
Karen and me at our motel. You need to
meet Karen anyway, and there's been
a few developments we need to talk
about.**

More silence. River thought about calling Reggie over the phone
again, but then a message came through.

**I swore I wouldn't tell you, but fuck it.
If I'm going to die anyway, I might as
well talk . . . they showed me pictures of
a woman. Her name was Maria. It was
bad, real bad. They gave me the photos
and asked me to show them to Jason,
saying it would be you next.**

"No," River cried. "No." She kept repeating this as she typed
her answer.

**Did you?**

**I had to. I couldn't keep that from Jason. For a
start, my face looked too bad for me to lie.**

**I need to speak to him,** River texted.

**I think you do.**

River checked her watch—7:15 p.m. The DC Jail was closed for visits, and she would have to wait.

**Until then, you're coming to stay with us at the motel. I'll text you the address. I won't take no for an answer.**

**I'm not going to say no. In fact, I'm already packing. See you in one hour.**

Karen had been reading the messages over River's shoulder and said, "Aren't you supposed to get your picture taken?"

"Yep. And I'm going to that appointment on my own," River said as she texted the motel's address to Reggie.

"What?" Karen protested. "I was thinking I could perhaps test this baby," she added, lifting a SIG Sauer M17.

River raised an eyebrow. "I thought you'd taken the Hippocratic oath."

"I'm not shooting first—that's my interpretation of it."

River said, satisfied, "That works for me, but I'm still going on my own. You need to wait for Reggie to turn up and then survey the layout of this place and the motel. I don't think these guys are going to give up until either we win or they win."

# Chapter Eleven

River decided to risk taking the motorcycle. It was much quicker, and now that she knew men were after her, she would make sure she took the proper countermeasures to avoid being chased and run over. If they decided to come after her with a gun, Pablo's pickup truck would make no difference. It wasn't armored, and even if it was, she'd seen what the right rifle with the right ammo could do to bulletproof vehicles.

River stopped just before crossing the 11th Street Bridge into Washington Highlands. She chose a secluded spot from which she could see traffic coming and going. She waited a moment, but nothing seemed off, so she took her iPhone out of her pocket and checked the directions to Eduardo's place. She doubted it would be a pleasant photo shoot, but she wasn't expecting to be treated like a top model, either.

She rejoined the traffic, crossed the bridge, and pushed the bike a little harder to get to her meeting. The building looked shabby, but less so than she'd expected. It was a low-rise with shops at street level and an entrance at the side. She rode the bike right to it, found something to tie it to, and secured it with a heavy chain. She walked to the door and checked for names on a column of buzzers. Only one buzzer had a label on it—THREE. The word had been written a while ago, and it had faded almost to nothing. Eduardo had said to press the only button with a label, so she did. The intercom came alive, and she heard static.

"Eduardo sent me," she said. The door clicked open onto a staircase. The smell of dampness and pot slowed her down. The single light bulb dangling from the ceiling threw some harsh light onto the stairwell. The paint was coming off the wall, and part of the banister was missing. She climbed the steps two at a time and at the top found herself facing a long corridor. A man in a black T-shirt and jeans was waiting for her at its far end. His bald head looked stuck on oversize shoulders, and River wondered whether her combat training would be of any use against a man his size.

She walked at a measured pace toward him. He turned to face her when she was a few steps away and said, "Security check."

River unzipped her jacket and lifted her arms at shoulder level. The man came closer and started frisking her. He took his time, and for a moment he locked eyes with her. She didn't flinch. His hand moved around her buttocks for a little too long.

"If you're going to get off on touching my ass, I'm going to start charging Eduardo for it."

He took his time stepping back, but there was a flicker of concern in his eyes. Eduardo must be the business if this mountain of muscle was worried about getting on the wrong side of him. The man moved aside, and she walked through a door that led to a large open space. The windows were covered with thick black cloth. In a corner a tall stool cast a long shadow on the floor. A gray sheet hung behind it, and a camera was ready for use at its side. A plump man with a thick mustache and thick dark hair walked toward River. He eyed her up and down, grinned, and extended a hand.

"Eduardo told me you needed ID photos."

River shook his hand and made sure he knew she had the strength to inflict damage if he had any misplaced ideas. His grin faded, and he pointed to the stool. She sat on it, and he picked up the camera. While he was adjusting the settings, River surveyed the space. There were props all over the room, but River couldn't quite tell what they were. She spotted a crate that seemed to be overflowing with clothes and what she thought might be a wig.

"I'll take a couple of shots and check them out."

"Wait," River said as she jumped from the stool and walked to the crate.

"I don't have all the time in the world."

"I know. People are lining up to get their photos taken."

River reached the trunk and noticed something she hadn't noticed before. Wigs arranged on a rack above it hung on pegs. The one she'd noticed must have fallen off. She chose a shoulder-length version with dark hair and returned to the stool.

"I want my photo taken with this one."

The man grumbled again but helped her fit it on so that the hair looked natural. He took a couple of shots and showed them to River.

"That works," she said. She dug into the pocket of her jacket and took out the $200 she'd brought with her. The man grabbed the money and slowly counted the bills.

"The ID will be ready tomorrow. Eduardo will contact you."

River turned back and made her way toward the door.

"Hey," the man said.

River stopped but didn't turn around.

"If you want to earn a bit of extra cash on the side—a looker like you, with a bit of makeup and not much else on . . ."

River shook her head. Sometimes guys just didn't get it.

"If I ever come back here, it will be because I didn't get my ID, and in that case I promise you that even the gorilla at the door won't stop me from breaking your fucking neck," River said over her shoulder.

Her answer was met with a stunned silence. She walked out the door, expecting to meet the gorilla again, but he had vanished. She retraced her steps and went outside to find that her bike was still there. The streets were getting quieter. The cold wind had picked up. Snow was coming. She freed the bike, gunned the engine, and made her way back. She needed another stop at the Walmart she'd patronized before, and then she was going back to the motel.

When she was done with her shopping, she rode her bike straight to Arlington and to the motel's door. Pablo came out and threw a key fob at her. She caught it and lifted her visor.

"What's that for?"

"Better you take the bike into the backyard."

River gave Pablo a thumbs-up, and she rode the bike down the side of the building and around the back. She opened the gate to the yard with the remote on the key fob and rode in. She parked and took out the large bag of shopping she'd secured in the bike's storage compartment. River glanced through the window of Pablo's apartment and noticed Karen talking to someone. She stood on tiptoe to look. Reggie was seated at the kitchen table, a bandage around his head and a pack of ice on his cheek. Karen had done a thorough job, it seemed.

River knocked at the window, announcing herself. Karen went to open the door and nodded her in.

"Reggie arrived fifteen minutes ago," Karen said.

"I see that." River walked past Karen and straight to Reggie. He tried to get up with a grimace, but River stopped him. "That's okay. At least you got proper medical attention."

"Much be'er than 'ospital," he mumbled. His lower jaw looked swollen, and an ugly bruise had already spread over it.

River dropped her Walmart bag on the table. She took a bag of groceries out, which she handed to Karen, and took out some clothes to replace the one Clery's thugs had torn to shreds. She'd splurged on a dark suit that was much more expensive that the one she'd originally bought for the purpose of visiting Jackson Laboratories and produced a black leather coat to go with it, which brought a smile to Karen's face.

"You're gonna look the part in that, Riv. Just be careful you don't get caught in the whirlwind."

"No chance," River replied. "I couldn't make it in a nice job with a nice guy in a nice apartment. I don't think the lobbying world is going to inspire me. I need the open roads."

She finally threw a box on the table, which Karen picked up. Karen was taken aback. "What now—you're gonna turn into a brunette?"

"I got my photo taken with dark hair. I don't know whether

this guy Clery has seen a picture of me, so just in case. Anyway, it's not a permanent dye."

"You're seeing Ja'on tomo'ow?" Reggie asked.

"First thing. I'll change my hair color after that."

Karen had taken the grocery bag to the small kitchen countertop. "I'll fix us some dinner."

River put the clothes she'd bought in the bedroom she and Karen were going to share now that they had another visitor. It was good of Pablo to be so accommodating, but she suspected he might actually enjoy the company. She came downstairs and helped Karen with the food, and they all sat around a big bowl of pasta with bacon-and-tomato sauce. Pablo had declined to join them but accepted a plate of hot food, which he carried back with him to the front desk. Reggie took a while to finish his meal, each mouthful looking more painful than the one before.

Pablo turned up with his empty plate and started brewing coffee for everyone. Karen and River listened to Reggie's slow account of what had happened. River paid even more attention when he described his meeting with Jason.

"I don't know, but . . . it's as if he wasn't su'rised."

"You mean he was expecting to be blackmailed into submission?" River asked. She was the one who was surprised.

Reggie nodded, and then Karen asked, "But what did he say?"

"No'hing." Reggie shrugged.

"I can't wait to meet this guy Clery," River said. "He must be a real piece of dirt if he thinks he can influence good people in that way."

"We still don't know whether he's the one trying to frame Jason," Karen said hesitantly.

River shook her head. "Too many coincidences. And remember he lobbies for the gun and armament industries."

Pablo brought a pot of coffee to the table with four cups. He poured himself one. "If you're taking on one of DC's lobbying firms, you need to be prepared for a real fight," he said as he was returning to the reception desk.

"We are," River said.

Pablo turned back and shook his head. "No, you're not."

He disappeared down the corridor, and they all looked at one another.

"What is he expecting? We call one of the SEAL teams and ask for help?"

Reggie nodded. "No' a bad idea."

River poured coffee into the remaining three cups and took her iPhone out of her pocket.

"I should fill out this online application form for the assistant job in Clery's office and be done with it," she said.

She found Clery's firm's website, clicked on the CAREERS icon, and frowned. The deadline was midnight today.

"Shit." River checked her watch. It was almost 11:00 p.m.

Karen and Reggie looked at her quizzically. What could go wrong now?

"I'm going to have to use my phone to fill in the recruitment form that Clery's firm requires. The deadline is tonight, in an hour's time. I wanted to go to the veterans' center and use one of the computers there, but that's not going to happen."

Reggie got up, hobbled to the backpack he had brought with him, opened it, and extracted a laptop from it. He returned to the dinner table and booted it up. He logged on and turned the device toward River.

"Here you go," he said.

"You genius!" River grinned.

She found the website and started filling in the details. The name on her ID card was Laura Crain. She asked Karen to create a Gmail address using the name. Karen got to it on her cell phone, found there were a few email addresses using that name, and suggested an alternative. River nodded and used the new email created by Karen. The job opening was for a junior intern, but candidates with the right experience were encouraged to apply. River drew on her military background to concoct a résumé she thought would appeal.

130

The clock was ticking, and River read the form one more time. It was 11:45 p.m. when she clicked the SUBMIT button and breathed a sigh of relief. She noted the name of the HR person she needed to call to confirm that it had all been received. Perhaps she could impress the guy enough to be considered for an interview immediately. River stared at the screen for a moment. She looked around and hadn't noticed that both Karen and Reggie had retired to their rooms. Pablo was seated on the sofa bed, nursing the last cup of coffee of the day.

"Are you sure you want to sleep on the sofa?" River asked.

"Always. I don't sleep so well these days, so I putter around, watch TV, make more coffee . . . been doing this for a while."

River nodded, closed Reggie's laptop, and made her way upstairs. Karen was already asleep in one of the single beds. River tiptoed around the room, got ready for bed, and slid into the clean sheets Pablo had provided. She didn't need to set an alarm. She would wake up at 6:00 a.m. the following day as she always did, no matter the season, the weather, or the time zone.

## Wednesday, January 19

The next morning, River slid into the jogging pants that had been spared during the raid of her motel room, put on a heavy fleece and some running shoes, and went out for her daily workout. She ran along a route that wouldn't take her back to Father Hopkins's center. She would visit later to discuss what had happened to Maria and what the police had said. But this morning, her priority was to speak to Jason.

When she returned from her three-mile run, everyone was up, and the place smelled of coffee and pancakes. Pablo was taking a plate with him back to reception. It was the first time she had seen him eat anything in the morning. Karen and Reggie were chatting. Reggie's face still looked swollen and painful, and one of his eyes was now completely closed. River greeted everyone, ran up to the minuscule bathroom, took a shower, and put on a pair of black slacks and a black sweatshirt. She applied a little makeup, just enough to bring out the color of her blue eyes and the slant of her cheekbones.

"Going to see Jason?" Karen asked.

River nodded as she picked up the cup of coffee Karen had just poured. "I don't want him to make any stupid decisions."

"I'm seeing him later this morning," Reggie said. "Detective Parker has to tell us whether he's decided to charge Jason, and then we have to reply with our own plea."

River put on her jacket and helmet, stuffed her iPhone in her jacket pocket, and was out the door. Karen ran after her and asked, "Should you really be taking the bike?"

"I'll keep an eye out for these people, but I figure that if they want to blackmail Jason using me, they need me alive. At least for a while longer."

River straddled the bike and rode it through the open backyard gates. She was on her way to the DC Jail just across Washington Highlands on the other side of the river. It had almost started to feel like a commute, and the thought made her both smile and shudder.

She rode along Potomac Avenue once more and parked the bike near the front of the Central Detention Facility at 1901 D St SE. A man was seated at the reception desk when she entered. She removed her helmet and walked up to him.

"I'd like to visit Jason Wayne, please. I am a friend."

The man took a good look at her and lifted a phone receiver.

"Have a seat. I'll make a call."

Another officer arrived. "Come this way," he said.

The officer led her through a gray corridor that resembled the one she had gone through before. A guard stood at the set of gates and asked her to surrender her phone. He ran a metal detector along her body as she stayed still, arm and legs outstretched. He nodded to the officer, and they both crossed the gate into the area where the cells were.

He chose a room, opened the door, and ushered her in. It looked very different from the one she had been in a couple of days ago, when River had first been allowed to see Jason. It felt more oppressive and stunk of sweat and stale cigarettes. She took a seat at the table in the center. It felt like an eternity had lapsed between her last visit and today's and she'd been forced into a world she wanted to forget existed. River had rehearsed what she would say to Jason but suddenly felt unsure. She pushed the feeling away and waited, alert to every sound coming from the corridor.

Voices made River rise from her seat. Jason appeared in the door frame and stopped. His face was closed to scrutiny, and for a moment she thought he might turn back, but she caught his eyes, and he moved forward, led by two prison guards. He dragged his stiff right leg a little more than usual as he walked to the table.

"I thought it was Reggie," Jason simply said as he sat down, his chains rattling on the plastic of the chair. One of the guards secured the chains to the table and moved away without a word.

"I made progress," River said as she moved forward to reach Jason's clasped hands. He withdrew them quickly and let them rest on his thighs underneath the table.

"It doesn't matter anymore, Riv. You should stop looking for something you're not going to find."

Jason's voice had the calm she'd known him to have when he prepared for something hard and painful. He wasn't upset anymore. He'd made a decision, and he was following it through, just as he had in operations he'd been part of in the past.

"If you think I'm going to stop looking for proof of your innocence, think twice," River said without anger. She was as determined as he was, and he needed to know it.

"When Reggie comes today, I'll tell him I'm pleading guilty."

River shook her head. "No, you won't." River took a few seconds to steady her voice, then said, "You won't, because you're innocent."

Jason's eyes blinked once. "I will plead guilty."

"Tell me you murdered this girl. Tell me you tied her to the bed and slit her throat open." River drove her eyes into his, waiting.

Jason said, "I tied Jane to the bed, and I used my KA-BAR blade to slit her throat open."

Jason's words froze River to her seat, and his cold delivery for an instant convinced her. He rose slowly and said again, "Stop looking for what you're not going to find." He then called the guards and said, "I'm done."

"No!" River cried, tears in her eyes. "What about all the other SEALs and Special Forces who are going to die if the truth doesn't come out?"

The two guards collected Jason, and the three men walked away, leaving the door open. River had stood without noticing. Jason's face had remained inscrutable, and she slowly slumped back into her chair. She wanted to scream and kick, shake Jason out of his stubbornness, but she was now alone in the room without a way to vent her anger and fear. She had to speak to Parker.

She left the DC Jail, got to her bike, straddled it, and gunned the engine with an angry kick. She rode down Potomac Avenue again, across the Anacostia River, and arrived at the District Seven Police Station on Alabama Avenue.

When she got inside, the same woman was at reception, and the moment she saw River she picked up the phone and made a call.

River came to stand in front of her. "Detective Parker. This is urgent."

Detective Parker walked through the doors of the station's back office within a minute or so. He looked more relaxed than River had ever seen him before. Parker must have thought that the case was almost wrapped up. She wouldn't contradict him. What mattered was that she got information out of Parker.

"You've spoken to Jason's lawyer?" he asked, indicating they should make their way to the back of the station.

"Yes. And I'd like to know how Jason feels about his forthcoming plea."

"So you know about the KA-BAR blade?" Parker looked surprised, perhaps thinking that River would give up Jason's case as soon as the weapon had returned a positive test for his DNA.

"I just want to understand . . ." She let the rest of the sentence hang. Parker probably thought she had decided that Jason must be guilty and she wanted to know why he'd acted the way he did. What she really wanted to know, however, was how his DNA could have ended up on the blade.

Parker shrugged. "What is there to understand?" He waited for her answer, smug yet patient. He'd wrapped up the case in record time. He seemed happy to give her time to process what he must suspect she'd heard—Jason was pleading guilty. River stopped before they reached their destination and turned around, casting a last glance at Parker over her shoulder, her face like thunder.

"He isn't guilty, and I'm going to prove it."

Parker's eyebrows rose, and he shook his head. "You're wasting your time," he said, still standing in the doorway of the station's back office.

"And you're risking your reputation," River replied over her shoulder.

She walked out of the Alabama Avenue station without listening to whatever it was Parker was trying to say to her.

*Just another SOB who would do anything to get a promotion or save his ass from demotion.*

She put her helmet on, straddled the bike, and gunned the engine. When she joined the road traffic she hesitated. Indulging in a wild ride might take the edge off her anger, yet it wouldn't help Jason or men like Jethro and his family. She made her way back to the motel at a controlled pace. She needed to find a way to delay Jason's plea.

# Chapter Twelve

August 2022
SEAL Team 1

I have gone back to see F several times at Walter Reed, but no matter what tests we try, there is no answer. I've been reading more books about brain injury and taking separate notes at the end of this notebook. F asked me to participate in a clinical trial for some new pills, but like the others they make no difference. He suggested increasing the dosage to see whether it will help. I can see it on his face: Every time we meet, he doesn't know how to help me, and that thought devastates him.

At least the books I bought are assisting me in understanding how and why the brain deteriorates. In a strange way, I find it comforting to know what might happen next, even though the prediction is bleak. The bouts of paranoia are getting more frequent, and according to these books, this indicates that a new stage in brain deterioration has been reached.

I don't know whether I should share this with the family. I've never wanted to worry them in the past, and it feels wrong to start doing it now. But containing my anger has become harder. I sometimes realize I must have had a bad patch because everyone around me is tiptoeing and avoiding contact.

J

*　*　*

Reggie was on his own when River returned to the motel. He had changed into a dark suit and was preparing to go back to the office, although he'd been working on his laptop. He'd called Thompson & Meyer to warn them that he'd had a "fall" and had had to be taken to the hospital.

"Can't you tell them you need to work from home so that you can recover more quickly?" River asked.

Reggie shook his head, still concentrating on his laptop screen. "They want to make sure I don't spend more time than necessary doing things other than work."

"Such as what? Having lunch and going to the bathroom?"

"Something like that."

River sat next to Reggie. He stopped reading the emails he'd opened and turned to face her. "How did it go with Jason?"

"Badly," she said with a short exhale. "In fact, very badly."

"He's going to plead guilty?"

River nodded. "He spooked me—only for an instant, but still. It's as though he's decided to play a part, to convince a future jury he's guilty."

Reggie dropped his chin to his chest for a moment, thinking, and then said, "Don't take this the wrong way, but . . . you're sure he's playing a part?"

She shuddered at the question. Jason's eerie calm had unsettled her, but she had seen him before at Camp Leatherneck, in Helmand Province, preparing for an op. He'd exhibited the same focused calm when committed to a course of action.

"It *is* a part, Reggie, and your job is to delay his decision about the plea."

Reggie chewed his upper lip. "What chance have I got to persuade him if you, whom he trusts the most, haven't been able to?"

"You need to tell him that I know about Maria, about the blackmail."

"Are you . . . are you mad?" Reggie stammered. "I've been beaten to a pulp once, and I don't want to get beaten again."

"Don't be silly. Jason is under restraints," she said, although she was certain that these wouldn't stop him from inflicting serious pain if he decided to.

"And what if he gives me the sack?"

"Tell him I'm only asking him to delay by twenty-four hours, and . . ." River hesitated to draw Lorrie into this, but said, "Tell him I've spoken to Lorrie, Jethro Carlton's widow. She, too, wants an answer."

Reggie stood up slowly. "Fine. But don't expect a miracle. Those photos of Maria were gruesome beyond imagination."

He got himself ready and finally left, still limping from yesterday's beating.

River made two cups of coffee and went to the front desk to check on Pablo, who was reading another newspaper. He didn't bother to lift his head but just said, "Nothing to report. I think it's the calm before the storm."

She put his cup on the desk and said, "I don't like the fact that the guys who were following me seemed to have suddenly disappeared, either."

She turned around, went back to Pablo's living room, and took her iPhone out of her pants pocket. She went to Chuck Clery's firm's website again, recalled the name of the HR person in charge of recruiting, found his number, and dialed it. The phone rang a couple of times, and then Don Bannon answered with a terse "Hello."

"May I speak to Don Bannon, please?"

"This is he," Don said with a little impatience.

"My name is"—River had to stop herself from saying "River" —"Laura Crain. I sent my résumé yesterday for the intern position with Mr. Clery's office. I submitted my application very close to the deadline because I've just returned from deployment. I hope you received it."

Don's tone changed immediately. "Let me check for you. Please hang on."

He came back a few seconds later. "We have received your résumé—many thanks."

River could hear in his voice that he was reading the document. "Very impressive," he said, confirming River's suspicions. "I have to be honest with you, Ms. Crain. We haven't received a lot of applications from military personnel—well, not as interesting as yours, that is."

"I was very impressed that your firm was willing to give someone with a little more experience the opportunity to apply for an intern job."

"Well," Don said, "how about we meet for a chat? I'm not saying you'll be selected, of course. We apply a strict set of rules when it comes to recruitment, but perhaps you could help me grade the other participants."

"If you think I can be of help, then I'm very happy to meet. And I of course understand your recruitment policy." River rolled her eyes and waited for Bannon to give her a time and a location.

"Our offices, 2:00 p.m."

River thanked him for the opportunity and checked her watch. She just had enough time to dye her hair and hope the color wouldn't make her look like a member of the Addams family. Whatever happened, she would then make her way to Capitol Hill to meet Don Bannon.

When Karen opened the door to Pablo's living room, she stopped dead. River smiled, enjoying her friend's confused look. River's transformation had worked beyond her expectations. The dark hair, the white shirt, and black suit over which she wore a leather coat gave River an edgy look that went with the stern feel of the outfit. The change was radical, and River was now certain no one who knew her would recognize her.

"WTF, River? You look . . ." Karen scratched her head, looking for the right word.

River grinned. "Different?"

Karen nodded and then said, "And really good, too."

River gave Karen a fist bump. "Hey, even in scrubs I used to look good!"

"But that was Jason chatting you up." Karen grinned back.

The banter suddenly stopped, and both women's faces dropped.

"I'm sorry, Riv," Karen said as she squeezed River's shoulder.

River shook her head, took a moment, and then said, "He's going to plead guilty, you know."

"But he isn't guilty. And doesn't he realize that the moment he pleads guilty and is found guilty, the people who are hunting you will finish the job? Whoever they are, they don't want you to find out the truth."

River cocked her head. "That's a great point you're making. Reggie is on his way to see Jason to try to persuade him to delay his plea. Why don't you give him a call and tell him what you've just told me? That may help."

"On it," Karen said as she fished her cell phone out of her backpack.

River walked to the reception area. Pablo slid his hands toward the left-hand drawer of his desk, where River knew he had a gun. River lifted her hands in mock submission.

"Don't shoot! It's only me—River."

"Shouldn't make me nervous like that," Pablo grumbled.

River smiled. "I'll give you notice next time I change my hair color."

She walked through the motel's sliding front doors and waved without looking back. She reached the street and noticed a black SUV parked a hundred yards away. She smiled to herself. They would have to wait for rather a long time before they saw River Swift walk out of the Arlington Inn. Instead, Laura Crain had just left and was on her way to an interview at Chuck Clery's firm.

River took the Blue Line and arrived at the Capitol South station. She left the Metro and turned right toward the address Don Bannon had given her. Chuck Clery's offices were impressive. She took a moment to survey the layout and spotted what might have been a suite of large offices at the top of the building. From there she was certain its occupants could both see the Capitol and the White House. She wondered whether Clery was there now. Anger pricked her heart, and she had to let it wash over her before walking into the building.

She proceeded to the reception desk and asked for Don Bannon. The receptionist gave her a chilly smile. River ignored the woman and went to sit in the corner of the reception area reserved for waiting guests.

A thick-necked balding man arrived within moments of the receptionist's call. He asked the woman at the desk a question and then made his way to greet River with an extended hand.

"Very good to meet you," he said.

His handshake was firm, and he held River's hand perhaps a little too long. She reciprocated with a firm yet controlled grip. She needed to get the job and didn't mind a little compromise.

"Thank you for taking the time," River replied.

Bannon led the way, and they took the elevator to the third floor. Bannon was making seemingly idle chitchat, but River sensed he was observing her. They walked into a large office, with a comfortable set of chairs and table in one of the corners.

"Let's sit and talk about your résumé and the role," he said as he pulled a chair out from the table and sat down.

River sat opposite him and noticed that Laura Crain's résumé was already on the table. River had never had to lie about her identity before, and she feared that she would slip up. Bannon skipped her early years at college and then medical school to concentrate on her military career.

"You were deployed three times? Once in Iraq and twice in Afghanistan?"

"That's correct, sir." River was reverting to the formal way of addressing people in authority. It felt somehow strange and yet comfortably familiar. If she dug deeper, she might have to admit she had missed it.

Bannon, for his part, seemed to enjoy being addressed in that fashion.

"How familiar are you with military armaments?"

River frowned but then nodded as she realized what Bannon was after.

"I am trained in several survival, evac, resistance, and escape methods, using any appropriate armaments for these purposes. I went through several months of SOF-specific operational and tactical training and participated in full mission profile exercises with other combat units."

River's vocabulary, which showed Bannon that she meant business when she spoke about her time in the military, impressed him. He straightened up and asked, "Are you familiar with heavy crew-served weapons?"

"You mean automatic grenade launchers, cannons, and mortars—and howitzers?"

"That sort of thing."

River wondered whether Bannon had been given a list of desirable weaponry to be familiar with or whether he knew what he was talking about. She shrugged and said, "These weapons usually need more than one person to operate them. So that's a negative, sir."

Bannon frowned, and River added quickly, "The SAW and rifles are operated individually, but the operator has an assistant who carries additional ammo and acts as a spotter."

"But you could recognize a lot of these and could learn about new ones?"

*He hasn't got the slightest idea . . .*

"Yes, sir. I'm certain of it, sir."

Bannon nodded enthusiastically. "Are you busy this afternoon? If not, I'd like you to meet someone else."

"It's fine, sir. I'll make myself available."

Bannon stood up and disappeared with a spring in his step. River waited a few seconds, then stood up. She walked to the door, opened it, and stood in the doorway. Bannon's assistant looked up after a moment and said, "Turn to the left, end of the corridor."

River thanked her for indicating where the restrooms were and took her time getting there, surveying the layout of the office. She suspected that all floors were designed with a similar footprint. She entered the ladies' room, noticing that only one stall was in use. She chose the stall next to the occupied one and waited. She heard the toilet flush and a tap being turned on and off. When the main door banged shut, she left the stall and went to the far end of the room. There were two small windows opening onto the sky but bolted shut.

A women entered and stopped. River turned around and smiled. "The weather is still holding," she said, looking once more at the sky through the small windows. The woman nodded and entered a stall. River washed her hands and then left. By the time she returned, Bannon was waiting for her, impatient.

"Mr. Clery is free for a few minutes. He'd like to meet you."

It was the news she'd been waiting for, and yet River had a sudden pang of doubt. Was she mad enough to attempt to fool a man as seasoned as Clery?

*General MacArthur would have said that defeat resides in two words—too late. Yes: too late to have misgivings.*

She followed Bannon to the elevator. He pressed a button, and the elevator started its run to the top floor. Bannon rocked to and fro, head held high, and then said as they were about to reach their destination, "If all goes well, we will want to verify your military record as soon as possible."

River nodded. That *would* be a problem.

They stepped out onto a floor that felt very different from the one they'd just left. River hadn't realized it before, but the third floor had a buzz to it. Here the atmosphere was more hushed, almost guarded. The decorations felt lavish, and River noticed that the offices looked much larger than even Bannon's spacious office.

A woman she suspected was Clery's assistant stood up. She eyed River up and down and seemed to think what she saw would please her boss. She nodded to Bannon, who withdrew, and turned to River.

"Mr. Clery will see you now."

She knocked at the door, an almost hesitant knock, River noticed.

"Bring her in," Clery shouted from inside.

His assistant opened the door but didn't enter. She stepped back, as though crossing Clery's office threshold might invite trouble. River walked in, and the door closed behind her.

Clery was typing on his keyboard and simply lifted a hand from it, beckoning River to step inside. He finished whatever work he was doing, then finally looked at her. River was standing still in the middle of the room, waiting, already feeling a dislike for the man in front of her.

"Take a seat, Laura," Clery said as he extended a hand toward the armchairs and sofas clustered at the far end of the room.

It took a few seconds for her to react to the use of her new name. She looked around, as though confused about where to go, to disguise her hesitation. She cursed herself. She had to be on the ball if she wanted to convince Clery.

She walked to the far end of his oversize office, but Clery stayed behind, almost certainly taking his time to appraise River's backside. She took her time, too, and when she reached the armchair she was aiming for, she took off her leather coat slowly, as though it were a dress. River had never really thought about what a man might find seductive in her, although she had a vague idea, but she gave it her best shot.

She then sat down, turning her gaze toward Clery. From the look in his eyes, River knew she'd been perhaps more successful than she'd anticipated. He didn't bother to hide his interest. He eventually rose from his seat and came to join her, choosing the sofa closest to her chair and spreading his arm over its back in a proprietary manner.

"Bannon tells me you've been deployed a few times," Clery said, his focus now shifting on what River had to say for herself.

"That's right. Once in Iraq and twice in Afghanistan."

Clery didn't smile, but something in his face changed, and River knew he needed someone like her. He proceeded to ask the same questions as Bannon did, but unlike him, Clery understood weaponry and armaments, including the ones River had only seen during deployment but never operated. She hadn't had time to check whether Clery had a military background himself. She would later try to find out.

"For someone who was only a medic, you seem to know a lot about the range of armaments at the disposal of the US military."

"Every medic like me is trained not only as a soldier but also as a support for special operations forces around the world," River replied proudly.

Clery grinned. It was his first smile, and she wondered whether that was a good thing. A ring of his desk phone made Clery frown. The phone only rang once, and River wondered whether it was a reminder from his assistant that River's time was up. Clery stood up, walked back to his desk, and picked up the phone.

"Add one more guest to tonight's event," he said. He put the phone down and turned to River, who had stood up and was slowly walking back to the center of the room.

"I'm meeting some lobbying clients this evening after 8:00 p.m. Martha has put you on the list."

Clery had sat down again and was already logging on to his computer.

"Thank you, sir. I'll be there."

*Oh, yes, I will.*

River turned around and left Clery's office. She was again sure that he took his time to check out her backside. River walked to Martha's desk. Clery's assistant had printed a document she handed over to her. The woman's attitude had changed, and River thought she read concern or even fear in her eyes. River picked up the document and scanned it in front of Martha.

"Is this a formal event?" River asked.

Martha hesitated, but then said, "Formal enough. You can't go in trousers, but a simple black dress will do. And don't forget an ID card."

River nodded. "How many people are invited?" she asked and then, mindful of not sounding too inquisitive, added, "I'm not so comfortable with a lot of people around."

"Forty or so people. You'll be fine." Martha hesitated and then unexpectedly grabbed River's forearm. "But if you'd rather not go, you can always call me to cancel at the number on the bottom of the page. I'm always around."

Martha's cheeks turned a light shade of pink, but then she straightened up and returned to her computer screen. River thanked her and walked to the elevator. She stepped into it as soon as it arrived and was out of Clery's building within minutes. She started walking toward the Metro station and took her cell phone out of her pocket to call Karen.

"I spoke to Reggie, and he thought it was a good idea. I haven't heard back from him, though," Karen said as soon as she picked up.

River gave a sigh of relief and said, "And I've got good news myself. Chuck Clery is a sleazy SOB—and I'm already invited to a party."

There was silence on the line, and River asked, "Are you still there?"

"I am, but jeez, this is a bit quick."

"I intend to go and give him a lot more than he bargained for."

"Do you have room for another guest?"

"It's not that sort of party on the surface of it, but I bet you once it gets going it's gonna be ugly. I'm going to need some help."

River gave Karen the address of Chuck Clery's mansion in Kalorama Heights.

"I need reconnaissance. I need to know as much as you can find about this house, and then I need you to find me some strong sleeping pills."

"Got it. And what's your next move?"

"I'm collecting my ID from Eduardo, and then I'm going to find myself a little black number."

"What?" Karen said, sounding puzzled. "You're after another gun?"

River chuckled. "It's a little black number you can wear, not a gun with a holster."

"You mean . . . a dress?" Karen almost sounded shocked.

"Yup. Short and tight-fitting."

# Chapter Thirteen

Clery left the office after the interview with Laura, the new recruit. He'd asked Bannon to expedite matters. She was knowledgeable and had the sort of cute little ass he liked to lay his hands on. But of course she also knew how to handle a gun, and the thrill of overpowering a young woman with Laura's skills gave Clery an extra kick.

For now, though, he needed to check on a thought that had been troubling him for a couple of days. Jason's girlfriend was proving a greater challenge than he'd expected, and every passing hour put his failure to deal with her on a collision course with his most demanding client.

And then the name Swift had rung a bell. He hadn't registered it at first, but as time progressed and Manolo kept missing his target, the name had started to play on his mind.

Clery arrived home and went straight to his study. He unlocked the door, stepped in, and locked the door again behind him. He looked around the room and walked to a series of bookshelves that covered one of the walls. Using his foot, he pushed aside the Persian rug that lay in front of it and uncovered the floorboards.

The slight discoloration of a couple of short planks told Clery where he needed to push. He pressed hard in a couple of places, and the planks moved sideways, uncovering an opening. Clery used the flashlight on his cell phone to get to the safe he had had installed there at the same time as the one in his DC office. He entered an eight-digit code and heard a discreet click. He opened the safe and removed a small laptop from it as well as a couple of old CDs. He hadn't looked at their contents for some time and wondered whether they were still readable. But the information he was after would be there. Of that he was sure.

Clery went to his desk, plugged the laptop in, and waited for it to come to life. The device wasn't set up to be connected to a router. Its only purpose was to view the sort of information that was too sensitive and damaging to be sent over the internet. Clery tapped the trackpad, and the screen came to life. He pressed a button on the side, and the CD tray slid out. Clery took the oldest of the CDs, labeled 2000–2010, and pushed it into the laptop. A series of files appeared, and he scrolled quickly through the dozens of names that had been saved there. There was no reference to the name Swift anywhere, and he wondered whether he was being paranoid.

He checked his watch. He had a little more time before his guests arrived. He opened the CD tray, removed the CD, and replaced it with the next-oldest one, labeled 2011–2020. Clery started to scroll down the list again, a little less eager, until names written in capital letters and boldface type startled him: JOHN & BEVERLY SWIFT: TERMINATED 2014 AFRICA.

Clery sat back, and a fine sheen of sweat developed on his forehead. He now recalled who these people were. Two medics who'd stumbled across an illegal network of arms traffickers, a network Clery used to ship armaments to warring African nations. The business had been incredibly lucrative, and he hadn't wanted to give it up just because a couple of do-gooders had found out about it. As it turned out, these do-gooders were a little more than that, and it had taken planning and the resources of a well-connected warlord to stage an ambush for the couple. It was essential that their deaths look like an unlucky meeting with a group of warring factions rather than an execution.

Clery recalled the event now with clarity. There were some loose ends he'd never been able to tidy up, and these had worried him for a while. As time passed, he'd manage to convince himself that the

149

story was dead and buried, as were the Swifts, but now it was rearing its ugly head. He opened the file and started reading through it, losing track of time. He came across the name of the warlord he had employed in the Democratic Republic of the Congo and jotted it down on a notepad on his desk along with the names John and Beverly Swift. He wondered whether the man was still alive. He hadn't heard from him for a while and hoped that, in a country where conflict erupted regularly, the man had been taken down by one of his many opponents. Clery would have to find out.

His cell phone rang, and the sound of it made him jump. He closed the file, ejected the CD, powered down the laptop, and closed it. He returned it to the safe hidden underneath the floorboards. He shut the safe, replaced the planks, and spread the rug back over them. His phone had stopped ringing, but he didn't need to answer it to know that his security team was informing him that his guests had started to arrive. Clery cursed. The memory of the Swift couple had put him in a foul mood. He would have to get over it quickly. New clients had been invited, and he needed to ensure that they had a good time and that he learned as much as he could about them.

He left his study, walked to his bedroom, went into the adjoining bathroom, and splashed water over his face. He grabbed a towel and pressed it against his skin.

"Shit," he muttered. "I hope this dumb fuck in the Congo is dead."

He dried his face and straightened up. He hadn't yet had time to read all the details about the Swifts, but he was sure that the couple had two children, a boy and a girl. What were the chances the young woman he was trying to eliminate was their daughter? Pretty high, he feared.

Clery took a moment to compose himself. He threw the towel into the sink and changed suits rapidly. His wife wouldn't be joining him tonight. Her holidays in Europe were always the perfect opportunity to throw a party at home, after which he could enjoy a bit of fun.

Clery checked his appearance in a long mirror and made his way to the first floor. His guests would be gathering in the great room, which spread across the back of the house and overlooked the garden.

When he reached the bottom of the stairs, a young woman wearing a tight-fitting black dress walked up to him and said, "We've started serving drinks and canapés, as you asked us to."

Clery nodded and made his way to the great room. He'd call Manolo a little later, as soon as the party got going.

Karen parked Pablo's truck two streets away from Chuck Clery's address. River and she had decided not to drive past his house. The old black pickup was too noticeable in this affluent neighborhood, and Clery's security detail might spot it and record the plate number.

River, sitting in the passenger seat, checked the contents of her evening bag. She was certain that she would have to open it and that whatever it held would be closely scrutinized. Karen had been busy getting her what she needed. Fortunately, she'd managed to find flunitrazepam tablets—also known as Rohypnol. She hadn't had time to fully explain to River how she'd succeeded, but Reggie had somehow lent a hand.

"This kid is not going to keep his Thompson & Meyer job if he keeps being *that* helpful to his clients," Karen said.

"You mean if he's prepared to do what it takes to prove his client is innocent?" River replied.

"We're talking a controlled substance."

"Reggie is just resourceful," River responded. "Don't worry. If I get caught, I won't rat on him."

"Speaking of which, are you sure you want to do this?"

"Oh, yes. I just wish I could take my gun with me."

Karen sighed. "Fine. I won't stay parked here. The pickup is too obvious, but I'll find a spot as close as possible to Clery's place. You call me as soon as there is trouble."

"First sign, I'll call you." She probably wouldn't, but she wasn't going to admit this to her friend.

River stepped out of the pickup, stood outside the door, and tugged at her black dress. She put her leather coat on, made sure her hair was loose on her shoulders, and walked toward Clery's house. She had chosen a set of high heels she thought she could manage, but they were proving a lot trickier than expected.

River turned the corner and spotted Clery's house from afar. The front was teeming with security personnel. She had opted to arrive a bit later than requested, hoping that Clery would by then be a little drunk and easier to handle. Despite the late hour, guests were still arriving and were being ushered into the house. The place was impressive, and although River had no idea which architectural style the property might be, it felt grand and dignified. The tall windows on the first floor were surrounded by lush ivy trimmed in the form of an arch, the design of which she'd never seen before. River slowed down and felt her stomach somersault. Perhaps Karen was right. Was she sure she wanted to do this?

She shook herself like a boxer ready to enter the ring. She would go in and see what she could gather. Then she would decide how far she would go. River resumed her progress toward Clery's residence.

As she approached, a couple of his bodyguards stopped in their tracks. She got a little worried, wondering whether her disguise was no longer working and she'd somehow been identified as River Swift, only to be reassured when she realized that the little black number—short, form-fitting, and stylish—was doing the trick underneath her open leather coat.

River smiled as she reached the first guard and said, "I have been invited by Mr. Clery. My name is Laura Crain."

The guard looked her up and down and gave her a grin. He seemed to agree with Clery's decision.

*So it's that sort of party . . . and it doesn't seem as if it's his first one.*

He didn't bother to ask for her ID but simply glanced over the invitation River had taken out of her purse. It was true—there was very little she could have hidden on her person, and her small evening bag wasn't big enough to hide a gun. Still, the inspection was a

152

little lax, she thought. River walked up the steps to the main entrance behind a couple of men who, she was almost certain, were speaking Arabic. She could hear them conversing in low voices, impressed, it seemed, by Clery's abode.

River stepped inside Clery's house and was welcomed by two other guards. One was holding a scanning device. She opened her arms and let him run it over her body. The second man was all smiles and asked whether she'd like to leave her light leather coat in the cloakroom. She shook her head, and the man looked disappointed. The security guard who scanned her asked to check her coat pockets and trim. He opened her bag and rummaged through it. He took her iPhone out and placed it in a small box.

"These are not allowed in here," he said tersely.

She would have liked to argue, but it wouldn't have achieved anything.

He turned his attention to a small glass vial that Karen had bought at the same time she bought the liquid it contained. He took it out of her purse. She tried to smile seductively and said, "A little perfume to freshen up with." He placed the bottle—which contained the flunitrazepam she'd crushed and diluted with water—back into her clutch. She thanked him with a nod and kept going until he couldn't see her any longer. She then stopped and leaned for a few seconds against a wall. That had been a little too close for comfort.

She followed the buzz of voices and laughter that came from the back of the house and found herself at the top of a few steps. These led to a spacious room that was tastefully lit by a mix of candles and soft LEDs. River was offered a glass of Champagne, which she accepted. She had no intention of drinking it, but it might help her fit in. She hadn't been to any gathering like this before. The closest she had ever come was when Father Hopkins, Jason, and she had been invited to celebrate the creation of the veterans' center at one of the DOD offices, and she was certain that the drinks there hadn't been this expensive or plentiful.

The party was in full swing when River entered the room, guests speaking loudly and enjoying the finger food served by white-gloved waiters. She was offered some hors d'oeuvres but politely declined. A few men turned their heads when she walked past, but she wasn't interested in a chat, either. She needed to find Clery.

She spotted him at the far end of the room, talking to a taller man. The conversation looked amicable enough, but perhaps not as friendly as the surroundings suggested. She could see tension in Clery's body—shoulders slightly up and his free hand clenching from time to time. He must have sensed that someone was looking at him because he turned his head to give the room a quick sweeping glance. River turned away and opted to walk toward one of the large French doors that led to a terrace. She couldn't quite make out the face of the man who was speaking to Clery, but she thought she recognized him from the gun-loaded photo earlier on. If she wasn't entirely sure about the identity of Clery's client, though, she was certain that Clery had spotted her, and she waited for him to finish his conversation. She opened her purse and slid the small bottle into her coat pocket, ready for use at the appropriate time.

A few moments later, she saw his reflection in one of the windowpanes. He was stopped by a woman who seemed eager to speak to him. He indulged her for a couple of minutes and then made his way to the place where River was standing.

"I'm glad you could make it, Laura," Clery said as he drew close to her, perhaps a little too close for comfort.

"I wasn't sure," River lied. She tried to sound shy. "It's not the sort of gathering I'm used to, and I didn't want to look out of place."

Clery gave her a broad smile. "There is nothing I can see that is out of place here."

She smiled back, feigning relief.

"Let me introduce you to a few clients," Clery said. He put his hand on the small of her back. River had to force herself not to push his sweaty palm away. They moved around the room, making small talk with a couple of men who, River thought, sounded eastern European. She'd heard the accent before, when her parents had spent time in Albania. Some of the other medics they were working with had the same singsong accent, which River thought was fun to listen to.

Clery didn't leave her side. He had taken possession of her the way he probably did all the other young women who were invited to his parties. They moved on, and he introduced her to a couple who were tanned and dressed in more casual yet expensive clothes. They got to talking about politics, and River simply nodded, not certain they would want to hear her views. As they started moving toward another group, River spotted the man Clery had been speaking to when she first entered the room.

She bent slightly toward Clery and murmured, "Who is this gentleman?"

Clery's hand slid away from her back, and he faced her to ask, "Why?"

River shrugged and gave him an innocent look. "You were talking to him when I first came in." She wondered whether she'd made a fatal mistake.

Clery's eyes bore into her, and it made River shiver. She remained as calm as she could with a quizzical look on her face. Clery shook his head and said, "Certain clients require delicate handling. You'll get to know them when you've spent a little more time with me."

River smiled her best smile. "Of course. I appreciate the fact that I don't understand the lobbying business yet."

Her reply seemed to satisfy Clery, and he relaxed. She dipped her lips into her Champagne, not wanting to look as though she wasn't interested in the drink. Clery grabbed a glass from a tray one of the waitresses was circulating with, raised it, and tapped it against hers.

"Welcome to the world of greed and power."

River flashed him another smile. She took another sip and then pulled a face as she dipped her lips once more in the liquid.

"It's a little warm," she said.

Clery turned around and summoned one of the waiters with a snap of his fingers. He wasn't looking at his glass, and River seized her chance. She dug into her pocket, flipped the small vial open, moved closer to Clery so she could hand over her warm Champagne to the waiter, and poured the drug into Clery's glass. She then swiftly replaced the vial in her pocket. The fresh glass of Champagne appeared. The waiter took her old glass away, and she raised her new glass to Clery. He smiled, lecherous, and took a large gulp of from his glass. River took a sip, too, and this time it was she who looked him in the eyes. Clery took another sip. His glass was almost empty. River bent toward him, her face close to his, and said, "It would be lovely to visit the rest of your house . . . it's sumptuous."

Clery gave her a hyena's grin and slid his hand once more on the small of her back, his thumb moving along her dress and her skin underneath. She kept smiling and managed to glance at her watch. Clery would start feeling woozy in about ten minutes. Another five minutes and he wouldn't be able to stand, and then River would start the interrogation. She couldn't wait.

They left the great room and walked past the couple of bodyguards who'd handled security earlier on. As far as Clery was concerned, they were transparent. He kept chatting up River as though they weren't there, and she grew certain that Clery used his powerful position to attract and abuse younger staff. He didn't bother to show her the first floor and moved immediately to the second floor.

The door of the first room they came across was open, and River noticed it was an impressive library. She left Clery's side and walked in.

"This is incredible . . . have you read all these books?" she asked, almost childlike.

Clery stayed in the entrance and replied, "A lot of them."

He leaned against the door frame until River walked out again, brushing her body against his. She sensed that he was already struggling with balance.

"So where is your study? The place where you conduct all this incredible lobbying business?"

Clery almost stumbled but straightened up to follow her. River was walking down the corridor, opening the next door. He caught up with her and grabbed her shoulder for balance.

"This study is really impressive," River said as she walked in.

"Not for everyone," he said, with the beginning of a slur.

He stumbled once more, over one of the rugs this time, and almost fell. River steadied him and said, "Why don't we go and sit down on one of these chairs?"

Clery shook his head, but she ignored him. He no longer was strong enough to put up a fight River couldn't handle. She just needed to get him where she wanted him to be before he collapsed and would prove difficult to move. She dragged him to the nearest armchair.

"What . . . do you . . . wan'?" he struggled to articulate.

"A conversation about someone you've been trying to hurt very badly."

Clery opened his eyes wide, and then his face contorted in a mix of anger and defiance.

"Ne'er . . ." Then his eyes rolled back into his head, and he collapsed into the chair. She reached into her purse again, took out a packet that looked as though it contained tissues, and extracted a pair of examination gloves. She put them on, then ran to a pair of curtains that were held by tiebacks and grabbed the closest one. She returned to Clery, slumped over in the chair, and tied his hands behind his back.

He winced as she secured the knot. He repeated, "Ne'er."

River slapped his face hard, and he came to, looking now lost and confused. She opened her clutch and took out a tube of lipstick. She opened it, but instead of a column of colorful waxy pigment, it held a cluster of small yellow pills. She shook out a few and held them in the palm of her hand.

"You see these, Chuck?" she said as she pushed her knee into his belly. "These are pills stronger than Rohypnol. You're experiencing what these can do to you in a small dose. If you don't talk, I'll make sure you swallow the rest, and you won't wake up."

River grabbed him by the hair and yanked his head up. He tried to scream, but only a garbled sound came out of his throat.

"No one can hear you. They're all too busy drinking your Champagne and eating your food. And I bet your instructions to your bodyguards are to not disturb you once you've taken your new recruit to the second floor."

Clery seemed to wake up again and he whispered, "You're a dead bitch."

River laughed in his face and said, "I'm the one deciding who lives and who dies now." She slapped him harder than the last time to keep him awake and asked, "Why do you want Jason Wayne out of the way?"

Clery looked confused for a moment, and River feared the drugs had worked faster on him than anticipated, but then he managed to say, "Never . . . tell."

"Oh, yes, you will," River pushed her knee deeper into his stomach and liver. He yelled and she put her hand over his mouth. "I can do this for as long as it takes, Chuck, and at the end you'll tell me what I want to know."

He shook his head, but already River could sense that he couldn't put up the fight a lucid man could. River delved into Clery's inner jacket pocket and took his cell phone out. She presented the phone to his face, and it opened. Clery didn't struggle. He just mumbled. She opened his calendar and checked for meetings. A lot of them were in person. Some of them were video conferences with participants clearly identified. But she found that Clery had blocked out time yesterday and simply put a *G* in the allocated slot.

"Who did you call yesterday at lunchtime?" she said as she showed Clery the phone. "Is it the man you didn't want to introduce me to?"

He opened his eyes a little wider and tried to grab his phone, but the rope stopped him. River was going in the right direction.

"If you don't tell me, I'll go and ask him myself."

Fear shot across Clery's face. "Gun rights organization . . . dange'ous," he slurred.

"Is he the SOB who tried to get me run over? Or was it you?" River said as she kept scrolling through his calendar. She didn't have to go far to notice other entries with the letter *G* on his calendar. Clery was due to call G at twelve thirty tomorrow.

"So you're supposed to call this scary guy back tomorrow. What happens if you don't?"

This time Clery shook his entire body, struggling with all his might and almost managing to shake off River. She tied the rope behind his back tighter and returned to her interrogation. She'd found his sorest spot yet—his fear of the man he represented and lobbied for.

The effort seemed to have exhausted Clery, and his head dropped to his chest. River checked her watch. She only had a few more minutes before the Rohypnol sent Clery into a deep and vulnerable sleep.

"What's the connection between this guy and Jason? Is it because he was making progress finding the reason why Special Forces operatives die by suicide?"

Clery shook his head, but his eyes said otherwise. River was getting threateningly close, and Clery would fail his client if she exposed the truth, just as Jason intended to. She recalled what she and her friend Frank Bruce had discussed at the Walter Reed research center.

"So your pal in the gun business is worried about the test results? Is that it? He doesn't want SEALs or Special Operations Command to know about it? Because . . . because"—River hesitated and then she said, incredulous—"it's bad for *business*?"

It no longer was anger that washed over Clery's face but terror.

"My God . . . you and this guy don't give a shit whether these elite men and women die. You're only interested in making money." River heard the ring of her voice around the room. She'd been shouting.

Clery groaned, and his chin dropped once more to his chest. River was about to ask her final question when someone knocked on the door and said, "Is everything all right, Mr. Clery?"

It was a man's voice, and River thought it must be one of the bodyguards. She pulled her coat off and lifted her dress to a level that might still be called decent. She yanked Clery's shirt open and went to the door. She opened it in one swoop and said, "Chuck and I are busy."

The man tried to look inside, but River remained camped in the doorway. "I'm not into a threesome, okay? And neither is Chuck, at least when the third one is a guy."

The man pulled back and nodded, looking a little embarrassed. River closed the door with a feigned harrumph. She stood a moment near the door but heard the guard's footsteps fading away. She returned to the chair where Chuck was tied up. His head had rolled to one side, and he'd started to drool. She slapped his face hard. His head rolled to the other side, and his eyes fluttered open.

"I need a name," she said. "Is it on your cell phone?"

Clery shook his head. She looked around the room and walked to his desk. She opened the various drawers and found what she was looking for. Clery had a couple of burner phones hidden in one of them. She took both out and checked whether they were locked. She presented the first to Clery and said, "What's the PIN?"

He mumbled a few words, but they were hard to understand. River only had a minute, maybe less, before the drug she'd given him incapacitated him fully.

"Again. What's the PIN?"

Clery gave her a string of five numbers and then stopped. His eyes rolled back into his head, and River knew she wouldn't be able to wake him up again. She ran back to his desk, found a stack of Post-its, and wrote down the numbers. There was one number missing to complete the PIN. She would have to try, hoping she wouldn't end up permanently locking the phones.

She picked up the first burner phone and entered the numbers Clery had given her. She then decided on the number 5, because it wasn't among the numbers she entered, and got a retry request. River grumbled a few swear words and thought about whether Clery would have chosen a number at random or whether he might have used a mnemonic device to remember his PIN. She noticed that the first number had been repeated. In a six-number sequence, it was easiest to repeat the first two. She tried it, and the phone opened.

She scrolled down the call list. Clery had only called one number from that phone. She checked the text messages. There weren't that many, but the questions were always the same. They were about the deliverables—the steps that were agreed upon between the two men. River looked at the dates and times. The conversation had started a few weeks back and had intensified in the past four days. River didn't know what she would do with this information yet, but she scribbled the number of the other man's burner phone on another Post-it. Then she turned to the second burner.

*Clery's a pragmatic sort of guy . . .*

River was right. He used the same PIN for both burners. Clery was in contact with only one man, a guy called Manolo. She checked the messages, and a shiver ran down her spine. The timing of one of the texts coincided with the botched attempt to run her over. Clery hadn't been pleased.

River looked at the man who wanted her dead and thought about cramming the rest of the pills down his throat. But no—she needed him alive for a little while longer. She jotted down Manolo's number, too, and stuffed both Post-its and burners in her clutch. She checked her watch. It was almost 2:00 a.m. Clery's guests would have almost all left by now. She, too, should leave soon. She glanced around Clery's desk, spotted a few words scribbled down on a notepad, and glanced at them.

The names at the top punched her in the stomach and forced her to sit down: JOHN AND BEVERLY SWIFT.

# Chapter Fourteen

River put her coat back on, left Clery's office, and reached the first floor in a hurry. She retrieved her phone from one of the security guards, then texted Karen as soon as she was outside. Karen arrived within minutes and was waiting for her in the place where she had originally parked Pablo's truck. When River reached the black pickup, she was shivering from head to toe.

She opened the door and collapsed on the front seat. Karen didn't ask any questions. She just took off, intent on putting as much distance as possible between them and Kalorama Heights.

Once they reached Dupont Circle, Karen asked, "You didn't—"

River shook her head. "I was so close and really tempted, but no. I didn't kill the douchebag."

Karen nodded, waiting for more without wanting to push. This was what River appreciated so much about Karen. She knew exactly when to push and when to be patient. She was a true *uuma*—a true friend.

"It's all about money," River finally said.

"What's not these days?" Karen said, shaking her head.

"Perhaps, but the fact that Clery has agreed to go along with this made me feel like exercising my knowledge of anatomy in a way not intended by our training."

"That could come at a later stage," Karen mused.

"Clery lobbies for a gun-rights group, and the guy who's his contact scares him."

"Wow—another psycho with a gun fetish. I thought we left those behind in Afghanistan."

"You forget that America has the highest number of guns per capita in the world."

Karen thought for a moment and said, "I suppose almost two guns per person for an entire population is rather a lot."

"Couple of guns for hunting and maybe a sidearm if you really feel you have to, but do you need machine guns or automatic weapons?" River said. "Anyway, it was harder than I thought to get Clery to talk. What I gathered, though, is that this client of his and his gun group don't want people to know about a study that links firing thousands of rounds in combat or in training with brain injury."

"They'd rather let SEALs die than let the truth come out?" Karen turned her head toward River and had to swerve around a car she almost hit.

"That's what I got. But think about it, Karen. It's not only the SEALs. It's all the special-ops people who are deployed regularly and train like mad when they're not. And then what about artillery crews and mortar teams?"

They both fell silent. River's mind was pulled back to the piece of paper she'd found on Clery's desk—the name of her parents along with the name of a man known in the Democratic Republic of the Congo as Dr. Death—an arms dealer. It couldn't be a coincidence that her parents' last post with Doctors Without Borders had been in the DRC. Then there was the way they'd died, gunned down in the village where they were finishing a round of vaccinations, along with many of the villagers. The police report had said that two warring factions had opened fire on each other there. But it had never quite made sense to River, and now . . .

She felt the light touch of Karen's hand on her forearm. They had stopped at a traffic light.

"Something else troubling you?"

"I need to think it through . . . but for the time being, I want to concentrate on Clery and his pal."

River pulled out the two burner phones she'd found in Clery's desk.

"Clery uses this one to communicate with the gun guy," she said, holding it in one hand. "And this one," she added, holding up the second phone, "to call his team of contract killers."

"Shit—you're joking."

"Not joking at all. I saw the instructions to get rid of me, and they were pretty clear. But we have a few hours to push these guys to make a mistake. I popped a couple more pills into Clery before I left—not enough to kill him, but I think he'll be gone until lunchtime."

"What's next?"

"A text to Clery's client to start with," River said as she opened the first burner phone and started typing.

She read the message she intended to send. She reread the messages that Clery had sent in the past. She'd managed to sound like him, she thought. Her thumb hovered over the Send button, and then she pressed it.

**Highly unexpected development regarding our business. Need to meet tomorrow. No phone call.**

"We're almost at the motel," Karen said as she turned into the road that led to it.

"Let's get a few hours' downtime and then see whether the guy responds to the text I sent."

Karen drove up the alleyway that led to the motel's backyard, opened the gate with Pablo's remote, and parked the pickup. They both got out and tiptoed into Pablo's living room. The old man wasn't asleep. He was sitting on the sofa with a blanket up to his chest and what River suspected was a cup of coffee. The TV was on low, more of a friendly presence than something to watch.

"I was getting worried," he said as they both came in.

River didn't have time to reply. One of Clery's burner phones buzzed. She checked the message. It seemed that Clery's client was suffering from insomnia.

**No. Too risky. Find a place secure enough for a call.**

River ran her hand through her hair. Whoever was at the other end of the phone didn't like doing Clery's bidding. She thought about what else she'd learned that evening. There must have been a reason why Clery had dug out the old story regarding her parents and the Congo. She couldn't think of anything else to say, and so she took the chance.

**It's about the old DRC file.**

The phone remained silent for a long while. River kept staring at the screen until she felt she was being observed. Both Karen and Pablo were looking at her, waiting. River shook her head and said, "I've blown it."

She felt tears of rage filling her eyes. The thought of hurling the phone against the wall crossed her mind. A message pinged.

**Fine. Pavilion Café, National Gallery, outside table, 8:00 a.m.**

**Understood,** she replied.

She looked into Karen and Pablo's expectant faces.

"He bought it. He thinks I'm Clery."

The three of them bumped fists. Pablo got out from under his blanket and went into the kitchen. Then he brought three shot glasses to the coffee table and poured tequila into each of them.

"What have I missed?" a sleepy voice said. Reggie stood in the middle of the room looking rumpled in his gray jogging pants and T-shirt.

River filled him in with the details of her evening—at least those details she didn't mind disclosing to Reggie and Pablo.

"Anything illegal I should be aware of?" Reggie asked.

River gave it some thought. "I'd say pretty much the whole of it."

Reggie shrugged. "You gotta do what you gotta do." He took the shot that Pablo handed him. They all raised their glasses and downed the tequila in one gulp. River pulled a face. Reggie spluttered a bit. Karen looked as though she wouldn't mind having another one, and Pablo smiled blissfully. They chatted a little more, and then River stood up.

"I need some shuteye."

She bade goodnight to the three of them. She got into the room she shared with Karen, stripped down to her underwear and bra, and slid into bed. She was already asleep when Karen got into bed herself.

## Thursday, January 20

At 6:00 a.m. River opened her eyes. She rolled onto her side and didn't bother to check the clock on her iPhone. She went to the bathroom for a hot shower, where she was relieved to find that the hair dye she'd used the day before came off—at least enough to ensure that she no longer was a dark-haired woman. She'd have to give it a go one more time before she returned to her natural color.

She lingered a little longer and finished off with a thirty-second cold-water blast. It helped chase away the aftereffects of the evening before and the impromptu tequila shot.

She returned to the bedroom. Karen had woken up, too, and was opening the curtains.

"What are you going to do? You can't go meet this guy," Karen said.

"I want to get pictures of him," River said to Karen as she was choosing which clothes to wear.

"You won't be able to approach him that easily. He's got to be on high alert."

"I'm sure he is, but I've got a plan to make sure that when he sees me coming, he'll welcome me with open arms," River said as she slipped into a pair of cargo pants and a sweater.

She went downstairs to prepare some breakfast. Pablo was already at the front desk. She opened the fridge and took out a carton full of eggs, some tomatoes, and a package of bacon that hadn't been opened yet. She placed a hand on the coffeepot. It was still hot. She poured a cup. She returned to the fridge and took out a loaf of sliced bread and package of croissants. Karen stepped into the kitchen, hair still wet from her shower, and said, "I'll take care of breakfast."

River nodded. She picked up Clery's second burner phone, entered the PIN, and accessed its texts. She read all the messages that Manolo and Clery had exchanged in the past three months. Some of them made for rough reading, but at the end she got the hang of the way Clery would give Manolo orders to maim or kill.

**New target—man—Caucasian—dark hair— late forties—contact point: Pavilion Café, National Gallery, outside table, 8:00 a.m. Shoot to wound ONLY. Acknowledge.**

River had checked the hours of the café. It opened at 10:00 a.m. The place would be nice and secluded—and empty at eight. This time the burner phone pinged back within seconds.

**Acknowledged. Nothing new on the other front. The two women haven't moved from the motel since we paid a visit to their room.**

The last comment brought a smile to River's face. "Oh, yes, they have," she whispered.

**Keep watching,** she replied, and waited for a moment.

Manolo followed orders without questioning, it seemed. River checked her watch. She had a little more than an hour to get to the Pavilion Café herself and decided that this time she'd do what she planned to do on her own.

"Whoever Clery's client is, he's got him scared, and that's a warning sign. I'm flying solo on this one."

Karen planted her fists on her hips, shocked. "I didn't know Afghanistan was a picnic and the Taliban a bunch of friendlies."

"I take your point, but I'm still going it alone," River said as she was getting ready to leave, grabbing a croissant out of the package. "And anyway, you've got things to do."

"Such as?"

"You need to call your dad," River said as she put on her leather coat. "And this time he's the only one who can help."

Karen crossed her arms over her chest. "Convince me."

"I'm going to send you the picture of this guy as soon as I have it, and I need to find out who he is through your dad. He might be the man I spotted in that photo with Clery, but I need to confirm that."

Karen grumbled a response, but River was already out the door, on her way to the Metro. She caught the Blue Line to the Smithsonian stop and arrived about fifteen minutes early. She couldn't be quite sure, but she thought she hadn't been followed. She crossed Madison Drive and walked past the Pavilion Café. It looked closed, and she exhaled a sigh of relief. She kept going and took a sidewalk that led to the back of the café. Three tables were huddled close to a line of evergreen shrubs. She could see why Clery's contact had chosen this spot. She didn't stop or even slow down. It was likely the man would ask his own men to do reconnaissance before he settled at one of the tables, waiting for Clery.

River kept walking until she reached Constitution Avenue. She then glanced at her watch. It was five to eight. She only had five more minutes to see whether her plan had worked.

Using the alleys that led back to the café would enable River to arrive shortly after 8:00 a.m. and watch the tables from a distance.

She followed Constitution Avenue and then turned right, retracing her steps. She slowed down almost to a halt, put on a pair of gloves she'd stuffed into her coat pockets, and then kept going. She would only need a few more steps before she could see the tables.

A man dressed in a thick black coat was walking the opposite way. He reached the café, slowed down, retrieved a cell phone from his pocket, and made a call. He'd almost gotten to the tables when he turned around. He waited for a few seconds, dropped the phone in his pocket, and took a seat. River recognized the man from the photo and the party right away. She now wondered whether Manolo was around or whether this man's own thugs had found him. She hesitated. If she kept walking, she would come between Clery's client and Manolo's bullet. But if she waited, it would look suspicious. She stopped to rummage through her pockets, pretending to look for a ringing phone.

A muffled cry and the sound of a chair screeching made River raise her head. The man was on the ground, holding his leg and now screaming. River ran toward him, phone in hand. When she reached him, she knelt and said, "I'm a medic. I can help."

"I've been shot," the man screamed as he held his thigh. "I've been shot."

"I'll call 911 immediately."

River held the phone up and snapped a couple of photos of his face without his noticing, then called 911. An operator responded within seconds.

"Nine-one-one, what is your emergency?"

"Someone has been shot outside the Pavilion Café at the National Gallery of Art. He's bleeding heavily."

She dropped her phone next to her after disconnecting, and her training kicked in.

"I know it hurts, but you need to let me look at the wound."

The man nodded while whimpering in agony. Manolo had done the job. His bullet had savaged the man's thigh, and part of the muscle was hanging loose, but he hadn't shattered the bone or the main femoral artery. She reckoned he'd used an AR15 fitted with a suppressor and perhaps a .223 Remington to minimize the impact.

River took the man's scarf off and bunched it up. She applied it to the wound and pressed on it hard. The man screamed again.

"I know, but I need to stop the bleeding until emergency services arrives," River said, and then asked, "What's your name, sir?"

Even through the pain, she read suspicion in his eyes, and he simply said, "Karl."

Now that she'd settled in a position she could hold and he had accepted the pain, she studied his face. Karl was beefy, yet in good shape. Unlike Clery, who looked as though he enjoyed partying a little too much, Karl looked after himself. She wondered whether he was also the sort of man who kept himself fit so that he could fight his way out of a possible ambush.

"Who do you work for?" Karl managed to say.

The question surprised River, and she had to think fast about a credible answer.

"Walter Reed, but I'm on my day off—at least I thought I was."

She applied a little more pressure on the wound, and Karl whined in agony. This might distract him from her answer, a strategy that seemed to work. Karl closed his eyes tight, as though it would help him deny the pain. River heard the wailing of a siren. The ambulance would be here any moment. She spent the remaining minutes committing the man's face to memory—his square jaw and thin lips, his thick hair closely cropped, almost military style, and his eyes, blue and unforgiving.

Two paramedics ran toward them. They dropped their equipment next to Karl and turned to River.

"We've got this. Thank you."

River nodded. She removed Karl's scarf and let the taller of the two apply pressure on the wound with a fresh cloth. She let go, scooping her cell phone up from the ground. The paramedic started to speak to Karl just the way River had done—asking his name, sounding in control. The second paramedic was preparing a fluid bag and the medical equipment necessary to bandage the man and ready him for transportation. River stepped away slowly. She could hear another siren, and this time it was the police.

She walked backward until she turned the corner into an alleyway. She ran toward the end of the sidewalk and folded Karl's scarf, covered with his blood, into her pocket. She might have left some DNA behind, although she'd been careful. She took her bloodied gloves off and folded them into her pocket, too. She kept going until she reached Constitution Avenue and jumped on the first bus going west. She waited until the bus reached the Lincoln Memorial and then got out.

Tourists were starting to arrive, and she milled about. She kept walking until she reached Arlington Memorial Bridge. She slowed down, took her cell phone out, and called Karen.

"I'm going to send you some images. The guy's first name is Karl, although I'm not sure he gave me his real name. This time you've got to ask your dad for help."

"I'll make sure he finds his name," Karen said.

"I'll leave it to you to fill in your dad about why this guy has been shot."

Lucas Robinson, Karen's father and chief of police in Kotzebue, might not appreciate the ploy that had brought River close to Karl. But Karen had always been able to get her father to come around whenever they disagreed. River hoped today would be no exception.

"I'll decide what I say to him when I've seen the photos you're sending me."

River was about to kill the call but then said, "And Karen—this guy Manolo knows what he's doing with a rifle."

"Contract killer?"

"Definitely, and I don't know what will happen when Clery wakes up, which should be an hour or so from now."

"Perhaps I should take stock of what Pablo has in his armory here at the motel."

"Good idea. I don't think Clery recognized me, but when he discovers that his two burner phones have gone missing and that Karl has been shot by Manolo, he's going to want to finish the job."

"You mean *us*?" Karen said, unperturbed.

"You got that right. And I guess Reggie might be on the list, too."

"I'll call him and tell him."

"If he's not in court, he may want to spend the rest of the day at the motel."

"I'm not sure, Riv. I'll speak to Pablo, but I don't want a shootout in a motel full of innocent bystanders."

"There is that," River said. She didn't want a shootout at the motel, either, although she hadn't yet thought through where they could hunker down if they needed to leave the motel. "I need to get to Father Hopkins's center before I come back to the motel," she continued. "I'll be back in an hour or so, and then we can decide what we do next."

River terminated the call and crossed Arlington Memorial Bridge. She caught the Metro and got out a couple of stations later. She would have liked to walk—not that walking in the middle of the city gave her great pleasure, but at least she could release some of the morning's tension. Instead, though, she jumped on a bus and got out only a few yards from the center. She hadn't yet spoken to Father Hopkins about Maria's murder in detail, and she wanted to understand why Maria might have been a target.

### NOTEBOOK—VIRGINIA

August 2022
SEAL Team 1

I've postponed writing about the latest episode for a couple of days. Even now that I've found the courage to do so, I feel sick.

Three days ago, I left the house for a two-day training course. This is because I accepted a new role, at least for the time being. I teach the tech members of the SEALs teams to fly drones.

These are getting more important in warfare and can achieve a multitude of objectives. I'm good at it, and that was one of my tasks in Team 1.

The trouble started when I had difficulty getting to the training ground. I've driven there hundreds of times, but I kept forgetting the route. At the end, I had to navigate with GPS. Then I blanked out. I must have been fine until the following morning, but when I woke up, I felt . . . empty. I don't know how else I can describe it. I couldn't remember how to fly a drone. I couldn't remember anything. I got so scared that I called home to talk to the only person I can turn to. She managed to calm me down. I cried on the phone.

Writing these few lines is unbearable, but I know I must if I am to make sense of what's happening to me. Now that I am aware of my own issues, I speak a little more with former SEALs. I realize that I'm not the only one experiencing these symptoms. But perhaps none of the people I've spoken to has reached the advanced stage of deterioration that I have. Or they don't want to tell me. I get that, and it is for them as well as for myself that I write these notes and work with F at Walter Reed.

The more I think about it, the more I believe that the only way to find out what's happening is to analyze in detail the brain of one of us, but for that, the person needs to be dead.

J

A young man was manning the reception desk at the veterans' center when River walked in. She didn't know him and approached with a smile.

"I'd like to see Father Hopkins if he's free. My name is River Swift."

The young man smiled back and picked up the phone. He announced River, nodded a few times as he was listening to Father Hopkins's reply, and then turned to River.

"Father Hopkins suggests you wait for him here. He says coffee at the diner next door would be a good idea."

River nodded and moved to the waiting area. She caught her reflection in the window that opened onto a small inner garden. She'd completely forgotten about her hair color. She hesitated. Even though she wasn't a brunette anymore, noticeable traces of the dark color lingered.

"River?" Father Hopkins sounded startled. She turned around and felt a little warmth rising to her cheeks.

"I know—I had a bit of a meltdown yesterday."

Father Hopkins shuddered. "So did I . . . with Maria's news, you know."

River took him gently by the arm and said, "Let's go and have this coffee."

They both walked out of the center in silence and went into Ruthie's All Day Diner. River saw Betsy, the young woman who had served her before, when she pushed the door open. Father Hopkins waved, and Betsy came to greet them with a smile. She stopped in her tracks, and then her smile broadened.

"I almost didn't recognize you," Betsy said as she pointed to her own hair.

"I know," River said with a chuckle. "I got a little mad yesterday."

Betsy led them to a quiet table at the back of the diner. River and Father Hopkins didn't need to see the menu. They ordered coffee and pancakes.

"I'm not sure you want to talk about Maria," River said once Betsy had left, "but it might be relevant to what's happened to Jason."

Father Hopkins sighed and took his time to consider his answer.

"I've got to admit that Maria hadn't, well . . . hadn't been herself in the past few days. She was forgetting things, nervous, and . . ." Father Hopkins hesitated and then said, "She was asking a lot of questions about Jason and you, ever since you turned up a few days ago."

Their coffee and pancakes arrived. Betsy arranged the food on the table. "Enjoy."

174

They both smiled and waited to be alone to continue.

"What sort of questions?" River asked.

"Why you'd returned since you two were no longer together, that sort of thing," Father Hopkins said before he took a sip of coffee. "I first thought it was because she'd taken an interest in Jase, although I'd never seen any evidence of that before. But you know I don't always get things right."

River could vouch for that. He certainly hadn't foreseen her canceling her wedding just a few weeks before it was scheduled to happen.

"But you don't think it's that?" River prodded.

"No. First because I told her off. Nicely, but still she kept asking questions. It was as though she was desperate for answers. And then there was this question about a notebook. That worried me somehow, and I was about to ask you, but then . . ." Father Hopkins's voice trailed off.

River frowned. "A notebook?"

"Yes. Maria wanted to know whether Jason had left a notebook behind."

"That's a very precise question. How did she bring that up?"

"She said she was wondering whether he may have noted his feelings about his life-changing injuries. A place where he might record his state of mind."

River thought about it some more. The questions sounded very targeted for someone who didn't know Jason well. "Do you think Maria knew there *was* a notebook? I mean, do you think she was looking for it?"

Father Hopkins helped himself to a pancake and cut a piece. He put his fork down, thinking. "You're right. I wouldn't have put it that way, but now that you say it, I'm sure she knew of this notebook and was looking for it."

River helped herself to a pancake, too, and then said, "I don't recall Jason ever mentioning a notebook to me, but he didn't always share his thoughts with me. I never prodded—perhaps I should have."

Father Hopkins shook his head. "Some people only share when they are ready to share, and there is no point in pushing."

"But sometimes it's hard to know whether you've missed an opportunity to talk. I've seen this so often with men who incur traumatic injuries," River said, now no longer sure she had an appetite for her food. Could she have overlooked something vital? Something that meant Jason was on edge but couldn't or wouldn't share?

"Do you think we missed an opportunity to talk to Jason?" Father Hopkins asked.

River smiled at his kindness. It was so good of him to include himself in a potential admission of failure. "I don't know, Father. I sincerely hope not. I guess this notebook will give us the answer."

They both toyed with their pancakes, and then River said, "I still don't get why Maria was so interested in—" And then the answer dawned on her. If someone had disposed of Maria after she failed to find the notebook, then it was likely to be Clery. And if it was, the notebook might have to do with brain injuries. Clery and Karl were desperate to make any evidence disappear, no matter what it cost.

"Something come to mind?" Father Hopkins asked.

"I need to think this through. I hope that's okay."

They both managed to eat some of their food as they changed the subject and chatted about the center. Father Hopkins left, telling River he'd think about the notebook. River waited until he'd returned to the center to make her call to Karen. She stepped outside.

"You need to pick me up from the diner next to the veterans' center—Ruthie's All Day Diner. Clery should be awake by now, and I think things are going to turn nasty when he realizes he's been set up. And I know what he's after."

"On my way," Karen said.

River heard the door of the diner open, and she turned back. Betsy was standing there with a bag of food. She'd boxed up the pancakes that neither River nor Father Hopkins had finished.

"I'd hate to see these go to waste," she said with a smile.

River nodded. "Thank you. I didn't think of asking."

"Anything else, let me know." Betsy handed over the bag and returned to the kitchen.

# Chapter Fifteen

The room was spinning when Clery finally managed to open his eyes. He tried to lift a hand to touch his head, but a stabbing pain in his shoulder stopped him, and he winced in agony. As his mind emerged from the fog of Rohypnol, Clery became aware of how sore his body was, and then he grew perplexed. He couldn't remember why he felt that way.

He rolled onto his side, looked at the time on the digital clock he kept at his bedside, and blinked: 10:07 a.m. He struggled to sit up and realized he was still in the clothes he'd worn the evening before. A spell of dizziness forced him to lie down again, and he looked for his cell phone. It wasn't in his pants pocket. He rolled onto his side once more and saw it next to the clock. At least it hadn't gone missing.

Clery finally sat up straight and swung his legs over the side of the bed. He grabbed his phone and called the head of his security team.

"Any incident I need to be aware of last night?" Clery said, his words sounding a little mangled.

There was a short silence, and then the man replied slowly, "You were with a young lady last night in your study." The man hesitated some more. "I found you in the early hours of the morning. We couldn't wake you up."

Clery's mind went blank again. He tried to remember who it

was he'd spent time with in his study, a place he would never use for sex, no matter how hot the woman was.

"What did she look like?" Clery asked, his mind still struggling to focus.

"Tall, brunette, in a very short black dress."

Clery tried to think back to a part of the day he could recall. He remembered opening the safe he had hidden underneath the floorboards of his study and finding information about a couple he hadn't thought about for years—the Swifts. He recalled jotting down their names and that of the arms dealer he had employed to murder them in the DRC.

He ran a hand over his face and then realized he was still on the phone to his head of security. "When did she leave?"

"With the last of your guests."

"Did you check her out?"

"There was very little she could hide under that dress," the man protested. "But she was checked thoroughly, like everyone else, on the way in."

"I mean on the way out." Clery's voice had risen a notch. What sort of fool was he to let a woman . . . and then the image formed in his mind. He saw the attractive face and the jet-black hair. He saw the tight-fitting dress and the engaging smile of Laura Crain. He stood up and killed the call to his head of security. Clery felt unsteady on his legs as he staggered forward. He clung to the bedside table for a moment, then walked as fast as he could to his study, using the wall for support. He reached the place and crashed the door open.

A curtain tieback lay on the floor next to one of the armchairs. Clery walked to it and noticed a few white dots on the rug. He bent forward and saw that they were small shirt buttons. He then looked at his shirt and realized that she must have ripped his shirt open, popping the buttons out and sending them falling to the ground. Yet he still couldn't remember the encounter. Clery stayed still a moment, unable to admit he'd been conned.

He looked around the room, walked to his desk, and sat down. He immediately noticed that someone had taken a pencil out of the pencil cup. He picked up the notepad on the desk and bit his lower lip. The page on which he had written the Swifts' names and that of the Congo arms dealer was gone. He yanked open his bottom desk drawer and ran his hand over its contents. He pulled the drawer fully out and tipped its contents onto the ground. His two burner phones were gone.

Clery collapsed back into his executive-style desk chair. Whoever Laura Crain was, she had broken his defenses, and he needed to make sure he took the situation back in hand. He was due to call Karl in less than two hours' time. He needed to act fast.

Clery moved to another drawer, from which he extracted a brand-new burner phone. He set it up and powered it on. He then laid it on his desk and took a moment to think. He couldn't afford another mistake.

Clery briefly wondered whether Laura Crain had anything to do with River Swift or Jason Wayne. He would have to address that question later. First he needed to clean up the mess he'd made. He could perhaps claim that the wretched notebook his men hadn't been able to find had perished in the motel fire he was about to ask Manolo to set. Clery shook his head. Lying to Karl wasn't a good idea. Very few people scared him, but Karl did.

Clery dialed Manolo's number, let it ring five times, and hung up. He repeated the process, a sign that he'd changed burner phones.

"It all went down smoothly this morning," Manolo said as soon as he answered the phone.

Clery felt his throat tighten in anger. "How so?" he simply said.

"The man you instructed me to target came to the meeting point just on time—8:00 a.m., at the Pavilion Café. He sat down at one of the tables in back of the place. I got a clean shot in the thigh. A woman rushed to his aid. He'll survive."

Clery's mind went blank for a moment. A sheath of perspiration suddenly covered his entire body. How could he ask Manolo who it was he'd told him to shoot without sounding like a fool?

"Describe him again," Clery asked.

Manolo seemed taken aback by the question. "As you said, man—Caucasian, dark hair, late forties, and going to an 8:00 a.m. meeting at the Pavilion Café."

"I'll call you back" was all Clery could say. He dropped the phone and grabbed the side of the desk with both hands. Fear had replaced anger in one fell swoop. Someone had contacted Manolo with Clery's own burner phone, managed to convince Karl that a meeting was necessary with the second burner, and then . . .

The thought made Clery sick. Laura Crain must have managed to get him to give her his PIN, or else she worked for one of the agencies—FBI, CIA, Homeland Security—and had a tech work on the phone, or even both. Clery managed a bitter laugh. The con man had been conned.

Clery had known that this moment might one day come, but he had assumed he might have gotten an inkling beforehand and had a chance to prepare accordingly. No such luck: This moment, the one in which his shady dealings had caught up with him, had been forced upon him by a woman, one he knew nothing about.

Clery fought off the shock of realization. He hadn't been completely idle, and a bank account in the Cayman Islands was waiting for him under an alias. A set of documents confirming his new identity was waiting for him in the Bahamas. But before he could go, Clery needed to tidy up some loose ends. He would have a final assignment for Manolo, make a final appearance at his office in DC, retrieve documents from his other secret vault, gather the vault he held in Kalorama, and head to the airport, where he would board a plane to Nassau.

Clery dialed Manolo's number again. "New set of instructions. Eliminate the two women, River and her friend, and anyone who stands in the way. Do it now. Find someone who can also finish off Jason Wayne."

Manolo seemed to think it through and then said, "The women

I can take down today. They still haven't moved from the motel. We'll find them there easily enough. Wayne might take a little more time."

"Money isn't an issue. Bribe whomever you need to. I want Wayne out of the way tomorrow at the latest." Clery hung up and thought about his upcoming call with Karl. He could try to explain, but what would be his excuse? A young woman had drugged him and used his burner phones to draw Karl into a trap? Even to Clery, this sounded like the worst possible admission of failure.

He picked up his iPhone and looked at the availability of airline tickets online. It seemed that there wasn't any direct flight to Nassau in the late afternoon. Clery swore and thought for a moment. He would need to use one of the private jet companies he traveled with regularly. He moved to his contacts page, found the name he was looking for, and called. A light jet would be waiting for him at Dulles at 6:00 p.m. It was the earliest they could do. He just had to try to stay alive until then.

Karen arrived at Ruthie's All Day Diner in Pablo's pickup. River got in, and they drove off.

"How many vehicles keeping an eye on the motel now?" River said.

"Funny you should ask," Karen said. "Another one just joined, I think, but then again surveillance isn't my field of expertise."

River checked her watch. "Clery has woken up. He's realized what I've done—or, rather, what Laura Crain has done—and it's showtime as far as he's concerned."

"Dad would laugh at me. I got into the military because I didn't want to become a cop. And here I am, dealing with contract killers."

"I'm not sure cops deal with contract killers that often," River said.

"You may be right. They're more often dealing with mass murderers."

When they drove into the alleyway that led to the motel's backyard, Karen opened the gate using Pablo's remote and parked the pickup inside. River jumped out, walked into Pablo's living room, and then went to the front desk. Pablo was on his own, reading a newspaper and drinking a cup of coffee.

"We need to talk," River said, sitting next to him at the desk.

Pablo nodded, folded his paper, and sat back in his chair. "They're coming?"

River was taken aback by the coolness of his remark. "I'm glad you're so calm about it, but I don't want bloodshed or a hostage situation developing just because you've helped us."

"I've not been taking any new guests in," Pablo said. "And the ones who are here I've moved away from the room I rented to you."

She crossed her arms over her chest and said, "You've thought about this in detail, haven't you?"

Pablo smiled. "You got that right, and since I've been managing this place for over ten years, I think I've got a solid plan."

River smiled back. "All right, let's have it."


"Another SUV just arrived," Karen said to River through the walkie-talkie Pablo usually used to call his maintenance guy. She'd moved to the second floor, where Pablo had freed a couple of bedrooms overlooking the main road and the parking lot.

"I don't see anybody yet," River replied. She'd taken a position on the ground, behind Pablo's pickup truck at the back of the building. She'd moved the truck to a spot where she could see the window of the bedroom she and Karen had used when they first arrived.

"They're all going to move at the same time," Pablo replied from the desk, using the channel the three of them had switched to. He had sent the maintenance man out for a few hours after River had told him she suspected that Manolo and his men would be back before the end of the afternoon. No one would be using the regular walkie-talkie channel but the three of them.

There was a moment of silence, and River used it to review the team's positions. From her second-floor post, Karen could see movement at the side and front of the building. She'd also know if their assailants were trying to use the fire exit. Pablo had blocked it, and it would take explosives to blow the heavy reinforced steel door. By the time they set them up and detonated them, if they were willing to go down that route, Karen would have taken a position at the top of the fire-exit corridor, ready for retaliation. She'd borrowed an AR15 from Pablo and had plenty of 5.56 NATO to keep her going.

River had Jason's Glock 19, stuck in her waistband against her back, and an M60. She hadn't had time to ask Pablo where he had gotten it but now wondered whether this was a Vietnam War heirloom. Pablo had assured her that the Pig, as it was then known, was in good condition and could happily be fired from the shoulder. She'd learned to fire a machine gun during her training but hadn't done so for a while. An M60 would be difficult to operate on its own, without an assistant gunner. Still, she was sure she could handle the Pig when the time came.

The walkie-talkie crackled. "They're coming," Karen said.

"I see them getting out of one of the SUVs, too," Pablo said.

River pictured him sitting at his desk, newspaper open, a walkie-talkie on one side and two Glocks ready for use underneath the paper—the most exposed of their positions, yet he'd insisted on holding it.

A couple of men turned the corner into the alleyway in which Pablo's truck was parked. River crouched behind it, turned the volume of her walkie-talkie down a notch, and glanced at their progress from her hiding place. They reached River's old bedroom window and waited a moment. One of the men tried to look inside, but Pablo had drawn the curtains, and the view was blocked. The other man took his cell phone out of one of his pockets and made a call.

A moment later, voices came over the walkie-talkie.

"We're looking for River Swift. She's expecting us," a man's voice said.

River imagined Pablo lifting his head to face the men, unperturbed. "Turn left, second room on the right—A3," he said.

River's heart tightened. Pablo had now seen their faces, and he wouldn't be allowed to live, but he'd convinced her that they would kill him after they'd gone into her old room. The priority was to eliminate her and Karen first. The assassins wouldn't want to attract attention by first gunning down the receptionist. Pablo must have been right, since she didn't hear any gunshots. Even a suppressor would have made a distinct cork-popping sound.

"I'm moving," Pablo said after a few seconds.

He was now taking up a position at the corner of the corridor that led to room A3 and the reception area. He'd put his walkie-talkie in a holster on his belt and held a Glock in each hand. Then he spoke the magic words: "Drop your guns to the ground or I'll shoot you dead."

The answer came in—a low *bapbapbap* of a couple of guns with suppressors. Pablo responded immediately with several rounds.

"River, they're coming your way. Two of them," Pablo said.

The men forced their way into her old bedroom and found it empty. She couldn't help smiling at the thought. The two men underneath her window looked at each other. It seemed that the use of unsuppressed guns hadn't been on the menu. The curtains opened, followed by the window.

River took up her position, fired a series of rounds from the M60 into the ground, and shouted, "You move one muscle, and I'll shred you to bits that I'll feed to my pigs." The impact of the 7.62 NATO had created craters in the ground around the men. One turned around to fire his gun. River fired another series of rounds and got him in the legs. He collapsed, screaming, and his mate raised his hands in the air.

The man who'd opened the window retreated, and River lost sight of him. She heard Pablo shouting once more, "You've got no way out. I just called the cops. You try to escape, and I'll shoot your asses down, so just drop those fucking guns."

River heard the distinct sound of the suppressors and then a return volley from the Glocks. Someone cried in agony.

"I warned you," Pablo shouted.

River gave a short exhale. Pablo was fine, and now she needed to deal with the two men in front of her.

"You there," River shouted. "Drop your gun to the ground slowly or you go down the same way as your pal."

The man bent his knees slowly and let go of his SIG. He stood up just as slowly. River broke cover and stood with her weapon aimed at the men. She could see in the second one's eyes that he'd never seen an M60 before and wondered who the woman in front of him was.

"Step away and lie on the ground, facedown, hands on your head."

River walked forward. The other man had curled up on the ground. He held his wounded leg, whimpering. His gun had flown to the side, and neither he nor his weapon was a threat to River.

"If you move a muscle or try anything, like using a knife on me, I'll finish you off. You get me?" River shouted. He nodded and waited. River dropped the M60. She checked the Glock in her waistband and walked to the man lying facedown.

"Move your legs out more, stretch your arms, palms up, and turn your head to the right," she instructed.

The man responded to her instructions with a slight slump. He'd been handcuffed by police before, and he knew what was coming. She took a restraint she'd prepared—a nylon cable—dropped to one knee, and moved the man's left arm into a wristlock. She slid the cable around his wrist and pulled tight. Still controlling him through the wristlock, she leaned forward and slid the cable around his second wrist, fastening the loop and securing the man's hands.

She stepped away just as police sirens sounded in the distance. River grabbed her walkie-talkie and said, "Karen, do you see anybody else coming out of the SUVs?"

"Nothing at all."

"Then I need you to babysit two guys for me."

Karen appeared at the far end of the alleyway within seconds. She ran toward River, took her own gun out, and stood next to the two men.

"You'll need to take cover and keep an eye on these two guys. Two more are stuck in our old bedroom. They tried to get out once through the window. They might try again."

Karen moved behind the pickup, and River called Pablo on the walkie-talkie.

"Pablo, I'm coming through the back," she said. She ran through the backyard and then down the corridor.

Pablo had his shoulder to the wall and glanced behind him to see who was coming. When he saw River, he turned his attention back to the corridor and peeked around the corner. He whispered as River got close, "One of them is badly wounded. Not sure about the other one."

"The cops are going to be here any minute," River whispered back. "I heard the siren."

"No, they ain't," Pablo murmured.

River frowned. "But you said—"

"We're gonna get them to speak to us first. Tell you what you want to know. Then we call the cops."

"I'm a medic," River murmured. "I'm supposed to help people get better, not torture them." She'd already done quite a job on Clery; perhaps this was enough.

Pablo nodded. "Don't worry. I'll do the persuading."

River wondered what this would entail and decided that she didn't like that idea, either. She asked in a soft voice, "You did Vietnam, right?"

Pablo nodded again. "Yes, ma'am—101st Airborne Division."

"Let me do the talking," she whispered, and then shouted, "My friend here thinks he'd like to interrogate you before the cops arrive. We've already gunned two of you down, one with an M60, and it's not a pretty sight. My friend's done Vietnam, and he'd like to revisit some of the interrogation techniques the VC used on him and his pals. That's fine with me. So you've got two ways it's gonna swing. You get out nice and easy and talk to us, or we get in, we hurt you bad, and then you talk to us anyway."

River thought she could hear whispers, so she added, "Don't

187

even think about escaping through the window. My other friend—the one you were supposed to murder with me—has got the M60. She's waiting for you, and she's pissed."

The sound of a gun sliding along the corridor was encouraging. "And the other gun . . . and your ankle guns. If I don't have four guns in the corridor when I break cover, me and my friend here go for option two."

River heard more metal sliding on tiles. Pablo looked disappointed. "You never know," she said to him. "Maybe they've got knives and you can give them a kicking for it."

Pablo gave her his second smile of the day and said, "That's a thought. I'll go and get the guns. You cover me."

"No," River protested, "this is my fight."

Pablo grabbed her shoulder and said, "Don't begrudge an old man a bit of fun. And anyway, my motel, my rules."

River dropped to one knee and took up a position where the wall met the corridor. Pablo lifted his SIG and broke cover, gun at the ready. River swung low and shot a couple of rounds that hit the floor near her old bedroom. There was blood on the tiles along with four guns. Pablo ran to them, used his foot to slide them farther away from the door, and stopped at the corner.

"Come out with your hands over your heads," he shouted. "You know what happens if you don't."

"Don't shoot," someone cried from inside the room.

"You come out nice and easy," Pablo shouted back. "I want to see your hands first, high in the air."

He took a step back and waited. River had a good angle, too. A pair of hands appeared out of the door. A small man stood in the door frame, and River shouted, "Keep going. You stop when I tell you."

He glanced at Pablo, more to avoid him than challenge him.

"Stop and drop to the floor," River shouted. She immobilized him just the way she'd immobilized the man in the alleyway, but this time she tied up the feet, too.

"C'mon—it's your turn, Manolo," she shouted.

188

She had a hunch that the smaller guy wasn't the leader of Clery's gang of murderers. The man on the ground looked surprised and turned his head to the door. River now knew she was right.

"Clery is dead. If not now, he will be soon. The man you shot this morning was Karl, his biggest client. Karl is not the sort of man who forgets, so the best you can hope for is to cut a deal with the police—tell them what you know and get into the witness protection program. The reason why you shot the wrong guy is because I sent you the text. I'll prove it to you."

River grabbed Clery's burner phone and sent a text. **Hello Manolo!**

"I also sent a text to Karl, and I'm happy to send him another one to tell him where he should send his men to collect you. So what's it gonna be?"

"I'm wounded," Manolo said from inside the room.

"Not so much that you can't walk out. I'm a medic, so don't try that shit on me. You got in there. Now you get out."

Pablo looked back at River. He was eager to go, but she shook her head and mouthed "No."

"Last chance, or I'll text Karl. You're not going anywhere. He'll find you in police custody wherever you are."

"How do I know you're not going to call him anyway?"

"You're just gonna have to trust me."

Manolo laughed, and River wondered why he still sounded so confident. She got closer to Pablo and said, "He's called reinforcements. He still got his cell phone. They're coming."

Pablo charged inside without warning. River heard a gun discharge. She shot in after Pablo, but it was too late. Manolo's eyes were already losing their focus, and his body slid sideways, leaving a trail of blood against the wall.

"No," River cried. She rushed to Manolo and pressed her fingers against his neck, yet felt nothing. The gaping hole in his chest should have told her he was already dead, but the thought of losing her only witness to Clery's dirty business was unbearable.

River slumped to the ground. For an instant she wondered

whether Pablo was in on it, cleaning up Clery's mess. A whimper from the corridor made her turn around. Pablo had gotten the man who'd been restrained to sit up. He had his gun to the man's head and said, "Are you ready to talk? Or do you want to go the same way as your boss?"

The guy nodded and said, "I'll tell you what I know. Just don't shoot me."

Pablo walked to the place where Manolo's body had fallen and took his cell phone out of his pocket. "First, call off your troops. They turn up, you're dead."

Pablo dialed the last number Manolo had called, stuck the phone to the man's ear. River watched as he managed to persuade Manolo's thugs to pull back. When Pablo hung up and took the phone away, River walked to the man and asked, "What's your name?"

"Carlos."

"And what do you know about Jason Wayne and why he's been set up?" River said.

Pablo cocked his gun and pressed the barrel against the man's temple.

"If you kill me, you'll know nothing."

"If you don't talk, we'll know nothing anyway," Pablo said.

"C'mon," River said as she prodded him with the toe of her shoe.

"Manolo didn't tell me why he was asked to frame Wayne. All I know is that it was Mr. Clery who asked for it to be organized."

"Who killed the woman?" River asked.

"I think it was Manolo."

Pablo pressed the gun harder against Carlos's head.

"I swear—I don't know for sure. I wasn't in the room. I was in the car, waiting for Manolo, another guy called Nas, and Wayne."

"But you saw them drag Jason out of the hotel, unconscious?"

Carlos nodded. "And then I drove them to an underpass in Washington Highlands. They dumped him there, but they weren't happy when they came back, because a couple of hoboes had seen them. They caught one a few days later, but one of them is still out there."

Pablo and River exchanged a look. The first piece of good news of the past few days.

"Anything else?" River prodded Carlos again with her foot.

"They were talking about a notebook. They haven't found it yet."

River pulled her iPhone out of her pocket, walked back toward Pablo's living room, and made a call.

# Chapter Sixteen

The phone rang a few times. River was preparing to leave a message when a breathless Lorrie picked up the phone.

"Carlton residence," she said. Her voice sounded overly formal, and River wondered whether she'd been expecting a call from a military official.

"Lorrie, I hope I'm not troubling you. It's River, Jason Wayne's . . ." River faltered. Who was she? His former bride-to-be? His friend? But Lorrie saved her the trouble and said, "It's good to hear from you. I had a message from Walter Reed hospital. I'm expecting a call."

River thought about offering to hang up, but she had to ask her question, so she apologized. "I'm very sorry. I hope you won't mind speaking with me while you're waiting."

"Please go ahead," Lorrie said. "If a call comes in, I'll hang up with you and pick up the other one."

"It's about a notebook," River said. She let the idea sink in a little. It was a sensitive subject—a diary that her late husband might have kept. Such a diary would be intensely personal, perhaps revealing Jethro's innermost thoughts, and River felt embarrassed about asking.

"Whose notebook do you mean?" Lorrie sounded perplexed.

"Jethro's. I know it's very personal, and again, I'm sorry. I wouldn't ask if it weren't important."

Lorrie seemed to be thinking for a moment and then said, "I

didn't find any notebook in his desk or his study." River sensed that Lorrie was pushing back her pain to answer River's question. "But I do recall him talking about notes he was taking."

There was another silence, then Lorrie continued. "I didn't think about it at the time, but it would have been typical of Jethro to record what he observed in detail. He was like that—he enjoyed understanding how things functioned, and I don't think it would have mattered to him whether the thing he was observing was himself and his own . . ."

Lorrie's voice trembled, and she stopped short.

"I'll call you back, if you'd rather—"

"No," Lorrie said, and the moment seemed to pass. "No. It's important. So to answer your question, I didn't find a notebook, but that doesn't mean there isn't one."

River could hear movement at the other end of the line. She thought Lorrie was walking. Then she heard what sounded like a door opening. "I'm in his office," Lorrie said.

The sound of a drawer being opened told River that Lorrie was searching for something.

"I found a list of books that Jethro had left behind. There's an annotation that I didn't pay attention to at the time. It says, 'Must include with notes.'"

River ran her hand through her hair. "Do you think Jethro may have given the notes he'd taken to Jason?"

"They were very close . . . Jase had been part of Team 1," Lorrie said. "Jethro would have trusted him enough to share his worries with him."

"Even more so because Jase had gone through a very bad patch after he returned from Afghanistan and discovered he would never join Team 1 again," River added.

Both women remained silent for a short while, and then River said, "Thank you for sharing with me. It helps."

"I'll let you know if Walter Reed sends me any meaningful information."

Lorrie hung up, and River heard sirens in the distance. This time she was certain it was the police, and they were heading her way. She returned to the corridor where she'd left Pablo and Carlos.

"I need to go to Father Hopkins's veterans' center. I'll leave it to you and Karen to handle the cops."

Pablo nodded, and River disappeared back through Pablo's small apartment. She grabbed her helmet and jacket, got on the motorcycle, and rode down the alleyway. She stopped near Karen. Her friend had secured both men and done a good job at controlling the extensive damage one of the men had sustained from the M60.

"I need to see Father Hopkins," River said after flipping her visor up.

"You go," Karen said as she cocked her head toward the main road. "I'll handle the cops, and I'll chase Dad about Karl's identity."

River revved the bike and joined the traffic on the road. Her mind was on her next task—finding the notebook that she now was almost certain Jethro had left behind. She swerved around the cars that were clogging the streets, eager to reach the center. Perhaps the notebook was there, and Maria had failed to find it, which had gotten her killed. It wasn't at Jason's apartment, not even in the hiding place where River had found his Glock. She didn't believe Jason would have left the notebook lying around and so dismissed the thought that the CSI team working with Detective Parker had found it.

Father Hopkins's center looked busy when she arrived. The parking lot was unusually full, so River parked her bike near Ruthie's diner. Betsy was opening the door for a man who was struggling to use his set of crutches. She spotted River and waved. River waved back and walked to the center. The same young man who'd welcomed her when she last visited was manning the reception desk. He looked a little frazzled, trying to respond to a group of men who were attending whatever event it was that Father Hopkins had organized.

She tried to be patient but couldn't help glancing at her watch.

The receptionist spotted the move and nodded apologetically. She smiled and pulled back. River took her cell phone out and thought about the call she wanted to make. It was worth a try. She found the contact information for Frank Bruce at Walter Reed hospital and dialed his number.

Frank picked up almost immediately and said, "How did you know I needed to have a chat?"

"I didn't, but since you're on the phone, why don't you tell me?" River said after finding a quiet place to talk.

"I can't speak to you about the specifics—"

"You mean the name and exact diagnosis?"

"Patient confidentiality," Frank replied.

"But you found something unusual in the tests you've been running on brain-tissue samples."

"You can say that again." Frank sounded bemused, and River took note. This wasn't a rookie researcher she was speaking with. It was one of the most senior figures in the Behavioral Health Clinic at Walter Reed.

"Do I need to call Lorrie?"

"Yes, but I'd wait a little while. I mean, I know you're racing against the clock, but still."

"Thanks, Frank. I'll bear that in mind. But I've got a separate question for you."

"Okay, shoot."

"Did either Jethro or Jason mention a notebook?"

"You mean like a personal diary?" Frank sounded surprised.

"Something like that."

"No. I can't recall our talking about one."

"And I guess there isn't anywhere they could have left such a document with you?"

Frank seemed to give it some thought but then said, "Again, no. Sorry I can't be of more help."

"It's all right, Frank. Your letting me know I need to get in touch with Lorrie, all in good time, helps a lot."

River hung up and returned to the reception area. David, the young receptionist—she could see his name now on a tag pinned to his T-shirt—was free.

"You have a big event today?"

"Yes, and I don't know the center well enough yet to direct everyone properly—a nightmare."

"Is Father Hopkins running the event?"

"It's about to start in a few minutes. You may be able to catch him before that."

River thanked him and darted toward the large conference room down the corridor. Father Hopkins was already seated. She wove her way through the attendees who were still choosing their seats and stood a little awkwardly in front of him.

"Would you mind if I looked around the center?" she asked. "I now think there *is* a notebook—the one Maria was looking for—and that it holds important information."

Father Hopkins frowned, but the room was almost ready, with only a few attendees still looking for a seat. The two other people who appeared to be chairing the panel with him also were taking their place at the long table. He nodded and said as he bent toward River, "Try not to be too obvious about it."

River nodded. She would be discreet. She left the room and went to what she thought was the most obvious place to look—Father Hopkins's office. The door wasn't locked. She recalled the morning when her jogging run had taken her to the center, and she'd noticed movement in the office. She was now certain it had been Maria. She also was certain that she'd disturbed her when she tested the doors to check whether the center had been broken into.

Father Hopkins's office was reasonably tidy, and River proceeded methodically. There were a couple of freestanding file cabinets that were locked. She would ask Father Hopkins to take a closer look at those when he was finished. After almost an hour of searching, she hadn't found anything.

She walked out of the office and into the kitchen. It was empty, and River rummaged through the cabinets. She walked around the rest of the center, but there wasn't any obvious hiding place she could find.

She wasn't thinking straight, she decided. Either Jason or Jethro would have left the notebook in a secure location if it was at the center—not in a place where someone might find it, if only by mistake.

River walked past the conference room, where Father Hopkins's event was in full swing, and arrived at reception.

"I'm going to Ruthie's diner," she said to David. "Would you mind calling me when the conference is over?"

David nodded and took down her number. She left the center and walked to Ruthie's, where she spotted Betsy again. River found a free table next to the window and sat down. She needed to think. She was getting close to amassing enough evidence to bring to Detective Parker—enough to ask him to reconsider Jason's murder charges. She was sure that Karen and Pablo would deliver Manolo's driver to the police and impress upon them the importance of this witness. And Pablo needed to be kept safe until she'd been able to speak to Parker. Then there was the vagrant who'd escaped Clery's men.

Betsy recognized River and came to take her order—another Cuban sandwich. River returned to her conjecture until her lunch arrived. Betsy was even more chatty than usual, and River didn't feel she could ask to be left alone. More customers arrived, and Betsy left River to her food. She took a mouthful of her sandwich, hesitated, but then called Karen.

"Hey. It was a good call to bail out," Karen said. "The cops who turned up got a bit confused about who was who. I thought they were going to cuff me and Pablo."

River smiled at the thought of the weapons on display. "You and Pablo were carrying some serious heat."

"Nothing they haven't seen before, right?"

"Yes, but not usually carried by the good guys, at least not in DC."

"You have a point. Anyway, I made sure that the cops spoke to

Detective Parker. Carlos is on his way to the Alabama Avenue police station. I then called Dad. We have a positive ID on Karl. His name is Karl Kruger, a dual citizen of South Africa and the United States and a serious motherfucker. Dad says Kruger's file is so large it crashed his PC. His main business is armaments. He belongs to several gun groups and is suspected of arms trafficking, although he hasn't been caught yet, and that is exercising quite a few agencies."

River lost her concentration for a moment. The note she'd stolen from Clery's desk was still in her coat pocket, and she could feel it begging to come out. Karen was calling her name, and River refocused.

"Sorry, Karen. Something crossed my mind. I need to speak to Reggie. I want him on Parker's case again about allowing Jason to be tested for Rohypnol."

"And to make sure Parker does his job and keeps Carlos safe," Karen added.

"That, too." River pushed her sandwich away. She was no longer hungry. "I still haven't found the notebook. Although I'm now sure there is one. I've been through Father Hopkins's center and found nothing."

"Have you spoken to him?"

"He was the one who mentioned it initially, and he has no clue. He's running a conference right now, but I hope I'll speak to him after it's finished. Two filing cabinets are locked. I need to check whether it's in one of them."

"Dad and I are having a call about this guy Karl Kruger again. He can't send the file, but he can give me a good idea about what to expect."

River tamped down the memory of Clery's notepad with her parents' names on it, then hung up and called Reggie.

"I have some news," River said.

"Me, too." Reggie sounded relieved, and she hoped he'd somehow managed to speak to Parker again.

"Has Parker changed his mind about Jason's blood test?"

"No such luck yet, but"—he paused for effect—"I've managed to convince Jase that he shouldn't plead guilty."

River let a small cry out, bringing her hand to her mouth to muffle the sound. "I'd almost given up," she said.

"Well, I almost did, too, but he thought about what I'd said. His guilty plea won't protect you. You already know far too much, and he saw the truth of that."

"Have you spoken to Parker about Jason's plea?"

"Not yet. He was out, but I'm not moving from the Alabama Avenue police station until I've seen him."

"And now," River said, "let me tell you about my morning."

She told Reggie about the attack on the motel, skirting around the gunfight a little, but she couldn't avoid mentioning that Pablo had gunned down one of Clery's men. She spoke about Carlos's expected confession and the promise that he would be protected if he gave evidence against Clery. She finished with a summary of what she was expecting Carlos would say.

"Wow, River. You've been busy." Reggie had let her speak without interrupting but then added, "How much of the information you got comes from official sources?"

"Good question. I'd say almost none," River said, biting her bottom lip.

"Then perhaps I can offer Carlos some help with representation. I'll tease as much as I can out of him in his confession."

"Is that . . . *legal*?"

"My representing Carlos? Yes. Squeezing him dry to get to the truth? Not so much." Reggie didn't sound that concerned, and River wasn't going to belabor the point.

"Update me after you've seen Parker," River said. She hung up and sat back. Clery had given his instructions and would be waiting for results. It'd been almost two hours since the attack had taken place. He might already suspect that it hadn't gone according to plan.

*If I were him, I'd run.*

River wondered whether he would have the time to get out of town. Karl Kruger wouldn't enjoy having been shot at and his operation compromised. She didn't care whether Clery lived or died as long as he paid for what he'd done.

A hand landing on her shoulder surprised her. Betsy was standing next to her with a concerned look on her face. "Didn't you enjoy the sandwich? I can get you something else if you'd like."

"I have a lot on my mind, and that has stolen my appetite," River said with an apologetic smile. "I'm looking for a document, and I still can't find it."

Betsy tilted her head and said, "I hope it all gets resolved."

River nodded her thanks. "Very kind." She needed to find Jethro's notebook, and she needed to start with the veterans' center.

## NOTEBOOK–VIRGINIA

### September 2022
### SEAL Team 1

I now have a plan.

I know it's inevitable. I'll soon be so out of control that I will commit an act that'll cost someone his life. I still have moments of lucidity, but they are less and less frequent. I otherwise spend my time experiencing mood swings the likes of which I've never felt before.

I have read enough about trauma and brain injury to suspect that the constant use of weapons and explosives has something to do with my condition. I wonder whether blast pressure affects the brain the way repeated blows sometimes affect the brains of boxers. Frank doesn't have an answer to that yet because the new research department that has been created to study PTSD has hardly received any brain tissue to study.

Frank has put me in touch with a group of former Marines who work closely with the armaments industry to make weapons safer. I've met one of them via video link. I no longer feel safe enough to meet people in person. I had to postpone our call twice. It was a real achievement to hold my own for the hour it took. But I told him all I needed him to know. He promised he would relay my concerns to the manufacturers he works with.

I have also spoken to Jason. Not much point holding back with him. He, too, needs to know. He came to the house when Lorrie, Tammy, and Muffin were out. I hardly leave my office these days. It feels more secure because I can shut the door when an episode comes on. I showed Jason the books, the notebook, and all the tests I underwent at Walter Reed. I'm not sure whether he suspects what's coming next. But he, too, must have thought about what it means to spend a life away from the best profession in the world—to serve one's country.

And like me, Jase is willing to die, but not the slow death of deterioration.

J

The new burner phone hadn't rung yet. Manolo had sounded confident, but now Clery wasn't sure. He couldn't fathom why his team of well-trained men couldn't deliver. But this was no longer important. He'd been spending the few hours after his call to Manolo storing information on flash drives—information he would use later to help himself stay alive. He started destroying the rest and was almost done when his iPhone rang. The caller's name was blocked, and he ignored it.

Clery had dismissed his staff and told them to take the day off. They all looked shocked at the thought, but no one had dared ask why, and Clery hadn't offered any explanation. Thankfully, his wife was still in Europe and out of the way, too. He just wanted to be alone—to pack a small suitcase, load his briefcase with papers and flash drives, and leave without witnesses.

Clery didn't call his usual driver. Instead he placed a call with a local limo company he'd never used before and asked for a car to pick him up in fifteen minutes. He hung up and was about to remove his SIM card from his iPhone when it rang again. The number was blocked, and Clery swore a couple of times until he realized what it meant. They were geolocating him, and they were coming for him.

His mind went blank for a few seconds. This wasn't the way it was supposed to go. He now didn't have time to wait for the limo he'd ordered. He left his small suitcase behind and grabbed his briefcase. He ran down the stairs to the first floor, went through the large kitchen, entered the pantry, and walked to the end. He flung aside a heavy piece of cloth that was used as a curtain and accessed a small door. It led to the part of the garden that ran along the property wall. He unlocked it and opened it cautiously. A rush of cold wind almost made him lose his grip, but he held firm and waited for a moment. All sounded calm in the garden.

Clery slid out the door, ran along the wall, and reached its far end. He slipped the briefcase strap over his shoulder, pulled at the heavy creeper that covered the wall, and uncovered a ladder. He'd just put his foot on the first rung when a couple of bullets flew above the top of the wall from the other side. They'd been fired from a gun fitted with a suppressor. He knew the distinct cork-popping sound.

Clery jumped back down. How did they know? In a panic, he ran to the opposite wall, managing to find cover behind the old trees that spread across the garden. There wasn't a ladder on that side of the wall, but he thought he could climb up the thick trunk of the ivy that grew on it. Clery found purchase along the bricks and started to climb. Nothing happened this time, and he thought that perhaps his pursuers hadn't managed to gain access to his neighbors' garden.

The sound of a door being opened and that of footsteps pounding the ground forced him to accelerate the climb. He almost slipped but recovered. His right hand reached the top of the wall . . . one more push. But someone was climbing the wall behind him. Clery slung his arm across the stones. A couple of hands grabbed his legs. He tried to kick, but the two men who were after him yanked him off the wall with a vicious pull. Clery fell backward and hit the ground with a thud.

\*   \*   \*

When he came to, his arms were tied behind him, and someone was shaking him awake. He was in his study, seated in his desk chair. Three men stood in the room, two on each side of him and one in front of his desk. The man on his left shook him again and said, "He's conscious."

The man who stood in front of Clery's desk nodded, took a phone out of his pocket, and dialed a number. He put the phone on speaker and waited. The phone only rang once, and then Karl Kruger's voice filled Clery's study.

"I'm in a great deal of pain, Chuck, but at least I'll keep my leg."

"Is it worth my saying that I didn't order the hit?" Clery said, keeping his voice as steady as he could.

"I already gathered that," Kruger replied. "Although my men didn't stop your hit guy in time, they managed to track him pretty fast once I instructed them to. In fact someone else has already finished him off at some motel. And why not finish me off rather than hurt me? But still, this is the sort of failure I can't let slip. I'm sure you see my point."

Clery's mind worked hard to find a compromise, but this time he couldn't see one.

"What are you going do?" he simply asked.

It was a stupid question, he knew, but somehow part of him couldn't accept the inevitable.

"I'm afraid, Chuck, you're not the only one who works for me in this town, so I need to send a message . . . and I need to make any evidence disappear."

Then Kruger's tone abruptly changed. He had been his usual self in their conversation—clinical, to the point. Now he enjoyed giving the order.

"Burn everything down," he said before the phone went dead.

Clery shouted and thrashed against the ties that bound him to the chair. One man slapped a piece of heavy-duty tape over his mouth. Clery moved his head, but another piece of tape came across

203

his mouth again. The two men on each side of him were wrapping the same type of tape around his legs and arms, securing him further to his desk chair. A strong smell hit Clery's nostrils. It was an accelerant that the third man was pouring over the carpet, the furniture, and the curtains. Clery screamed in terror, but the sound of his despair hardly broke the barrier of the tape.

The two men who had tied him to the chair left. The third one looked around the room. He seemed satisfied with his work and walked to the door. Clery screamed again as loud as he could, trying to catch the man's eyes, but he never looked at him. Instead, he took a box of long matches out of his jacket pocket and stood outside the door, making sure the fluid was as far as possible away from his feet. He struck a match, let it catch properly, and threw it into the middle of the room.

# Chapter Seventeen

Father Hopkins walked into the diner as River was about to leave. He settled at the table where River was sitting.

"Have you found anything useful?" he asked.

"Nothing at all. I'm now certain that the notebook Maria mentioned is Jethro Carlton's. I called Lorrie, and she's sure it's not at their home, but she confirmed that Jethro was taking notes on his condition. The notebook isn't at Jason's, either. I thought perhaps one of them had entrusted it to you or even hidden it at the center."

River had wondered whether Father Hopkins had been holding back information—not out of malice but in an effort to protect details that might have been shared with him in confidence.

"Neither of them told me about a journal or notebook, and that's why Maria's mentioning it sounded odd to me," Father Hopkins said. He shook his head. "Do you think that's why she was murdered? Because she was looking for this book?"

"I can't be absolutely sure, but I think so."

Father Hopkins slumped in his chair. "Matthew 9:13—'Go and learn what this means: I desire mercy, not sacrifice,'" he said. "But sometimes I desire sacrifice rather than mercy—a terrible admission for a man who seeks to serve God."

River replied, "'God delights when truth reigns in our inmost being'—Psalm 51, I believe. There is no point in denying that injustice and greed provoke anger and challenge us. We simply need to acknowledge it. I'm a medic. I save people's lives, yet I'm prepared to do what it takes to get Jason the justice he deserves."

"What else can I do to help?"

"I noticed two cabinets that are locked in your office. Perhaps you could check them to see whether the notebook is in there."

Father Hopkins rose slowly and nodded. "I'll call you if I find anything."

River stood up, too, and they both walked to the door. She turned back and waved at Betsy, who returned the wave with a smile. Outside, the sky was low, and she shivered as she fastened her coat. The wind had turned much colder, and snow was on its way. For the briefest of moments, she thought about Alaska and the blizzards she'd witnessed since she moved to Kotzebue. Even these felt more welcome than a snowfall in DC.

Her cell phone rang. She fetched it out of her pocket and answered.

"You've got to come to the Seventh District police station," Reggie said. "Detective Parker wants to speak to you."

River heart somersaulted. "Is this about Jason?"

"No. It's about Carlos. Parker has lost track of the police car that was taking him to the station."

"How can that be?"

Reggie lowered his voice. "Fuck, I don't know, but Parker looks pissed and perhaps even worried."

"This is our only witness when it comes to Clery," River lamented. "Parker and his cops can't be *that* incompetent."

"That's been my worry all along. He's crap at his job and needs to score a big win."

"I'm on my way. As quick as I can."

River put her helmet on, fired her bike, and joined the traffic. She checked her side mirror more times than she normally would. Karl Kruger might prove a more formidable enemy than even Clery was. She rode through traffic, swerving between cars and trucks. She finally crossed the Anacostia River and reached Alabama Avenue a few minutes later.

Reggie was waiting outside the station when she parked the bike. He waved at her and jogged toward her.

"They found the car," he said as he reached her.

River removed her helmet and asked, "Are they alive?"

"The two cops who were taking Carlos to the station are dead. No sign of Carlos."

River slammed her fist on the seat of her bike. "This is never-ending. Parker has got to get his ass in gear and stop thinking he knows better than anybody else."

"I sort of told him that, although perhaps a little more diplomatically."

"I'm no longer inclined to be diplomatic."

"What do you want me to do?" Reggie asked as they started walking toward the police station.

"We need Parker to focus on this guy Karl Kruger. He's got to be the one behind all this. I thought we were going to have a lot more time. He was shot in the leg, and the wounds looked bad."

"Hang on," Reggie said, slowing down his pace. "Have I missed a chapter?"

"You might have. I told you that Clery was acting on behalf of one of his clients. I've managed to identify him as Karl Kruger, arms dealer with a history of trafficking. Karen is getting more information from her father, the chief of police in Kotzebue."

"I know I keep asking the same question: Do I need to know—"

River shook her head and interrupted Reggie. "You do keep asking, and the answer hasn't changed. It's confidential."

Reggie rolled his eyes. "And how are you gonna persuade Parker to look into this guy Kruger if you can't reveal how you know his name?"

River paused for a moment. "Bearing in mind that Carlos has disappeared and that the likelihood of his being alive is small, I'll tell Parker that Carlos mentioned it."

"And what if Carlos turns up alive?"

"I'll improvise." River turned back toward the police station. "Let's go."

When River entered the police station, she didn't have to ask for a meeting with Parker. The receptionist who'd helped her on her other visits picked up her phone and made a call. Detective Parker must have been waiting for it. He walked through the doors of the station's back office a minute later. He went straight to River and offered the beginning of an apologetic smile.

"Reggie tells me you lost two of your men and a key witness," River said as she came to stand in front of Parker. "I've very sorry about the two police officers who lost their lives."

Parker's face fell, and he shook his head. "Two good guys I've known for a long time."

"Let's go somewhere else to discuss this," she said, now more sorry than angry.

Parker led the way to one of the meeting rooms, and both River and Reggie followed. He entered the room, went to the water cooler, and poured a glass he drank on the spot. He refilled it, poured another two glasses, and put them in front of River and Reggie.

"Please take a seat," Parker said, seemingly ready to acknowledge the fact that he needed some help.

"I'll tell you all I have gathered so far, Detective Parker, on the condition that you don't ask about my sources," River said as she sat down.

Reggie frowned, but River ignored him. She needed Parker on board if they were to catch Clery and Kruger.

"Carlos was prepared to reveal the names of the men who framed Jason."

River took a sip of water and waited a moment. Parker's jaw clenched, but he sat back and then nodded. "Who are they?"

"Before I tell you, I'd like to make a couple of requests," River said. "First, I'd like Jason to be tested for Rohypnol in his system."

Reggie straightened up. He seemed to understand what River

was doing. If Parker agreed, she had a solid witness in Reggie to remind Parker of what he'd promised to do.

Parker waved his hand in the air, dismissive. "Rohypnol only stays in a victim's blood for twenty-four hours and in the urine for sixty hours, sometimes a little bit more, but we are way past the window of opportunity in both cases."

River nodded. "That's true for a blood and urine samples, but that isn't the case for a hair sample. So I suggest you get your CSI people to take a sample of Jason's hair and start testing."

Reggie took a small notepad out of his satchel and started writing. "Let's set a deadline of the end of today for the sample taking," he said.

Parker's eyes went from River to Reggie and back to River again. His gaze narrowed, but he gave a short nod.

"Detective Parker agrees to the proposed deadline," Reggie announced as he scribbled a note on his pad.

"How about the names of—"

River raised her hand, interrupting Parker. "I also want you to ask your CSI to comment on the killer's dominant hand if you haven't already."

"What's that about?" Parker drummed his fingers on the table.

"Well, Jason is left-handed, not right-handed. I'm almost certain that the shape of the knife wound will show whether the murderer was right-handed or left-handed. You'll agree it's an important test?"

Reggie took a note and tapped his pen on his pad a couple of times.

"Fine," Parker grumbled.

River waited a moment, thinking. She leaned forward, forearms on the table and hands splayed over its top. "Two people have framed Jason. The first man is Chuck Clery. He is a lobbyist here in DC, and his clients are in the gun industry. The other man is Karl Kruger. He is a member of a few gun-rights advocacy groups and an arms dealer. He smuggles a lot of armaments to Africa but hasn't yet been caught by any agency."

Parker sat back and crossed his arms over his chest. "And I'm supposed to believe that Carlos volunteered this information to you?"

"Detective Parker, two of your colleagues are dead, and Carlos has disappeared. Shouldn't you be questioning these two men before they themselves disappear from DC? Both know by now that the motel assault has failed and that two officers were driving Carlos to your station. I doubt they'll be hanging around for much longer."

"Why would these two have wanted to frame Jason?" Parker's arms were still crossed over his chest.

"Because Jason was about to expose the reason why so many Navy SEALs and other Special Forces troops have died by suicide over the years, a reason that has something to do with the repetitive use of weapons. Gun-rights groups don't want to hear this."

"And you've got evidence that proves it?"

River moved forward a little more. "The results of brain-tissue analysis are in, and the lab at Walter Reed doesn't make mistakes."

Reggie stiffened up and then coughed. River was taking a gamble, and Reggie didn't approve.

Parker leaned forward, forearms on the table, too. He stared at River and said, "I'll find out more about these men and will pay them a visit if I uncover more evidence. But I can't just speak to them based on your account of what a potential witness said. And if I find out that you're sending me on a wild-goose chase, I'll arrest you for obstructing this investigation."

"Making threats won't get us any closer to finding the real culprit," Reggie protested.

"I'm not making threats. I'm telling you the way it's gonna be if you waste my time. You know the way out."

Parker stood up and walked out of the room. River and Reggie waited until he disappeared.

"What now?" Reggie said.

"I need to make a call to Lorrie, Jethro's wife. I don't really want to do this, but I need to know whether I'm right about the repeated use of firearms during training and deployment."

Reggie reached the door and turned back. "Why don't you use this room? That'll be more private than calling from the sidewalk."

He left, and River took her iPhone out of her pocket. She scrolled down her contacts list and found Lorrie's name. Her thumb hovered over the Call button, but finally she shook her head and pressed it. The phone rang a few times, but then Lorrie answered. She must have recognized River's number because she said, "Walter Reed has sent me the results."

River bit her bottom lip and then said, "Are you okay, Lorrie?"

"I can't pretend it isn't very tough, but now we know. Jethro had damage to his brain's glial cells, a condition called astroglial scarring. Frank explained that these glial cells have many tasks and are essential for good brain function."

"Did he say what caused this condition?" River managed to ask.

Lorrie sighed. "Frank needs to carry out further tests, but the likely explanation is that shooting ammunition and detonating explosives create microbubbles that burst in the brain and, in the long run, damage it."

River sat down again. She so wished she could be near Lorrie to comfort her.

"I can't thank you enough for giving me this information."

"This is what Jethro would have wanted. He would have wanted his teammates, his colleagues to be safe. Making sure this issue comes out will do exactly that."

"You have my word. I'll make sure it becomes public and that the military notices."

Lorrie hung up, and River stayed motionless for a while. She now had two reasons to help Jason prove his innocence. First, he *was* innocent, and once released, he would become a formidable advocate, speaking for the Special Forces and making sure their training and deployment were safe.

River stood up, walked out of the interrogation room, and almost bumped into Detective Parker. His face was drawn, and his brow was furrowed.

"Bad news?" River couldn't help asking.

"Clery's house is on fire, and we can't find Kruger."

River shook her head. "This guy Kruger is the one you really want. He's got dual South African and American citizenship. I'd make sure the airports around DC know you're after him. I'd alert Customs and Border Protection, too."

Parker didn't seem to mind her telling him what to do this time. He took his cell phone out of his jacket pocket and started making calls. River waited until Parker had finished and then said, "Keep me posted in case I can be of further help."

River left the police station and found Reggie making a call. He hung up as soon as he saw her.

"There's something else I didn't tell Parker," she said. "A couple of vagrants witnessed Jason being dumped by Clery's men. One of them has been silenced, but one is still alive. We need to find him."

"Why not tell Parker?" Reggie asked as he rubbed his hand over his short hair.

"Because I don't trust that guy. I don't want to show my hand fully. What if he screws up, just the way he did with Carlos? And what if Kruger has a way into this police station?"

"Good point."

"Any idea how we go about it?"

Reggie thought for a moment. "Leave it to me. I may know someone who knows someone."

River cocked her head. "Care to give me an inkling?"

Reggie sighed. "My elder brother has his struggles."

River sensed he'd rather leave the explanation at that. She just nodded.

"Then I'm going back to the veterans' center. I can't shake the feeling that the notebook is close to that place."

River parked the bike outside the veterans' center and walked into its reception area. She took her helmet off and stood in front of David, the new receptionist. He was nursing what River guessed must be a cup of hot chocolate. He put the cup down and smiled at her.

"Father Hopkins is in his office, I believe."

River smiled back and made her way to the rear of the building. Father Hopkins had shut his door, so River knocked and waited.

Father Hopkins took time to reply. "Who is it?"

"River."

She heard a few hasty steps, and the door opened abruptly.

"Can't find anything," he said as he stood in front of her.

River peeked inside his office—it was chaos. He stood aside to let her in. Father Hopkins must have checked every file he possessed. Papers and folders were scattered everywhere. She stood in the middle of the room.

"At least we're sure the notebook isn't in your office."

"I can guarantee that," he said as he was starting to gather the files again and put them back where they belonged. "But I've been thinking. What if Jethro gave this notebook to someone he thought was trustworthy but whom none of us would suspect? It could be someone here at the center. We have a lot of regular volunteers. I could draw up a list." Father Hopkins stopped for a moment and then continued. "Or it could be someone outside the center, even."

River frowned. She hadn't thought about that. Jethro wouldn't have wanted to talk about his condition to many people, but he didn't need to be specific about the contents of the notebook in order to entrust it to someone.

And then it came to her. She turned around and broke into a run. She hurried out of the center and kept going until she reached Ruthie's diner. She barely slowed down as she pushed the door open.

"Is Betsy still here?" River asked one of the waitresses.

The young woman appeared in the doorway of the diner's back room. She had her coat on and was about to fasten it with a belt. She stopped and walked toward River.

"I'm on my way out, but I always have a moment for you and your friends."

"Let's get a table at the back," River said, moving toward the booth she favored.

They both sat down. River thought about how to broach the

subject she wanted to discuss. Perhaps a simple question might elicit a simple answer.

"Did Jethro Carlton ask you to keep something important for him? Something he would have wanted you to give only to people he trusted?"

Betsy cocked her head. "Why would he do that?"

River had expected a straight answer to her question. She sat back in her seat.

"Because . . . because he wanted to protect his family," River said, the idea just occurring to her.

Betsy dropped her chin, thinking. "I hope you don't mind my saying so, but I need to decide whether I can trust you." Betsy lifted her head. "I think I can. I've been watching you. How you're trying hard to help Jason. Jethro and he were real close. They used to come here tons."

Her voice drifted. She must have realized it. "What is it you're looking for? Jethro said that whoever asked would know what the item was and why they wanted it."

"A notebook," River said as she leaned forward. "It contains important information about . . ." River hesitated, wondering how much Jethro would have revealed to Betsy. "About his medical condition."

Betsy nodded. "I know where the notebook is."

River closed her eyes for a moment. She was almost there. "Can you show me?"

With River following, Betsy stood up, walked to the center, and entered. She greeted the receptionist with quick smile and carried on toward the back of the building. She stopped in front of the chapel, composing herself, it seemed, before setting foot into a place of worship, and then pushed the door open.

The chapel was empty, so she walked along the side aisle to the sacristy. River followed and stopped on the threshold. The room was small, and she wanted to give Betsy space.

Betsy walked to a tall and slim armoire. She opened it, knelt, and began to rummage at the bottom of it. River heard the creaking of wood. Her heart had started to beat hard against her chest, and her mouth had run dry.

Finally Betsy took a plastic bag out of the armoire. It was folded around a bigger item inside. She stood up, walked to the door, and handed it over to River.

River took it with both hands as though it were a fragile item she didn't want to drop. She went to a row of chairs outside the sacristy, sat down, and slowly unfolded the bag. She found a leather-bound notebook inside, opened it with reverence, and read the name that was penned on the first page.

### JETHRO CARLTON

River's eyes welled. Betsy stood inside the sacristy, watching River from the door. She turned her head and disappeared into the corridor. River closed the book again. She didn't want to be the first one to read Jethro's notes. She took her cell phone out of her jacket pocket and searched for Lorrie's name. She pressed the number with a fast tap and listened for the ringtone.

"Have you found something?" Lorrie simply said. It seemed that she expected River to deliver on her promise.

"I found Jethro's notebook. I haven't looked through it, though. You should be the one," River said, trying to steady her voice.

Lorrie gave a small cry, and River heard what sounded like muffled sobs. River said nothing; she didn't want to create more despair for a woman who had already gone through so much. The line was silent for a moment. Perhaps Lorrie had muted her phone. She then returned and said, "Thank you. I'd like to do that—be the first one to read it. Or at least start. Where are you?"

"We found the notebook at the Ashton Veterans Center," River said.

"I'll be with you as soon as I can," Lorrie said.

"Are you sure? I could bring it to you."

"Positive. I'm on my way."

# Chapter Eighteen

September 2022
SEAL Team 1

Today's call was unexpected. A man named Clery got in touch with me. He wants to discuss my concerns about the repeated use of weapons and explosives. I didn't want to speak to him directly, but my former Marine contact in the armaments industry assured me he is well-connected and can make things happen. I was expecting a text asking for a convenient time to talk, but instead he called without warning and wanted a full-blown conversation on the subject right then.

I pushed back, pretending I had an urgent appointment to go to. Still, I still couldn't shake the guy, and we spoke for fifteen minutes. We agreed on another call after that, but I somehow don't like him. I've learned to trust my instincts when it comes to people. It's born of experience in an environment where teamwork is essential for survival. This man isn't a team player, and I'm questioning his motivation for the call.

A situation like this shouldn't cause me any issues. I'm not deployed. I'm not risking my life or the lives of my teammates, but Clery has unsettled me so much that I spent the better part of the day in my office. I couldn't think straight, and it was a struggle to formulate why it was I didn't like the man. I ended up calling Jason and talking it through with him. Didn't mention Clery's name. We finally agreed that it must have been the nature of his questions that disquieted me. I made a quick note of what we'd spoken about as soon as I hung up.

Clery's call was about evidence and whether other SEALs had experienced the same issues. But what seemed to worry him most was whether I'd voiced my concerns with other people. I tried to reveal as little as possible, but I found it hard to hold back. I started having a searing headache, and I had to ask him to call later. Our conversation is now fuzzy in my mind, but Jason is right. His questions weren't aimed at understanding my condition. They were aimed at discrediting my views.

I must find a way to keep these notes secure. I don't want to tell Lorrie about them. The less she knows, the better. I need to find someone trustworthy yet who's not close to me . . . I can't think. I'll need to come back to it later . . . too much.

J

Betsy walked out of the sacristy and came to sit next to River.

"You may wonder why Jethro trusted me with his notebook," she said.

River just nodded, still overwhelmed by the find.

"My brother died by suicide a few years back. He was part of a mortar team and highly respected by his teammates. Suddenly everything changed. Well, I shouldn't say suddenly. We all had noticed his mood changes, but they weren't that bad, so we ignored them. And then in the space of a few months, he just couldn't cope with the slightest confrontation. He almost killed one of his neighbors. A few weeks later, he took his own life."

River pressed her hand into Betsy's. "I'm so sorry. I didn't know."

Betsy dropped her gaze and sighed. "Some days, I still can't believe he's gone."

River squeezed Betsy's hand a little harder. "Thank you for helping Jethro and Jason—and me. It's going to make a difference."

Betsy gave River a weak smile. "I hope it will." She squeezed

River's hand back, stood up, and left the chapel slowly. River, Jethro's notebook balanced on her knees, watched as she walked through the door. She picked up her cell phone and called Karen.

"News?" Karen said.

"I've found Jethro's notebook."

"That's a relief! Where was it?"

"In the center's sacristy, wrapped up in a plastic bag at the bottom of an armoire."

"I thought Father Hopkins didn't know where the notebook was."

"He didn't. Listen, before I get into the whole story, I'd like you and perhaps Pablo to come to the center. Too many people are after that book. We don't know where Clery is, although my guess is that it doesn't look good for him. Parker told me his house is on fire. Kruger is on the run, though. He's wounded but still dangerous, so I'd like some backup here."

"I'm on my way—and I'm sure Pablo won't want to miss the excitement. He enjoyed this morning's action, and he's ready for a rematch."

River hung up and sat still for a moment. The center would soon become less busy, but it would stay open until 9:00 p.m. River rose from her seat. She picked up the notebook, checked the Glock in the waistband of her pants at the back, and walked out of the chapel. She found Father Hopkins in his office, still clearing the mess he'd created while looking for the notebook.

"Is there any event taking place here this evening?" River asked.

"No. I don't hold any events after something as involved as what we hosted this afternoon. Why?"

"I'd like to use the center to protect Lorrie Carlton—and this," River said, holding out the notebook.

Father Hopkins opened his eyes wide, momentarily lost for words. "Where was it?" he said.

"In the sacristy. What matters now is that this is a hot property. Karen and a friend are on their way here, and so is Lorrie Carlton."

"You want to use the center as a sanctuary?"

"I do. Please—at least until we've found a man who's on the run and very dangerous."

Father Hopkins dropped the pile of documents he was holding onto a chair and started toward reception. "I'll ask David to leave early. I don't want him around in case things go bad."

"Anyone else around? And how about you?"

"They've all left, but you may want to look around and make sure. As for me, I'm sticking around. A few thugs aren't going to scare me."

River left Father Hopkins and walked to the back of the building. She checked every room, and by the time she was done, David had left and Karen and Pablo had arrived. Father Hopkins locked the main door behind them, and they all gathered in his office.

Both Karen and Pablo were carrying a couple of cases containing weapons, and River could tell that Karen had done exactly what she had done herself—stick a gun in her waistband at the back. Father Hopkins didn't object. River wondered if, for once, he wouldn't have minded joining the fray.

"I'll get some coffee going," River said as Pablo and Karen were settling into the office. She went into the kitchen, dropped the notebook on the kitchen table, not wanting to let it out of her sight, and opened the cabinets, taking cups and coffee out. She poured some water into the coffeemaker and waited for the coffee to brew. Her cell phone rang. It was Parker.

"Have you found Kruger?" she asked, hopeful.

"We're tracking a car registered under his name. It's going in the direction of Dulles International. I'm just waiting to have enough police cars in place before we stop him."

"Where exactly is the car?"

"Why do you want to know?"

"Because I want to be there when you stop this guy." River sensed Parker's hesitation. "You owe me. You wouldn't have had a clue if I hadn't given you his name."

"Crossing the Potomac, almost certainly following Interstate 66," Parker grumbled.

"Make, model, and color? Plate number?"

"Mercedes S-class, dark blue. Plate number HH-888," Parker said, now sounding worried. "What are you gonna do?"

"I'll stay way behind, but as I said, I want to be there when you arrest him."

River hung up without waiting for Parker to complain. She returned to Father Hopkins's office and found that Karen and Pablo had already taken over the place. Father Hopkins had piled the documents he was meaning to file in a corner. He was at his desk, drawing a map of the building and answering questions.

"The police have found Kruger," River said. "I told Parker I was on my way. He didn't like it, but I'm not willing to risk another clusterfuck on the part of these guys."

"You're joining the chase?" Karen asked.

"I wish I could wait for Lorrie to arrive, but I don't trust Parker. I've got to be on his back, and then he'll have to focus." River handed the notebook to Karen. "I opened it only once, to check that it contained Jethro's name. Lorrie is on her way. I thought she should be the first one to read it."

Karen simply nodded, and the two men remained silent. There was no need to acknowledge that River had made the right decision. River walked back to the reception area. Father Hopkins followed her. He unlocked the main door as River was putting her helmet on and said, "Do I need to say it?"

River shook her head. "I intend to be there when Parker frees Jason and Kruger gets what he deserves."

She walked to her bike, fired it, and dashed onto the road. If she pushed the bike just a little over the speed limit, she should arrive just in time to catch Kruger's Mercedes as it crossed the intersection of Interstate 66 and Route 120.

River had hit rush hour. Cars were crawling along the streets of Arlington, and she tried to recall the layout of the area so that she could use the back roads. She was reasonably successful until she hit Virginia Square. She started pushing the bike into traffic and weaving her way between vehicles. She used the shoulder to overtake a truck, glancing at her watch a few times to gauge her progress. Her chances of catching Kruger's Mercedes were quickly vanishing. She slammed her fist on the fuel tank as she came to a stop. A couple of cars had run into each other, and the owners had stepped out of their vehicles, shouting.

*I don't have time for this crap.*

She revved her engine and started riding the bike on the shoulder of the road. Cars used their horns to complain about how close River came to hitting them, but she ignored the noise. She couldn't let Kruger escape, and although she should have let Parker deal with him, she didn't trust him to do the job. She kept going at speed until she spotted the highway on-ramp. She pushed the bike harder.

As River rode over Interstate 66, she spotted a car that matched Parker's description. She couldn't read the license plate from her position, but the dark blue Mercedes was going in the direction of Dulles International.

She veered into the feeder lane and found herself on Interstate 66. She sped up to catch the Mercedes she'd spotted earlier. Another car, dark gray and unmemorable, came alongside her and matched her speed. The window on the passenger side rolled down, and Parker's face appeared. He didn't say anything but indicated with his hand that she should drop back. River nodded. At least she was on the right road. The car in front must be Kruger's.

She pulled back and changed lanes so that she could still keep track of Kruger's car. The flow of cars slowed down, and a toll plaza appeared in the distance. River slowed the bike to a crawl. It was the ideal trap. The steel gates in front of the Mercedes and Parker's car, together with other unmarked police cars, would make it impossible for Kruger to escape. River's stomach fluttered. She was so close to her goal.

The roar of a car engine made her stand on the footrests as she kept the bike slowly moving along. Kruger's Mercedes swerved out of the lane it was in and sped toward the gate to the far right—the one that opened automatically for E-ZPass users. The Mercedes cut in front of another car. The other car's brakes screamed as the driver sought to avoid Kruger's vehicle. The Mercedes accelerated and squeezed through the toll gate in an instant.

"No," River screamed inside her helmet. She sat down again and gunned the engine. Parker's car was stuck in the wrong lane. It would have to wait a minute or so before it reached the toll gate Kruger had used. The car that had almost hit Kruger's reached the automatic gate and slid through. River got to the gate just in time. The steel arm had lifted to let the car pass. It was about to come down, but River slipped underneath it before it closed.

The road in front of her was now less busy. She accelerated, riding "death alley"—splitting the lanes between the cars. The Mercedes had almost disappeared in the distance. Whether Kruger had spotted them or he was late for his flight, his driver had been asked to forget about the speed limit and reach their destination fast. River kept pushing the bike and gaining on Kruger's car. The two police cars were also gaining in the distance and were now using their flashing lights.

The Mercedes accelerated again, and River found it hard to keep up. The police cars had disappeared from her side mirrors. Kruger's car jolted to the right in one crazy maneuver and rushed down the exit-only lane. It disappeared, and River thought she may have lost it. She cut across the lanes, too, almost hitting a large SUV, but she managed to turn into the exit-only lane just in time to see Kruger's car make a right onto another busy roadway.

She couldn't tell whether Parker and his crew had realized that the Mercedes had left the interstate. She caught up with Kruger's Mercedes, then pulled back a little. It was speeding along as though the police were still following. But the direction they were traveling in felt wrong. River was certain they were moving away from Dulles International. Perhaps Kruger's plans had changed after he'd spotted the two police cars.

The Mercedes went through a set of traffic lights. River had to stop but then accelerated once more. Kruger's car was now moving deeper into the side streets of the neighborhood they'd just entered. It felt almost random, and River wondered whether they'd spotted her. The car kept speeding along the streets, almost running into pedestrians. It took a final turn and found itself stuck behind a delivery van.

It was her only chance. As the Mercedes started to reverse, River slid the bike sideways to a stop. She dropped it to the ground and went down on one knee. She grabbed her Glock and aimed it at the car. She fires three times, hitting the rear tires. The explosion sent the car swerving against an SUV that was parked on the side of the street. River ran toward the car, gun aimed at the rear window. She fired and hit the top corner. To her surprise, it shattered, and someone inside screamed, "Stop."

"Then get out with your hands over your head. Same for the driver," River shouted. She kept the gun trained on the car and added, "Open the doors slowly. First the passenger and then the driver."

The back door opened slowly. A raised hand appeared, then a foot. A small, pudgy man with gray hair stepped outside the car. His face was ashen, and by the dark spot on his trousers, River judged that he might have wet himself. She thought for a moment that she had somehow gotten the wrong car. But the license plate was right: HH-888.

"Any other passengers in this car?"

The man shook his head. He said something inaudible, and River moved her gun to get a better aim. The man's arms shot up even higher, and he shouted, "No. I swear—only me and the driver."

"Whoever is driving this car, get out," River shouted.

The door opened, and a man of color in a suit stepped out. He looked far more relaxed than the passenger.

"Are you carrying a gun?"

The man shook his head.

"Slowly take your jacket off. One wrong move, and I'll shoot you down."

He did as he was told. River couldn't see a holster or a gun on him. "Both of you get into the middle of the road and lie on the ground, feet and arms spread apart."

As they were dropping to the ground, River went to the back of the Mercedes. From there she could see inside the car. The passenger was right: It was now empty. The realization punched her in the gut. It had all been a decoy. Kruger had never been in the car and had gained invaluable time over her and Parker.

Detective Parker was pacing up and down the street. River had called him as soon as she realized that Kruger wasn't in the Mercedes. Parker's car and the other two unmarked police cars had arrived ten minutes later. He'd been on the phone to contacts at every airport around DC and with Customs and Border Protection ever since. Karl Kruger had vanished without a trace.

River guessed that a man like Kruger would hold a variety of passports and that he must have used one of them to sneak out of the country unnoticed. Even with the severe wound inflicted by Manolo's rifle, he'd slipped through the net. She had to give him credit: Kruger was a serious opponent, the likes of whom she hadn't encountered for a long time.

She thought about calling Karen to check on the center, but she was still seething about being conned and didn't want to vent her anger in front of Parker. She might say something she would regret. Parker finished another call, hesitated, but then walked to her.

"We haven't found any trace of Kruger so far. Border Protection has told me that facial recognition will take time to yield results—"

"Got it," River said as she zipped up her coat. "You've lost him, and no one has a clue how to find him."

Parker opened his mouth a few times—a fish out of water—but in the end he had nothing else to add.

"How about Clery?"

"The firefighters who put down the blaze recovered a body."

"And?" River said in exasperation.

"The person had been tied to a chair."

"So Clery is dead," River said.

"But we still have Kruger," Parker said, trying, it seemed, to sound hopeful.

"Call me if you've got a sighting."

River left Parker to his search. It was time to return to the center and then call Reggie. Her last-chance witness was out there, and she needed to track him down.

When River arrived at the center, a new vehicle was parked outside the building. Lorrie must have arrived. River left her bike next to Pablo's truck and sent a text to Karen.

**Back at the center**

A moment later, Karen was opening the main door and letting River in.

"Did you get Kruger?"

"No. This SOB sent us on a wild-goose chase. It wasn't him in the car we were chasing," River said as she removed her helmet.

Karen shook her head. "I wish Dad could get involved."

"So do I. Did you get more information?"

"A lot more—and it's scary."

River bit the inside of her cheek. The piece of paper that bore the names of her parents was still in her coat pocket. She resisted the urge to take it out and ask Karen more about Kruger.

"Perhaps we can talk about it later. I see a car next to Pablo's. I guess Lorrie is here."

"She arrived shortly after you left and has gone to the chapel to read Jethro's notebook."

"Didn't she want to take it home?"

"I didn't ask, but she said she wanted you to be able to use it. I got the feeling she needed to read through it, to discover it first. It's one of the last things Jethro left behind."

River nodded and sighed. "I know. I simply wish I didn't need to gain access to Jethro's notebook so quickly."

Karen and River fell silent. They went into Father Hopkins's office, where the small team had hunkered down, but Karen didn't stop there.

"Where are you going?"

"To the chapel," Karen said. "Lorrie wanted to see you as soon as you were back."

They both made their way to the chapel. Karen knocked at the door and waited.

The door opened after a moment, and Lorrie stood in front of them both. Her eyes were red-rimmed, and she was holding Jethro's notebook to her chest. Karen withdrew without a word and River stood, unable to speak. Lorrie broke the awkward silence.

"I've almost finished Jethro's book," she said in a trembling voice. She cleared her throat and continued, "I don't think I can go ahead with the last few pages. But I'm happy for you to have the book now and use it to clear Jason."

She handed it over to River, who took it out of her hands with care. River folded her arms around Lorrie's shoulders and whispered, "I'll take good care of it and return it as soon as I can."

Lorrie squeezed River back and said, "I know. You're like Jason. Never break a promise."

Except that perhaps she had, and River felt her gut clench at the thought of Jason. Lorrie stepped away and walked slowly toward the reception area. "Call me if you need anything else," she added.

"Thank you," River said, the notebook now squeezed against her own chest. She waited until Lorrie had turned the corner, then walked back into the chapel. She sat down. Now she had to decide whether she should go through Jethro's notebook or try to find the vagrant who'd witnessed Jason being dumped.

# Chapter Nineteen

Snow had finally started to fall out of a starless night sky on DC. It had begun as a slow flurry, but it was now beating against the visor of her helmet, making it hard to ride at speed. River was due to meet Reggie at a homeless shelter in Washington Highlands, but crossing the Potomac had been painfully sluggish.

Reggie was standing outside the shelter when she arrived, stamping the ground with his feet so he could stay warm. He walked to her as she was parking her bike and said, "You'd better move the bike closer to the shelter and secure it to one of the bike hooks. I told a couple of the volunteers inside to look after it."

"Is the guy we're looking for inside?" River asked.

Reggie shook his head. "He doesn't use the shelter any longer. That's what tipped me off to the fact that he could be the man we're looking for. I thought about it and figured that someone who's scared of being gunned down is going to keep a low profile. On the other hand, he still needs food, and he can't panhandle anymore because he doesn't want to be seen, so his only hope is to use the mobile soup kitchen these guys run."

"Where is the soup kitchen?"

Reggie pointed to the corner of the street on which they stood. "We need to walk to the Anacostia riverbank. It's there at the moment but will be moving in thirty minutes or so."

Reggie took the lead. He started walking toward the corner, turned into a much narrower street, and crossed it. They both stayed silent, River aware that the houses on both sides looked old and shabby. As they progressed farther down the road, the streetlights became sparse. Many of them weren't working.

Snowflakes whirled in the air, and River shivered. They reached another corner, and Reggie stopped. "Do you have your gun with you?" he murmured.

River moved her hand to her back and said, "I do."

"Just checking," Reggie replied as he turned into an alleyway that led to the river.

He stopped again just as they reached the end of the alleyway. "There are a lot of homeless folk around here. Most don't want to come to the shelter because they don't want to be identified."

"Why not?" River asked.

Reggie shrugged. "Lots of reasons—they owe money; they do drugs; they deal a little, too. Some just don't want to interact with anyone."

"How do you know of this place?"

"My sister works at the shelter, and she sometimes helps with the mobile soup kitchen."

"That's very generous of her," River said.

"Perhaps, but it also helps her keep an eye on our eldest brother." Reggie surveyed the area for a moment, then started to walk faster. "I can see the lights of the food truck. Let's go."

The ground became uneven, and River could see that the area was used as a dumping ground for trash. The smell of rotting garbage drifted in the air. River rubbed her nose a couple of times, hoping the stench might go away.

They reached the banks of the Anacostia, and River spotted a small truck in the distance. Its side was open, and a couple of volunteers were serving food to a line of people. Most of them seemed to be wrapped in a blanket or, in the case of one lucky man, a bedspread. The line was starting to grow, and Reggie slowed down.

"Both of us can't be asking questions," Reggie said. "These people will freak out if we do."

"What do you suggest?"

"I'll go to the truck. My sister is here tonight. I'll speak to her. The people who line up should be okay with it. Then I'll see whether I can ask questions."

"Do you need to offer cash?"

Reggie shook his head. "Not a good idea. These guys will tell you anything you want to hear or make up a story for a few bucks. Keep an eye out from a distance and see who turns up."

River situated herself behind a cluster of trees, where she could observe the line without being seen. The snow had stopped, but the low clouds that scudded across the moon told her it would be only a short reprieve.

Reggie walked to the truck, raised a friendly hand, and called his sister's name from a distance. A few of the people who were shuffling forward stopped and stared, undecided, it seemed, about Reggie's arrival. His sister called Reggie's name in return and waved back. River couldn't hear exactly what she said, but it appeared as if she introduced her brother to the crowd, and everyone relaxed. The shuffle forward for food started again as Reggie helped his sister and another volunteer distribute the meals.

He was doing a great job of it, River noticed, exchanging a few words with each person he handed a bowl of soup and a sandwich to. It obviously wasn't the first time he'd served food to the needy. Reggie had mentioned his brother: River's own brother was a doctor in a small practice in Utah. They hadn't spoken much since the death of their parents. River ran a hand over her face. This wasn't the time or the place, and she pushed the thought away.

As the line kept moving forward, River noticed that one homeless man in particular had somehow fallen behind. The man behind him had spoken to him angrily and jumped the line, leaving the other man even more hesitant. And then another man did the same. The laggard drifted further down the line.

River spotted a way to move forward and get closer to the truck without being noticed by hugging a line of trees that ran parallel to the Anacostia's bank. She went slowly to avoid scaring off the small crowd. The man had now stopped falling behind. Reggie kept distributing food and chatting with the people who came to him. River wondered whether the laggard had first seen Reggie as a threat but then decided he wasn't a danger after all.

River was about to move a little closer toward the food truck when she noticed movement behind her in the alleyway she and Reggie had walked down earlier. Someone was standing where the small street met the riverbank, in the shadow of a large tree trunk. He was dressed in black. His puffer jacket was open, and he wore a beanie that had been pulled low over his forehead. He took a step back, hiding further in the shadows, and stood still, observing the small crowd shuffling forward. River retreated into the shade of the trees. She cursed her lack of vigilance. She'd assumed Clery was dead and Kruger out of the country, but either of the men could still have given instructions to terminate the last witness in the Jason Wayne murder case.

She turned to Reggie. He had stepped sideways, in the direction of the man who'd fallen behind. She couldn't be sure, but Reggie seemed to be speaking to him, perhaps offering food. River turned her attention to the man who had just appeared at the top of the alleyway. She crouched to the ground. She spotted a couple of dumpsters overflowing with garbage and a wrecked car that hadn't been cleared from the street. It would have to do for cover.

River crept along slowly until she reached the very last of the trees. There was a gap of a few yards between it and the dumpsters. Snow covered the ground, and she wasn't sure what lay underneath its thin blanket, but at least it would muffle the sound of her footsteps.

She cast an eye toward the newcomer. He hadn't moved, but he was now surveying the line of homeless people with a small monocular the likes of which she'd seen used by Special Forces on reconnaissance missions. She decided against a belly crawl to the dumpsters and instead crouched and ran the short distance. She slid against the metal and waited a few seconds. She then kept moving and reached the far end of the second dumpster. She risked a peek around the corner. The man was still there, concentrating on his task.

The newcomer straightened up. He'd noticed something or someone of interest. River took the Glock out of her waistband and slowly racked the slide to minimize the sound. She crouch-ran along the body of the car and dropped a knee to the ground when she reached the trunk. She risked a peek once more, and this time, the man was looking through his monocular again and reaching for something in his jacket.

River trained the gun on him and took cover behind the car. She then shouted, "Put your hands over your head or I'll gun you down."

The reaction was instantaneous. The man dived to the ground and started shooting in her direction. River slid along what was left of the body of the car, then threw a piece of junk she found on the ground in the air. The man discharged his gun a second time, giving River the exact spot she needed to aim for. She returned fire and hit the man a couple of times. He didn't shout, but she heard the distinct groan of someone who'd been trained to take pain.

"I've called the cops," she shouted again. "Give it up."

She moved away from her position. The man returned fire once more, hitting a spot in the wrecked car just above her shoulder. River ran along the dumpsters, away from the car. She took up a position behind the last dumpster again and saw him stand up and limp as fast as he could toward the tree that he'd hidden behind earlier. She aimed low and managed to hit him once more in the leg. He fell to the ground, and this time he cried out. She must have shattered a bone, and she reckoned he would now find it impossible to run or even walk.

River turned her attention to the food truck. Everyone had fled. The truck's shutter was down, and she gathered that Reggie's sister and the other volunteer were hiding behind it. River crouch-ran again to the line of trees she'd used for cover. The man had stopped shooting. When she reached the last tree, she checked on his position. He wasn't on the ground, and she couldn't see whether he was hiding behind the tree he'd used before.

She pulled her cell phone from her jacket pocket and called

Parker. His line was engaged, and she left a message. She turned her attention to the truck. It was about twenty yards away. She'd already fired seven rounds and had eight rounds left. She shook her head. It wasn't a good idea to break cover, but it might be the only chance she had to find the last witness.

River started running toward the truck. She fired at the tree behind which the shooter was hiding. The return fire came too late and too low. She was already behind the truck. Reggie's sister and her colleague looked more annoyed than terrified.

"What's happening? We lost all our regulars," Reggie's sister simply whispered.

"Someone is after one of the homeless people. Reggie and I are trying to find him. I think it's the shy one who almost turned back."

"That would be Charlie," the other volunteer said. "His lost his best pal a couple of days ago. Fell in the river."

"Charlie bolted as soon as the shooting started, and Reggie went after him," Reggie's sister added.

"Which direction?"

"Along the river, like everyone else, and then it's anybody's guess. There are quite a few side streets along the Anacostia's banks."

River nodded. "Stay behind the truck. The guy is badly wounded, so he won't go very far. I've called the cops."

River started running along the riverbank. She replaced her gun in her waistband and pulled her cell phone out to call Reggie. The phone rang a few times and went to voicemail. She killed the call and tried again. She was coming up to the first side street and could see a jumble of footprints in the snow. The group had broken up, some continuing along the riverbank, others taking the first turn they'd found.

"River," Reggie said on the phone, sounding out of breath.

"Where are you? I'm coming up to the first side street."

"Keep going. I'm with Charlie."

River sped up and almost fell. The ground had become slippery with the snow. Reggie had told her where to go, and she now needed to pace herself. A few minutes later she spotted them, Reggie standing up and Charlie crouched on the ground, arms around his folded legs. Reggie waved at her. She forgot about pacing herself and ran to them. When she reached Reggie, he opened his arms and gave her an unexpected hug.

"Man, I thought that guy was going to gun you down."

"I survived Afghanistan and Iraq. I'm sure I can survive a shoot-out on the banks of the Anacostia."

Charlie lifted his head, and even in the dark, River could tell he was terrified. River crouched next to him and said, "I hear you lost your best mate."

Charlie's jaw trembled, and he started to cry softly. "Dumbo never saw nothing. He was just old and scared," he managed to say.

"I'm really sorry about your friend. It's not fair." River put a hand on Charlie's shoulder. He recoiled, but she just left her hand there and squeezed gently. "I mean it."

Charlie must have believed her, because he relaxed and wiped his nose on the sleeve of his coat.

"Is it about what I saw in the underpass five days ago?"

"That's right. The man you saw being dumped is my friend Jason. If you come with us to the police, Reggie and I will make sure you're protected."

Charlie gave her an odd look. "Who's gonna believe the likes of me?"

"The police will, and they'll listen. That's the reason why these people killed your friend and want you dead, too. Because what you saw is important."

He wiped his eyes with the back of his hand and nodded. "Don't have much choice," Charlie said. "If I stay out here, they'll get me."

Charlie started crying again, and this time it was Reggie who crouched and laid a hand on his shoulder. River stepped away and made another call to Parker. It went through immediately.

"I got your message a moment ago and was about to call you back," he said. "I've sent two police cars to the address on the riverbank. They've just arrived and are looking for the gunman."

"Good to know," River said as she kept walking toward the river. "I found someone else who can help with the case."

Parker took a moment to reply. "Is it a credible witness?"

"This man saw Jason being dumped in the footpath. He can tell you that Jason was unconscious, and so if you combine this with the results of the drug test on Jason's hair—"

"Stop," Parker said. "I know what you're driving at, but I still need to interview your man before I come to any conclusions."

River bit her lip. She could have told Parker he was behaving like an asshole, but she chose the more diplomatic approach. "You're right. The name of my witness is Charlie. We'll be on our way to the Alabama Street station. You haven't confirmed, though. Have your CSI people taken a sample of Jason's hair for analysis?"

"They have," Parker grumbled.

River punched the air and hung up. She turned around and walked back to the spot where Reggie and Charlie were now standing.

"Detective Parker is waiting for us," she said.

Hesitation crept up again on Charlie's face.

"Reggie and I still don't know who's out to get you, Charlie. This is your best chance. You said it yourself."

He nodded and looked at River and Reggie in turn. River extended an arm toward the path that followed the river. "There are a couple of police cars waiting for us back there. Reggie and I won't leave you until we know you're safe."

Detective Parker's face dropped when he walked into the meeting room in which River, Reggie, and Charlie were waiting for him. Parker seemed not to have expected to have to deal with a homeless man as a witness. The three had sat down, and they stood up as one.

"Have your officers managed to find the gunman?" River asked.

"He didn't surrender easily, so now he is in the hospital in critical condition," Parker responded.

"At least he won't be having a go at Charlie anytime soon." Reggie shrugged.

"Charlie has been a witness to what happened to Jason," River said.

"So he was the target?" Parker asked as he indicated they all should sit down.

Reggie and River exchanged a look of disbelief, and Charlie turned to River, terrified.

"His friend was gunned down and dumped in the Potomac because of what they saw," River said, squaring up to Parker. "Why don't you ask Charlie to tell you his story and then verify whether a body has been found that corresponds to his friend's description?"

Parker's jaw clenched, but he seemed to think he wasn't in a position to be too picky. He'd lost two officers, and Carlos's whereabouts were still unknown. Parker called for someone to set up an interview room. He finished his call and stood up.

"I'll take it from here," Parker said. "Follow me."

Reggie stood up and placed a protective hand on Charlie's shoulder. "Charlie has appointed me as his legal representative. I shall therefore accompany him—if you don't mind, Detective Parker."

Charlie looked at Reggie and then River. River nodded, and he relaxed a little.

"Fine," Parker replied stiffly, "but you're the only one. Ms. Swift will have to wait." He walked to the door and left it open.

"I know it's late, but ask whether Parker has gotten the results from the lab," River said to Reggie. "I'm going back to Father Hopkins's center. The notebook is there, and I need to go through it."

Reggie nodded. He then turned to Charlie and said, "Let's go and tell Detective Parker what you saw five days ago."

Charlie stood and started shuffling forward. River nodded encouragingly when he looked back at her—a lamb to the slaughter. At least she was confident that Reggie would be on his side, unlike a state-appointed attorney who might be there only to collect his fee and nothing else.

River waited until Reggie and Charlie disappeared down the corridor before leaving the police station. Snow was now falling heavily again. She would have to take it easy on the bike, but somehow she didn't mind. The thought of going through Jethro's notebook filled her with dread. She knew how the story he recorded in his notes would end, and it seemed somehow wrong to be searching through it for clues. Still, she was certain that Jethro would have done anything in his power to help his teammates, and that included Jason. His notebook was part of that help, and it was the expression of Jethro's bravery, too.

She straddled the bike again, fired it up, and slowly merged onto the road. The front wheel slid a few times, but River steadied the bike again and kept going, across the Anacostia River, past the Capitol, across the Potomac, and then straight to Arlington.

When she arrived, the center looked closed, and she sent a quick text to Karen. Father Hopkins arrived at the main entrance and unlocked it.

"I'm sorry I'm keeping you so late, Father. It's almost midnight," she said with an apologetic smile.

"Don't worry. I'm so glad we found Jethro's notebook and that the center was the place it was kept safe."

They both went into the kitchen, where Karen was chatting with Pablo about Kotzebue.

"I'm glad I left to join the Corps. But then, after a few years away, I found I was missing Kotzebue's winters." Karen turned her head toward the kitchen door.

When she saw River, Karen got up, went to the counter, and brought a fresh pot of coffee to the table together with a clean cup. She poured coffee in it without asking and handed it over to River.

"You look tired and cold."

River grabbed the cup and took a sip. She closed her eyes and groaned. Karen was right. She was tired and cold, but she had one more task to accomplish before the night was over.

"Dare I ask whether you found the person you were looking for?" Karen said as she returned the pot to its base.

236

"We did, although it almost turned into a disaster," River said before she took another sip.

Karen shook her head. "I spoke to Dad about Kruger again. He'd gathered he was wanted—but perhaps not as wanted as he actually is. Kruger is one of the main arms traffickers in Africa. He sells arms to various militias that spread unrest on the continent, but he also works for Russia, it seems, and has links to Iran. Not one agency has been able to nail him—not the CIA, not MI6 . . . not even Mossad."

"So it's fair to say that he's not going to let go of this story just like that," River said as she finished her coffee.

"That's exactly what Dad said. He told me we should be cautious, and he's not the sort to advise caution."

River drew up a chair and sat down. "And now we have a homeless witness we need to protect. Reggie knows he's got to persuade Parker to put Charlie in a witness protection program, but I don't trust Parker to do that efficiently."

"I'll look after him for as long as it'll take," Pablo said. "We did a good job this morning stopping Clery's men. With a bit of improvement, the motel can be turned into a stronghold."

"And what about the customers?" River said.

"What about them?" Pablo asked.

"Don't you have a business to run?"

Pablo shrugged. "In life, you've got to get your priorities straight."

River couldn't help but smile. "I'm glad one of those priorities is to keep a key witness alive."

# Chapter Twenty

October 2022
SEAL Team 1

The day has almost come.

I had another appointment with Frank at Walter Reed hospital—although Frank doesn't know it yet, it is our last. The meeting outcome was predictably disappointing.

Clery, the man who called me a few weeks ago, insisted we meet. I didn't want to, but I relented. I don't trust this guy, but I also don't know whether it is my paranoia speaking or my clear mind. We met at Walter Reed. We went over the same questions, but this time he wasn't so negative. He sounded a lot more inter-ested in considering the issue. He also mentioned that one of his clients is keen to find out more. As it turns out, Clery is only a lob-byist. His client is directly involved in armaments and has a lot more sway. I'm willing to let Clery's client speak to Frank. But I want a name. Whoever his client is, he won't get access to my notes or records unless he comes clean. They must have been desperate, because Clery came back with a name: Karl Kruger. Although I'm sure he'll find out soon enough that I am about to give Frank exactly what he needs—the brain tissue of someone

238

he's been trying to treat for months and on whom no drug or psychological treatment has worked.

Jason knows as much as I think he can stomach, and I've decided not to give him this notebook. If I do, he'll know what my plans are, and I don't want him to try to stop me. I've been lucky in my search for the right person to entrust the notebook to. Betsy at Ruthie's All Day Diner is kind and honest. If I tell her not to look into the book, she won't. There is a story about her brother, but I can't recall. I've eliminated Maria at the center from consideration. I still can't quite figure out why, but I trust what's left of my old instinct. Tomorrow I'll visit Father Hopkins and have a coffee at the diner if all goes well. It'll be my last outing before I put a gun to my heart and press the trigger.

I am calm as I write these lines because I now know it is the only way. In my moments of clarity, I have considered what the future holds for me, and it is bleak. But overall, I can't stand the thought of hurting my family . . . leaving them behind is unbearable, and yet I can't guarantee I won't one day hurt them. For a while I had hoped I could perhaps still see my kid grow up and accompany her in life, but it just can't be.

What I do next will at least give me one last moment of pride—to serve and contribute to the effort to keep my country and my teammates safe.

J

Water dripped over River's face, all the way down her neck, and then onto her T-shirt. She splashed her face again and swallowed the bile that had risen to her throat. She'd seen Father Hopkins go back to his office after she finished reading Jethro's notebook. She'd rushed to the kitchen, dropped the notebook on the table, and gone to the sink in fear she might be sick. She didn't want to leave the notebook unattended and didn't mind showing Karen and Pablo how overwhelmed she felt. She fumbled to find a hand towel and wiped her face with it.

River sat down, and Karen put a glass of water in front of her friend. River nodded her thanks and took a sip. She closed her eyes and after a moment said, "Jethro mentions both Clery and Kruger in his book."

Karen tilted her head to the side. "But how did they know Jethro had a notebook?"

"Through Maria. Jethro must have told her he had one but didn't leave it with her at the end. He had mentioned notes about his condition to Clery anyway, so he knew he had to find these. I guess Clery tried to threaten or bribe people who were close to Jethro."

"It's lucky she didn't realize he handed it over to Betsy," Karen said.

"Jethro was extra careful, but perhaps not always as sharp as he might have been. His mental state . . ." River took a moment to find the right words. She didn't want to give the wrong impression of a man who'd been brave and selfless. "He knew he wouldn't get better, and at the end, he knew exactly what he was doing," she chose to say.

The three of them remained silent for a while until Pablo said, "What do you what us to do?"

"We need to get Jethro's notebook to Detective Parker," River said, looking at her watch. "It's very late, but I don't think he'll have gone home yet."

Karen and Pablo rose. River went to tell Father Hopkins they were leaving, promising she would call him with an update in the morning. When the three of them got outside, snow had now piled two inches thick on the ground. River would have to give up the bike. Karen and she got into Pablo's black pickup truck, with Pablo behind the wheel, and they made their way to the Alabama Avenue police station.

River called Reggie. He and Charlie had just finished the interview with Parker, who'd agreed to find a safe house for Charlie. Parker was busy with the formalities, and by Reggie's reckoning it would take him a while. River hung up and started taking pictures of Jethro's notebook pages. She'd need this for the conversation she was planning to have with Parker.

The journey was slow, and underneath the apparent calm in the pickup, River could sense they all were jumpy. They still didn't know for sure whether Kruger had left the country, and even if he had, the near disaster at the food truck told them he had a lot more resources at his disposal.

As soon as Pablo parked, Karen got out and scanned the area. She nodded to River, and they both went into the police station while Pablo stayed in the truck. Reggie was waiting for them. He'd gotten himself a burger and Diet Coke.

"Had to refuel after tonight's events," he said, glancing at the cardboard box containing his half-eaten meal. He dried his fingers on a paper napkin and stood up.

Karen eyed Reggie's half-finished dinner but kept quiet.

"Where is Charlie?" River asked.

"He's just been taken to a safe house. He was worried about going on his own, but I managed to persuade him."

"You're sure Parker knows what a safe house looks like?" River couldn't contain her sarcasm as she approached a receptionist.

Reggie followed her. He then moved in front of River to ask for Detective Parker. The man took his time, and Reggie took his cell phone out.

"Do I have to call him myself?"

The man grumbled something inaudible and placed a call.

A few minutes later, Parker appeared at the entrance to the corridor leading to the interrogation rooms. Dark rings had formed under his eyes, and his hair stood on end, as though he'd spent the better part of the evening with his finger in an electrical socket. He sighed and walked over to River, Reggie, and Karen.

"Charlie's been taken by a team of officers specializing in witness protection to a safe house," he said.

"As long as they get there in one piece, that sounds good."

Parker's face tightened, but he didn't answer back.

"I've come to bring you another key piece of evidence. It should help establish motive," River said.

Parker seemed to take a few seconds to register the news. "What is it?"

"The notebook of Master Chief Jethro Carlton, a Navy SEAL who took his life three months ago and the man who gave Jason the information he needed to go after Clery."

Parker opened his hand, but River shook her head. "I'd like to do that inside the station, please."

Parker didn't resist. He turned back and made his way to the door that led to the first floor of the building. He let River and Jason in. Karen sat back in the waiting area. He entered an empty room, flicked the OCCUPIED sign on, and indicated they should go in.

"Before we speak about the notebook and its contents," River said, sitting down, "I'd like to know whether you've had the results from Jason's hair test."

Reggie was about to say something, but Parker held a hand up. "I want to make sure the results have been confirmed by the CSI team."

"A prelim will do," River said. "I used to perform autopsies for the military police. Never liked it, but I'm not completely ignorant about the way evidence gathering works."

Reggie arched his eyebrows in a didn't-know-that way. Parker's chin sagged to his chest. He then lifted his head and said, "Prelim shows the presence of Rohypnol in Jason's system."

River closed her eyes for a fraction of a second and added, "And the knife-slash direction?"

Parker cleared his throat. "More likely than not, a right-handed man."

Reggie stood up and laid his hands on the tabletop, body forward. "Now that you have Charlie Baynes's witness statement and Master Chief Carlton's notebook, as well as the test results you've just mentioned, I request that you release Jason Wayne immediately."

Parker stood up and leaned forward, too. "Not until I have the CSI lab confirm its findings," he said through gritted teeth.

"It's got nothing to do with preliminary findings, Detective

Parker," Reggie said. "It's got everything to do with the fact that you haven't got anybody else as an alternative suspect—or, rather, that the probable perpetrator has almost certainly left the country."

River blinked. She hadn't expected Reggie to slaughter Parker that way so soon.

Parker's face turned pale, and he thumped his fist on the table. "You have no evidence that Karl Kruger is involved."

River opened Jethro's notebook to the appropriate page and slid it across the table. It landed in front of Parker, who picked it up and started reading. He slowly sat down as his eyes followed the lines that Jethro Carlton had penned only a few days before his death. Parker's eyes widened as he came across Clery's name and then Kruger's.

River gave him a moment to weigh the revelation and then said, "I am going to leave Master Chief Carlton's notebook with you. I have a copy of the book just in case it goes astray. His wife has read the book, too. Mr. Cameron and I are going to retire, but we'll be ready tomorrow morning to collect Jason Wayne at the DC Jail after you've confirmed he can be released. If we turn up and he's still in your custody, I'll send this book to every single contact I have at the DOD and the DOJ and let them know the kind of injustice you're perpetrating on a combat veteran."

River stood up. Reggie was already at the door. He opened it, and they both left without a word. Parker didn't call them back, and River wondered whether he was stunned or so pissed off he couldn't speak. They walked to the reception area, where Karen was waiting for them. She must have gathered by the looks on their faces that the meeting with Parker hadn't gone smoothly. The three of them left the station and got into Pablo's pickup truck.

River sat in the front passenger seat and let her head drop against the headrest. Pablo started the engine, and they left. They'd been driving for a while before River finally said, "I'm glad I left my gun behind. I might have been tempted."

Reggie leaned forward and stuck his head in the gap between the two front seats. "Words are mightier than the sword, and you sure got him in the gut."

River turned her head to face Reggie and managed a small smile. "We'll find out how right that is tomorrow morning."

## Saturday, January 22

River was leaning against Pablo's old pickup truck, waiting. She straightened up as soon as Reggie appeared at the door of the DC Jail. Her heart banged against her chest, worried he might be alone. It had taken all day Friday for Parker to relent, but a call from Frank at Walter Reed hospital had convinced him that River wasn't bluffing when she told him about contacting her most senior connections.

Reggie waved at her, and a few seconds later, a man dressed in civilian clothes that looked a little too baggy for him appeared behind him. Jason looked gaunt and tired, but his face lit up when River waved back at them. Reggie turned around and shook Jason's hand. He waved again at River and started to walk in the direction of the Metro station.

Jason stood for a moment, and River wondered whether she should wait or go forward and greet him. He stepped down the few steps that led to the street and accelerated his walk, making his slight limp more pronounced. River did the same, and they found themselves in a tight embrace. She pulled back a little and lifted her head. His arms were still locked around her waist as his eyes searched her face.

"I thought Parker would never let you go," she said.

Jason gave her a smile and loosened his hold. "He didn't know who he was dealing with."

River returned his smile and took his arm, leading him to the pickup truck. "Let me drive you back home."

Jason threw the small bag he was carrying in the back of the vehicle and got into the front passenger seat. River started the truck, and they drove off. The snow that had fallen was almost gone; only a few blackened lumps remained on the sidewalks. They stayed silent for a while. River cast an eye toward Jason a few times, gauging his mood. He would want to talk, but perhaps not just yet. He seemed to be simply savoring his freedom.

Traffic picked up a little as they were about to cross the Potomac. Jason glanced through the window and shook his head. They were getting closer to Arlington and to the memories of what had unfolded in the last seven days.

"Thank you for all you did," Jason said, stretching his hand to squeeze hers.

River squeezed back. "I couldn't let these guys accuse you of something you would never do—not you."

Jason nodded, and River let go of his hand to change gears. She glanced at him. He looked hurt by the gesture. Still, Jason moved sideways so he could look at her better and said, "I know you're a free spirit, River, but if you ever get tired of running, you know where to find me."

River's throat tightened, and she took a moment before answering. "I know, Jase. I just need to clear my life of a few ghosts that I didn't realize had been haunting me for a long time."

They fell into an easy silence until they reached Jason's apartment, in Arlington. River and Karen had spent the previous day cleaning it of the dust and grime that the CSI team had left behind. Reggie had called late Friday evening to let them know that Parker had finally relented and that Jason would be released on Saturday.

One of the conditions that had made River smile was that she not enter the DC Jail but wait outside. She and Karen had gone shopping to fill Jason's fridge. They'd even bought a bottle of Champagne to celebrate. But now that she and Jason had arrived back at the apartment, River wasn't sure she should go in. She parked the old truck, and they both got out. Jason gave River a quick hug and stepped back. She handed the apartment keys to him and said, "I'll be in touch in a few days' time."

Jason managed a smile. "I'm not going anywhere, at least not until Parker catches the SOB who framed me."

Unsurprisingly, Detective Parker had been "economical" when

it came to telling Jason the truth. Reggie would no doubt update him about the suspected escape of Karl Kruger, and she would call Jason, too, to fill in the gaps. River thought she might perhaps even do more than just call, but for the time being she needed to be on the move again.

Jason walked to the front door of his building. He went in but didn't turn back. River waited until she saw the light go on in his living room. She got into the truck and left for the motel. She'd return Pablo's vehicle, and then she'd catch a cab to Ronald Reagan airport. From there she'd be on the flight she booked the day before. She wasn't going back to Alaska with Karen, and yet she couldn't wait to get out of DC. As the tires caught on a small patch of snow, she wondered whether she would ever find enough peace to sometime return.

# Acknowledgments

It takes many people to write and publish a book, and for their help and support I want to say thank you to the following individuals:

Barbara Clark, my editor, for her immense knowledge of good language and of what makes a good story great; Lizzie Gardiner, for her expertise in design and for producing a book cover no reader can ignore; Susan Hood, for her proficiency in typesetting and knowing what it means to work with grace under pressure; and Sarah Chassé, for her precise proofreading.

Appreciation also goes to the friends who have patiently read, reread, and advised on all matters connected with my book, including my friend and *uuma* Karen Thompson, who generously shared her Inupiat stories, her language, and the ways of the frozen lands; Kathy Vanderhook and Karen Christensen, two most wonderful supporters, on whom I can test my storylines; and, of course, my very cool ARC team.

**Coming Soon from Freddie P Peters**

Also Featuring River Swift

*Savage Peace* (fall 2025)

*Trip Wire* (spring 2026)

# Dear Reader . . .

I hope you enjoyed reading *Kill Switch* as much as I enjoyed writing it!

Perhaps you would like to know more about my other series: If so, check out the Nancy Wu Smart Woman Crime Thrillers at https://mybook.to/NWCT and the Henry Crowne Paying the Price Thrillers, also featuring Nancy, at https://mybook.to/HCPTP.

Don't forget that by going to https://freddieppeters.com and joining Freddie's Book Club you can gain access to the backstories that underpin the series, learn about my creative process and how the books are conceived, and read opening chapters of each book and the prequel to the Henry Crowne series, *Insurgent*.

And now it's time for me to ask you for a small favor. Please take a few minutes to leave a review on Amazon, Goodreads, or Book-Bub. Reviews are incredibly important to authors like me. They help readers decide which book to choose next, increase the books' visibility, and help with promotions. Thank you so very much.

I look forward to connecting with you!

*Freddie*

Printed in Dunstable, United Kingdom

66652904R00147